The Southern Trust Conspiracy

Patrick Weill

Weill & Associates

E-book ISBN: 978-1-959866-18-3
Paperback ISBN: 978-1-959866-19-0

For Lulú

Contents

Main Characters

The Heroes

Sean Choi: A technology analyst working for the district attorney's office in San Diego, California, Choi is a gifted electromechanical engineer and computer programmer.

Chief Deputy DA Lynn Peters: One of five senior prosecutors for the San Diego District Attorney's Office. Hard-driving and ambitious, she directs several units, or teams of lawyers at the Hall of Justice, one of which is the Major Violators Unit. She is romantically linked to Dom Taylor (see below).

DA Investigator Dominick Taylor: A decorated former soldier and once a high-ranking police officer, Taylor now works in the Hall of Justice, usually with Choi, whose desk is next to his.

Deputy DA Dea Bladet: A seasoned prosecutor with fiery red hair and a sharp tongue. She leads the Major Violators Unit and has a history with Johnny Roche (see below).

Deputy DA Johnny Roche: A strong and well-liked prosecutor who previously served in the MVU but now works in Economic Crimes. In the present case, he teams up with Dea Bladet and Cammie O'Mara.

Deputy DA Cammie O'Mara: Relatively young and new to the DA's office, this talented and determined attorney joins the Major Violators Unit early in the story. She, too, is romantically involved with Dom Taylor.

The Villains

Vincent Tyson, Attorney-at-Law: A famous criminal defense attorney based in Los Angeles and San Diego, Tyson is around sixty years of age. In addition to his legal work, he manages a team of hired killers, each with their own specialty.

Dr. Millie Haukea: The defendant in the trial described in this novel. Thirty years of age or so, Millie is originally from Hawaii. Years earlier, she committed a series of murders on that island state, but Tyson took her case and saw to her acquittal. She is a doctor of pharmacy and Tyson's protégée. Poisoning is her area of expertise.

Asher: Tyson's digital mercenary. A technical expert, genius programmer, and designer of explosive devices. Sean Choi's rival.

Dane: A muscular specialist in staged accidents and suicides. Also a pilot and good with guns.

Kang: A master of martial arts and Vincent Tyson's live-in masseuse.

Morgan: An expert in disguise and impersonation. Ex-military intelligence.

Voss: Tyson's sniper. Also ex-military.

Igmar: Tyson's enormous butler. Highly protective of his employer.

Other Major Players

The Honorable Andrew Toles: A large Black man close to Tyson's age, Judge Toles presides over the present case and colludes with Tyson to rule in Millie Haukea's favor.

Dulce Garcia: Sean Choi's wife. Like Choi, Dulce is an accomplished computer programmer, and she is paralyzed from the waist down.

Lieutenant Ragasa: The leader of the San Diego Police Department's SWAT team. He and his men guard the courtroom throughout this dangerous trial.

Detectives Jeff Walker and Tony Park: Close friends of Lynn Peters, Dom Taylor, and Sean Choi, these two lawmen were witnesses to the crimes Millie Haukea committed on Oahu years earlier. Walker is married to Choi's wife's sister, which makes him and Choi brothers-in-law.

1

THE OPERATIVE WORD

Shaking her head in disgust at the latest antics of the so-called richest man in the world, the Sovereign turned away from the news and strode over to a window, sweeping her sharp gaze across a chain of snowy mountains. Then she dropped her eyes to the frozen lake below and the frosted trees surrounding it. Just outside the window, thick icicles framed this hostile landscape, the sight of which was, for her, the highlight of each and every one of these meetings.

"I can't stand that clown," said one of her co-conspirators in reference to the same individual, the one generally considered to have amassed the greatest fortune on the planet, but who in reality was simply the person held up for the population to love or hate.

A concordant murmur rose up from among all those gathered around the long conference table, who knew firsthand that the truly ultra-rich preferred to remain in the shadows.

This relatively lighthearted moment had come on the heels of a discussion about a politician whom this group had been planning to install as the President of the United States, but the fool had died in the most appalling display of weakness that the Sovereign—who was invariably referred to by that name, and her face never shown to anyone who did not absolutely need to see it—had ever witnessed. She spun on her heel to return to her chair at the head of the table, and as she did, she nodded to another one of her allies, vowing to herself that from then on she would keep a closer eye on her pawns.

The man she'd prompted with a nod—code name "the Chancellor"—was a thin-faced man in his forties. He was impeccably dressed, immaculately groomed, and his features showed no trace of emotion. Seated in the center of the men and women on the left side of the table, with a massive LED display mounted on the wall behind him, he actually *was* one of the world's richest men (*but not the richest person in the room*, thought the Sovereign with great satisfaction).

The Chancellor cleared his throat and said, "On to the next item of business, which involves one of our West Coast corporations." He pressed a button on a remote control, calling to the screen a chiseled face, that of a man in his sixties dressed in a dark suit and tie. "This is Vincent Tyson. In case you haven't heard of him, Tyson is well known throughout the State of California for his impressive record as a high-profile defense attorney. But he's found himself in a spot of trouble."

At that, the two men standing guard at the door looked to the Sovereign, their unspoken question being whether it was time to dispose of the Chancellor, but she shook her head imperceptibly. *Not yet.*

***

Having agonized over what she was about to do, Chief Deputy District Attorney Lynn Peters finally reached for her desktop phone and punched in an extension.

"This is Cammie O'Mara," came a younger woman's voice on the line.

"Good morning," said Lynn Peters crisply. "Do you have a moment?"

"Yes, ma'am. Be right up."

Peters pictured Cammie sashaying confidently from her office to the elevators, catching everyone's eye with that beaming grin and her perfect rear end swishing from side to side. As bright as any other person working at the Hall of Justice, this new deputy district attorney wasn't nearly as loyal as Peters had initially expected. The latter felt a selfish pang of regret for having hired the girl when she spotted her through the window, sweeping past the executive receptionist with a winning smile.

There came a knock at the door. "Come in," said Peters.

Cammie did just that and settled herself primly into a chair on the other side of her boss's desk. Her glossy black hair fell straight past her ears, almost to her shoulders, and her fine features expressed an innocence that Peters now found false.

"I can't believe you've been here for three years already," the blond-haired chief prosecutor began, forcing a smile.

"I *know*," said the younger attorney. "It's all gone so fast."

"Ha! I'll bet."

"Gotta start somewhere. I know *you* paid your dues."

"Yes, I did. At any rate, you've done an outstanding job," Peters said. "How'd you like to work in the Major Violators Unit? Dea Bladet could use your help."

Deputy District Attorney Cammie O'Mara's face brightened at once, but it didn't stay like that for long. Shortly thereafter she was sitting at a table in the corner of the same office, scribbling on a yellow legal pad while Peters briefed her and DDA Dea Bladet (pronounced *blah-day*) on the facts of the case at hand.

"The lead prosecutor is the U.S. Attorney's Office," Peters informed them. "They've filed separate actions against Southern Trust—one up north and another down here in San Diego—and instructed us to coordinate directly with the LA County DA's

Office. Until recently, the charges were only political and financial—money laundering, bribery, that sort of thing—so John Roche over in Economic Crimes was handling it on our end, but—" Peters stopped to shoot Dea Bladet an irritated look. "What?"

The head of the Major Violators Unit, whose striking red hair matched her passion for justice, among other pursuits, had turned to Cammie to flash her a suggestive wink at the mention of DDA Roche. Quickly Bladet apologized for the interruption.

"Anyway," Peters went on, "now that seven key witnesses have been silenced—five in LA and two down here—the judge has declared a mistrial. USAO has launched a new investigation and appointed me the task force liaison for San Diego."

"No homicide charges yet?" asked Bladet.

"Not even a suspect," said Peters briskly as she came to the part she'd been dreading. "Now, you will be working with Dom Taylor, an investigator with whom I believe you are well acquainted." This last remark, while true for both of her deputy prosecutors, had been aimed at Cammie and coupled with a four-second stare. "I have a conference in a few minutes, so I'll leave it to him to fill you in on the rest."

Take it easy on her, Peters told herself as she shut the door behind her subordinates a little too hard. *It's your own damn fault.*

***

"It's her fault," affirmed DA Investigator Dominick Taylor. "Lynn's the one who broke up with *me.*"

"Wouldn't the anti-fraternization policy apply to everyone?" asked Sean Choi, a technical analyst assigned to Taylor's office.

"You mean does it apply to me and Cammie O'Mara. No. Absolutely not."

Choi's face was narrow and delicate, his body skinny, but his gaze was as sharp as a razor's edge. He leveled a skeptical pair of eyes on his friend and mentor.

"It *doesn't*," Taylor insisted. "First of all, it's an anti-harassment policy, not an anti-fraternization policy, which establishes guidelines rather than official rules."

"Found it," said Choi, after using his tablet to search for the document in question, quoting some of its text. "Personal relationships between employees, particularly those involving supervisory roles, are strongly discouraged as they may create conflicts of interest, favoritism, or disrupt workplace harmony."

"*Supervisory roles* being the operative term. Plus, these *guidelines* aren't enforced or even discussed until you get up into the higher ranks. The political ones."

"Like a certain chief deputy gunning for assistant DA."

"Exactly." Out of the corner of his eye, Taylor detected movement on the far side of his interior window, so he heaved his powerful frame out of his chair and strode to the door to open it for Bladet and O'Mara.

Minutes later, Cammie O'Mara was scribbling on the same yellow legal pad as before, and as Taylor spoke, every so often she'd look up at him with an inviting expression. "Southern Trust," she repeated, taking down the name of the investment firm facing legal action. "Got it. And what was the name of the first victim again? The one with the shellfish allergy."

"Ronald Green," said Taylor. "He was the firm's private equity director. His whole table was served the same steak tartare mixed with tropomyosin and ricin. But he wasn't the first victim. Remember, the LA branch was hit first and much harder."

"The ricin made everyone sick but the tropomyosin killed only Green," noted Bladet. "Clever."

Taylor nodded. "It was. Threw Green off for long enough that he didn't think to use his EpiPen."

"What do we know about the killer?" asked Bladet, recrossing her long and muscular legs. The red-haired prosecutor was clad in a navy-blue pant suit that made no attempt to hide her impressive figure.

"Not much. She used a fake ID when she got the job just before the event, wore gloves while serving the food, and kept her face turned away from the cameras the entire time."

"She must have cased the Convention Center beforehand," said Cammie, glancing up from her notes with that look again. Taylor paused for a moment to reflect upon their budding relationship. He was smitten, but she was pretty young.

"Were there any pictures taken at the event?" Bladet wondered. "You know, by the organizer or the attendees."

"Good question," said Sean Choi. "That's one of the things we're going to look into today. Now, as for the second murder, Michael Schmidt was the head of business development for Southern Trust San Diego. He died yesterday in his office from respiratory failure secondary to acute nicotine poisoning. The tox report showed six hundred times the amount normally found in a smoker's body, and chemical analysis of his cigarettes revealed a similar altered concentration. That means someone switched out his smokes with doctored ones, but again the killer was careful. CSI found no useful prints and the surveillance system recorded nothing. The cameras had been malfunctioning for several days."

"Right," said Bladet.

Cammie scrunched up her lips thoughtfully. Then she said, "It's not easy to tamper with cigarettes while preserving their original appearance."

"Nor to enter a busy building undetected in broad daylight," added Choi. "That's what's remarkable about all this. The LA murders were made to look like accidents. There was a fire, a stray bullet in a drive-by shooting, failed brakes on a car, an apparent suicide, and a boating collision. With no evidence left whatsoever."

"We're dealing with professionals," DAI Taylor said, grabbing his coat from the back of his chair. "But there's always something you can learn from the scene, so Choi and I are going out to see what that is. In the meantime, I suggest y'all meet with Johnny Roche, who should be able to bring you up to speed on the mistrial. Also, head over to the intake unit to see if there's been any charges filed that match these MOs. We'll be searching the databases. And let's meet back here later today, if we can."

If would turn out to be the operative word.

2

DEAD ENDS

DAI Dominick Taylor, formerly *Lieutenant* Dominick Taylor less than a year before, had commanded Oceanside PD's Special Enforcement Section, and prior to his law enforcement career served as a soldier in the U.S. Army's Special Forces. So he knew what it meant to kill a man, and as he drove an unmarked SUV to his next destination, he felt guilty for having taken pleasure in that act on more than one occasion. Taylor was an outdoorsman, skilled in the operation of many types of vehicles, and still competitive in the fighting ring even at forty years of age. He was the kind of guy who, in order to maintain peak performance, relies on the regular company of other aggressive men. *And often the company of an attentive woman*, he thought, grinning as he hung a right. But now, in his capacity as a district attorney investigator, most of his colleagues were either assertive, ambitious, and single-minded females who were even busier than he was, or, if male, they were academic types who'd never held a gun or even wanted to. Sean Choi was a rare exception to that rule. Yes, the dark-haired analyst was currently sitting next to Taylor in the front passenger seat while using a tablet, most likely digging up some obscure fact or little-known detail, but Choi had proven he could handle himself when things got serious.

As Taylor crunched to a halt in the Convention Center's parking lot, he decided that this new chapter of his life would be good for him, that it would bring him balance, and that he needed to stop mourning the loss of his previous authority. *At least*, he consoled himself as he stepped out of the unmarked SUV, *I still get to wear a badge, carry a firearm, and drive a pursuit-rated vehicle.*

"You were quiet on the way here," he mentioned to Choi as they set off for Hall C. "What were you looking up?"

"Oh, I was checking out your Police Interceptor's specs. Four hundred horsepower, with a top speed of one fifty. Not bad!"

Taylor nodded pensively as he strode along. "No, it's not," he agreed.

They found the building they were headed for and went upstairs to the office of David Englander, the catering manager, a large individual who frowned at their arrival and reluctantly motioned for them to have a seat. When they asked Englander about the first of the two murdered witnesses, he replied, "When I got there, the paramedics were already treating the guests at table twelve. People were sweating, having trouble breathing, and throwing up. Except for one of them, who was lying face up on the floor with his eyes wide open. I'll never forget it. I asked how he died and they said 'anaphylaxis,' whatever that means."

"It's a severe allergic reaction," Taylor explained. "What can you tell us about the server?"

"It's all in my statement."

"I know, I read it. Your assistant hired her six days before the incident, and you never met her? What kind of background checks do you perform before letting a new server work such an important event? If any."

"I didn't send her application to the FBI, if that's what you mean. Plus, her references checked out. What do you expect for sixteen bucks an hour?"

"Is there anything else you can tell us?" Choi asked as he laid out five photographs taken by dinner guests showing the suspect in the background. She was overweight, with long blond hair and a fair complexion. "Whatever comes to mind, even if it doesn't seem important."

"No, not really." Englander swung his gaze back onto Taylor. "Okay, I never talked to Clarissa, or whatever her real name is. But I *can* confirm that's her. Listen guys, I'm not trying to be rude, but I'm way behind schedule, so if there's nothing else…"

***

Deputy District Attorney Cammie O'Mara felt as though she'd finally made it to the big leagues, and not for the first time; joining the Major Violators Unit was just one more milestone in a long series of significant accomplishments. But it hadn't been an easy road. At the moment, she and her new unit leader, DDA Bladet, were striding toward the Economic Crimes Division. Along the way, they passed the Misdemeanor Unit. Cammie poked her head in and waved to her former associates.

Like her boss, Lynn Peters, Cammie hadn't come from money; she could, however, claim an impressive legal lineage. Most of the men in her family had studied law, and some of the women too. Fortunately or unfortunately, the colossal failure of her father being a story in itself, Cammie had been forced to claw her way back up the economic ladder. As she and Bladet rode the elevator down to the sixth floor, she recalled the pain of working full time while earning straight As in school, with the added obstacle of sexism and discrimination at every turn. Eventually she'd been awarded a number of heavily contested scholarships, and this financial aid had led to her fast friendship with Lynn Peters. *Too fast*, Cammie joked darkly to herself with no smile whatsoever; that bond was all but broken.

The elevator doors glided open and Dea Bladet took the lead, bustling toward one of the doors up ahead. "You'll like him," the red-haired prosecutor said as she held it open. "Johnny Roche is a living legend."

"In our family we say *rahsh*, with the same long 'A' sound as in *John*," the attorney they'd come to see explained a few minutes later.

"It's French, right?" Cammie asked as she shook his hand. "I think it means 'rock.'"

"*C'est vrai*," he replied, nodding. "*Très bien.*"

"*Merci*," she returned, and he motioned for them to follow.

As they came into his little office and sat at his desk facing him, Bladet turned to Cammie. "Johnny and I go way back," she explained, then launched into the when, where, and how of that earlier association.

Cammie preferred to study the man for herself rather than endure Bladet's windy explanation. He was five foot ten or so, with thick sandy-blond hair, aquatic blue-green eyes, well dressed but not a dandy, trim, athletic looking—

"Mostly up in LA," were the words that finally shook Cammie out of her careful assessment, and they'd been spoken by the legend himself. "Southern Trust's offices down here are more like a satellite branch, secondary to the main operation. That's why only two of their executives were called to testify."

"And now you're at a dead end," quipped Bladet.

"It's an apt description," he conceded. "We'd just reached a non-prosecution agreement with Southern Trust in exchange for testimony against a corporation for which they were providing financial services, but now, with their employees and key witnesses out of the picture, there's no one left to prosecute. Not with what we have right now."

"Who was defending them?" Cammie asked.

Roche scowled. "Vincent Tyson. I just got off the phone with him."

Cammie felt a chill run down her spine. That name was familiar to her, of course, and well known throughout Southern California due to the regularity with which it was mentioned on the news and printed in the papers. She figured Roche had to be relieved about the mistrial, at least a little, since Tyson rarely lost a verdict.

"Well," said Bladet, "here's hoping something shakes loose here in San Diego and puts you back on track."

Roche nodded gratefully.

"And if you've got the time," she went on, "we're about to head over to intake to check for similar MOs."

"Sounds good," said Roche.

As Cammie and Bladet strode down the hall together, with Roche following closely behind, Bladet said, "Johnny used to work with me in the MVU, but we got into too much trouble together." She smirked. "And Lynn decided to separate us." Then she turned to Roche and asked, "How did she put it?"

"I believe Lynn's exact words were, 'The Major Violators Unit isn't supposed to be *made up* of major violators,'" Roche said, grinning sheepishly when Cammie looked back to show she was listening.

Cammie shot him a frown, then faced forward again and thought of Dom Taylor, wondering how he might be faring on his end of the investigation.

***

Having gleaned nothing useful from their interview with the catering manager, Taylor and Choi next headed for Southern Trust, walking there under the gentle sun of a spectacular winter's day—if "winter" were the right word for the time of year that spans from November to February in San Diego.

"Mike went downstairs for a smoke," the murdered witness's secretary told them with tears in her eyes. "He came back up all sweaty and dizzy, and five minutes later he...he was shaking on the floor like he was having a seizure or something. And by the time the ambulance got here, he was dead!" She began to cry. An uneasy silence followed, which Choi broke by grabbing a box of tissues and offering it to her.

The only person who'd come to work that day aside from the distraught secretary and the receptionist who'd greeted them on the way in was the office manager, who showed Taylor and Choi to the IT room. There, it took Choi little time to confirm that no security footage had been recorded for at least a week before the fatal incident. "How convenient," Choi muttered.

"Here's my card," said Taylor, giving it to the office manager. "I need you to put me in touch with whoever's in charge."

"I guess that'd be Vincent Tyson," she replied. "Our lawyer."

"Fine. Tell him to give me a call, if you would."

Once he and Choi had exited the building, Taylor checked his email, hoping to find a message from SDPD with information on any poisoner matching the facts of the case. And he did. A Major Wyans from Hawaii had seen the BOLO notice and responded with information about a suspect in a series of crimes committed ten years prior. Taylor thumbed in a quick reply before he and Choi headed back to the Interceptor and drove to a restaurant for lunch—sushi, which Taylor hated, but he'd lost the coin toss.

After the meal, on the way back to the DA's office, they were idling at a light on Fourth Avenue, at the top of the hill that leads back into the heart of downtown, when Taylor felt the gas pedal lock down and the Interceptor surge forward, accelerating at the vehicle's full capacity!

Taylor stomped on the brakes but they didn't work. His heart pounded frantically in his chest as he jerked the now resistant steering wheel left and right to avoid the cars ahead, and his black

SUV careened down the incline into the busiest part of the city like a roller coaster car in freefall.

Choi spun toward Taylor with wide, fearful eyes. "We've been hacked!" he said. "Someone's got remote control."

The speedometer read ninety-five as the Interceptor barreled through the A-Street intersection. Fortunately, the light was green. And by the time Taylor tried the door handle—to no avail—they were at a hundred and ten.

***

Way ahead of you, champ, thought a killer for hire, addressing Taylor in his mind. A smirk slowly curled his lips as he calculated the earnings he'd be raking in once his payment for the job began to compound with seven percent interest. Simultaneously, on his tablet, he was monitoring the signals transmitted by the OBD-II device he'd installed in Taylor's Interceptor while the investigator and his assistant had been busy with their meetings. Straddling a stationary motorcycle, this digital mercenary watched the black SUV from the bottom of the hill while entering commands intended to block whatever countermoves Sean Choi might think to make.

***

"The door handles are disabled!" Taylor shouted, still wrestling with the wheel.

Choi barely registered these words. Laser focused on his own tablet, the young analyst felt certain that an ill-intentioned programmer was relaying instructions to the Interceptor's CAN bus system through a secret backdoor. In response, he entered a series of commands that told his portable computing device to scan for wireless signals. With his eyes still on the screen, he barked, "Look down to your left! Do you see anything plugged in to the diagnostics port?"

"No," said Taylor, as the heavy vehicle roared on toward the next intersection, gathering speed with each meter traveled.

Damn. It's hidden inside the dashboard, Choi thought, searching his mind for a possible solution.

Thirty feet ahead, the light was red with several cars stopped at the line. With only ten feet to spare, Taylor wrenched the wheel to the right and bounced up onto the curb, speeding past a group of pedestrians to the right and to the left blowing by all those stopped cars, somehow also avoiding a collision with one of the vehicles driving crosswise. Now at a hundred and twenty, the Interceptor was screaming through the central part of the city, where a construction project had narrowed the street from three lanes to two.

Yes! Choi exclaimed mentally when he finally managed to connect to the Interceptor's onboard LTE system, but then Taylor crashed into a sturdy construction sign, one of those flashing arrows mounted on wheels, knocking that heavy piece of equipment into a chain-link fence.

"How we doin' buddy?" Taylor asked tensely. His jaw was set and his eyes single-focused on the road directly ahead.

"I need one minute."

"You've got twenty seconds."

They were the longest and the shortest twenty seconds of Sean Choi's life. His fingers flitted over the keypad in a blur as he attempted to override the CAN bus and kick out the bad hacker, but the system still wouldn't let him in. Then there came an ear-piercing metal-on-metal screeching sound as the Interceptor scraped roughly against something to the left, but Choi didn't dare look up to see what it was.

"Ten seconds," said Taylor.

Trust yourself, man, Choi thought. *No one's faster than you.* He sent one last command, and it did the trick. "Hit the brakes!" he shouted while trying the door handle to his right. The door came open.

As the massive rear end of a delivery truck came rushing into their field of view, Taylor did as he'd been told, and cranked the wheel ninety degrees, sending the Interceptor into a spin. He dove out just before impact, as did Choi, who protected the tablet as he slammed into the asphalt and rolled clear of the cars coming from behind.

"Stay here!" barked Taylor, heaving himself to his feet and sprinting after someone on a motorcycle. Meanwhile, Choi sat up to enter another series of commands, this time to disable the Interceptor's LTE system, thus cutting off the hacker's connection before he or she could erase the evidence of his or her intrusion. That done, Choi hustled over to the crash site to see if anyone was injured or needed help. With his heart thudding hard in his chest, he provided whatever assistance he could while hoping for his best friend's safe return.

3

PRO MALO

"That's odd," said Dea Bladet, pocketing her cellular phone. "Taylor's not picking up."

It was nearly time for her, Cammie, and Johnny Roche to call it a day. For hours they'd been poring over incoming police reports and recent cases filed, scanning for a match between those and the MOs employed in the San Diego Southern Trust murders, having found nothing thus far.

But as Cammie sat in a chair staring at a computer screen, her stony expression changed into one of guarded interest. Then it grew into a smile and her eyes came alive. "Check this out," she said to her colleagues, who left their monitors to peer over her shoulder. "Grimes Pharmacy is being charged with gross negligence in the death of one of its employees. The deceased's medication was incorrectly filled—she was given a high-dose barbiturate instead of a mild sedative."

"Have any of the employees been charged?" asked Roche.

"No. This is a corporate liability case, so they're just listed incidentally. The manager's name is Millie Haukea."

"Sounds Hawaiian," noted Bladet.

***

Ten years earlier, Millie Haukea had been lying on a bunk in a prison cell, attempting to quiet her anxious mind but with little success. She'd only recently begun to practice meditation there at the Oahu Community Correctional Center, where she was in pretrial detention for a series of murders to which she had already confessed. Not only that, but her DNA matched the genetic material found on the victims, so Millie was looking at life in prison without parole.

Her peace and quiet was intruded upon by the familiar sound of hard-toed duty boots clomping in her direction. Irritated, she opened her eyes and frowned at the sight of a broad-shouldered female correctional officer looking in at her from the other side of the bars.

"Get it together, Haukea," barked the guard. "You've got a visitor. Says he's your lawyer."

Soon Millie was in full restraints, shuffling toward an interview room where the guard sat her down before a handsome older man dressed in a silk-linen suit and tie, all black but for his white cotton shirt. His jaw was square, his shoulders broad, and with inscrutably dark eyes he regarded her with a strange air of appraisal. As the guard secured her wrists to a steel ring on the table, Millie met his gaze evenly, then curiously, since as far as she knew she'd been assigned a public defender, and this man was definitely not an attorney for the poor.

"Hello, Ms. Haukea. My name is Vincent Tyson," he said once they'd been left alone. "Victor Lager spoke highly of you."

At the mention of her former lover, who had leapt to his death to escape prosecution for his own crimes, Millie was swept away by a flood of strong emotions, relief being paramount among them.

"Assuming you agree," the lawyer went on, "I'll be taking your case pro bono. For free."

Over the following year, Tyson successfully argued that Millie's confession had been coerced, which made it inadmissible in court, then proceeded to discredit the forensic evidence by suggesting that her DNA had been mishandled and contaminated by police investigators, and he supported that claim with testimony given by a well-paid expert witness.

Early in this process, Millie began to wonder why Tyson was pouring so much time and effort into her defense, since, if billed at the normal hourly rate, his services would have cost her a fortune. Then, while in a confidential attorney-client conference in the same interview room as before, he provided some insight as to his motivation.

"We're only days away from a favorable verdict. I know it," he told her. "But that's not guaranteed. Suppose I make a terrible mistake in my closing argument. The jury could still convict you. And even if you walk, you'll never pass a background check unless I pull some strings. Listen, I represent many interests: from international corporations to private individuals—different kinds of clients, all with top-tier power and influence. In other words, there are people who can clear your name that owe me favors."

Now Millie understood. This wasn't pro bono. Pro *malo* was more like it. But shady transactions were nothing new to her; she'd grown accustomed to such arrangements. *So what does he want in return?*

"Besides my legal work," he proceeded with an ice-cold smile, "I also manage a team of sorts, one with an open spot that needs filling, and I think you'd be a perfect fit. With the right training, of course."

And so it was agreed. After an apparently impartial jury of Millie Haukea's peers found her not guilty on all counts, Tyson petitioned the court to seal the case records, arguing that her acquittal meant she was legally innocent, and that keeping them open would serve no public good. The ruling judge found in his favor, possibly influenced by a large deposit made into his offshore account.

A media blackout on the matter was also essential. Tyson bribed and pressured journalists to take down their articles, sued media outlets for defamation, thereby forcing them to remove their stories, and through a court order he suppressed any further news coverage, citing "privacy concerns."

The final brick in the wall had been to silence a few key witnesses through nondisclosure agreements and other means, while threatening legal action against the Honolulu Police and the Office of the Prosecuting Attorney for defamation, forcing those organizations to distance themselves from the case.

Now, ten years later, as Millie Haukea carefully tended to the plants in her garden, a wide range of natural products she'd been taught how to use, her thoughts revolved around her formal training in pharmaceutical science. She currently held a doctorate and worked as the manager at Grimes Pharmacy, where her co-worker had died by a one-in-a-million coincidence, and that unlikely turn of events would eventually set the stage for her second murder trial.

***

"Vincent Tyson is well known throughout the State of California for his impressive record as a high-profile defense attorney," said the Chancellor, "but he's found himself in a spot of trouble."

The stony circle of power brokers sitting around the conference table kept their eyes on the monitor as he called a second image to the screen.

"Let me explain. Tyson's second source of income is a team of trained assassins, each of whom is highly skilled in a single field. Meet Morgan, for instance, an expert in disguise and impersonation." *Click.* "And this is Asher, his technology specialist."

On the Chancellor went, introducing his co-conspirators to Kang, a master of martial arts dressed in black tactical gear, Voss, a shaven-headed man with a bushy black mustache whose abilities involved firearms and explosives, and Dane, a thick-chested, curly-haired killer who could stage any kind of accident or apparent suicide while leaving no unintended forensic evidence. "The last member of the team," the Chancellor continued, "is Millie Haukea. Our immediate problem is that Haukea was implicated in the death of one of her co-workers at her cover job. Not directly and not by her own doing, but it could certainly come back to haunt us." *Click.* "Secondly and much more serious is that a finance company in San Diego called Southern Trust was charged with a number of illegal activities last January, and most of these crimes were committed on behalf of one of our West Coast corporations. My concern was that several Southern Trust executives had agreed to testify against our corporation in exchange for immunity, so—"

"Just one question," said the Sovereign from the head of the table. "Who made the mistake of hiring Southern Trust?"

"I did," said the Chancellor. "But then I hired Tyson to silence the witnesses and provide legitimate legal services if need be. Unfortunately, there are still a few tricky issues that need to be resolved. This next slide shows—"

"We'll take care of it," the Sovereign cut in, flitting her eyes toward the guards at the door. They flew at the Chancellor, injected him with a sedative, and dragged him out of the room.

With this object lesson on the price of failure, the Sovereign declared the meeting adjourned, but not before reminding her associates that each of them would now be receiving a higher share of the profits. As they filed out of the boardroom with no handshakes or parting words, she rose from her seat and stepped to the window for another refreshing glimpse of the inhospitable wilderness outside.

4

CRIMINAL DEFENSE

Despite the speed at which Dom Taylor's big legs powered him through the downtown streets, the suspect on the motorcycle left him behind. Cursing bitterly, Taylor slowed to a walk, then stopped to put his hands on his knees and catch his breath. Banged up, bleeding, and dizzy after the ordeal of the runaway Interceptor, he saw no way to continue the pursuit, so his adrenaline-fueled energy began to wane.

But when a motorcyclist came grumbling up on a Harley, Taylor saw an opportunity. Stepping into the street to flash his badge, he said, "DA's office! I need to borrow your bike."

"But I'm out on my Thursday ride," the motorist complained.

"I'll bring 'er back," Taylor assured him.

So with a twist of the throttle Taylor blasted off, thinking the suspicious rider could very well be the hacker who had tried to murder him and Choi. With no bulky sides of the SUV to steer clear of cars and pedestrians, he flitted in and out of traffic easily as the warm air rushed past his body. Before long, he caught sight of the suspect about a hundred yards up ahead. The man's ride had no license plates and looked like a slower model, and the rider was looking down at a screen mounted to his handlebars as he zipped through a green-lit intersection. It had to be the hacker!

Taylor rolled the throttle back to give his bike more fuel, and the heavy machine leapt forward like a racehorse nudged with cowboy spurs. He had almost reached the light when green turned to red with no intervening yellow, and a wall of cars drove forward to block his path. The hacker glanced back once, then raced away, much to Taylor's disappointment.

***

That evening, after having his Interceptor towed to Guardian Fleet Services, Taylor was sitting glumly in the auto shop's reception area when Choi came in through the door with a box of parts tucked under his arm. Not through the front doors, but via the mechanics' entrance to the garage. "The OBD-II port was tapped," said Choi. "But I pulled every control module and data logger just in case—engine, telematics, security, the MDT interface, all of it."

Taylor rose to offer a grateful hand. "You saved my life, brother. Again."

"I'm still in your debt and you know it," Choi replied, catching Taylor's gaze meaningfully as they shook. "Are you okay here? I'd like to get started on this right away."

Two cups of coffee later, someone else arrived to shake Taylor out of his melancholy, this time through the front doors. It was Chief Deputy Lynn Peters, with whom he'd only exchanged a few work-related words since they'd broken up.

"Heard you had a hell of a day," she said, looking great as always. Yet her tailored blue sport coat and simple black blouse showed a focus on substance over style. The same was true for her lustrous golden hair, which she'd had cut since he'd seen her last. Taylor reckoned this new look would save her fifteen minutes in the morning.

"Please don't get up," she said, dropping into the seat beside him. She ran a clinical gaze over his scrapes, bruises, and the egg-sized lump on his head. "You should have gone to the hospital."

"Too much work to do," he said, looking away. Then he placed his elbows on his knees, hung his head, and studied his shoes as the sounds of the city filtered in through the front doors. A young group of people strode by, trading lively remarks. Apparently headed for some exciting destination. Then came the sharp hissing of air brakes on a bus. Next there was nothing at all but the feeling of being watched.

"Can we talk?" she asked softly.

He didn't look up.

"I know you think I'm mad about Cammie, but I'm not. Well, not anymore."

I loved you.

"This is all my fault, and I want to make things right, if I can."

Taylor finally turned to meet her imploring blue eyes. She needed to explain. So he listened, with every bit of empathy he could muster as she delved into her past and all the reasons why. It was enlightening, he had to admit, but when she came to the part about David Goode and how hard she'd fallen and still pushed him away, Taylor's interest dropped off a cliff.

"And I did the same thing to you," she said in conclusion, full of regret.

Of course Taylor forgave her; deep down he'd always known they weren't a good match, she with that all-consuming drive and he with a deeply rooted need for affection. Which led him to reconsider his budding relationship with Cammie, yet another ambitious professional. And fifteen years his junior.

Thus ended the whirlwind romance of Lynn Peters and Dom Taylor, although their professional dealings would continue for some time, and they'd always be friends.

"I've got good news," she told him suddenly, patting his hand. Then she stood to pull a file folder out of her bag. "I just got out of a meeting with DA Sellers, who's authorized us to retrofit the Interceptor with any modifications needed to keep you and Choi safe and put these crooks away."

That *was* good news. Taylor even cracked a smile for a change.

***

The digital mercenary known only as Asher sped north along the coast as the sun drifted down to the horizon on his left, still burning hot, sparkling in reflection on the vast blue surface of the sea. While discouraged by his failure to send Taylor and Choi to an early grave, he did feel proud of having intercepted the streetlight's signals and spoofed the commands, all while operating his motorcycle, and since he'd left a surprise for Sean Choi in the Interceptor's electronics, the mission hadn't been a total disaster.

At Solana Beach he veered right onto the exit ramp, leaned into a left turn to motor over the freeway, dropped down into a sprawling seaside community, and wound his way to a gated checkpoint. There Asher waved to the guards, who let him pass, then rolled onward through wide and perfect roads to a stately beachfront home.

"Well," said his boss's gigantic butler as he swung open the door. "Judging by your expression, I assume you failed miserably. Just as I expected."

"Shut up, Igmar," said Asher, striding past the grinning blond monster and out to the terrace, where Tyson was eating his supper by the pool. The sun had set by then, so the back yard was lit up artificially. This made it hard to see—but not to hear—the waves crashing rhythmically on the beach below.

"Steak?" Tyson asked, gesturing toward an empty seat at the table.

"No," Asher replied, dropping into the offered chair. "I can't eat."

Tyson nodded, then took a morsel with his fork and popped it into his mouth.

"I'll get 'em," Asher promised. "Tomorrow. But I'll need Morgan's and Millie's help to do it."

"Done. Now what's this about *more* bad news?"

"Taylor has an email in his inbox from Major Wyans of the Honolulu Police."

Tyson slowly set his silverware down. "Is that right."

"And Wyans attached Haukea's file to the message."

"In violation of his nondisclosure agreement," Tyson added, wiping his mouth with a linen napkin. "Has Taylor opened it yet?"

"No."

"Can you show me the file?"

Asher powered on his tablet. Once Tyson had seen enough, the two men plotted a suitable consequence for Wyans and also a strategy to either recover the file before Taylor could open it or put anyone who'd already done so to death.

***

The next morning, Dom Taylor's cell phone rang, dragging him out of a bad night's sleep. It was early, two hours before he was due to arrive at the office. Looking around his bedroom, he satisfied himself that the area was secure, then let go of his pistol under the pillow to take the call.

"I traced the hacker's tablet to a condo in Mission Bay," Sean Choi blurted out with no preliminaries, "and it's active as we speak. I just sent you the location. Should I meet you there?"

"No, I'll call SDPD for backup."

Ten minutes later, Taylor was parked one block away from the target location and growing increasingly concerned that the suspect who'd made a fool of him the day before might bolt out the back door before SDPD finally got their asses in gear. *I'll just take a look*, he decided, shutting his car door softly and walking toward the condo in question as if he were simply out for a morning stroll.

The sun was just starting to peek over the eastern hills, and with only a few birds flapping in the pink cloudy sky and no people around, he was able to listen for noise coming from the target residence. There was none. And as he passed, he peered through the windows, seeing nothing out of the ordinary and no one at home. Thus, still furious that the hacker had tried to kill him and his closest friend, he stormed up to the front door and rapped his knuckles on it. "District Attorney's—"

That final syllable never came out, as it was choked back by a storm of fire that ripped the door from its hinges and hurled Taylor's body into a wall across the street.

***

While Taylor was driving to Mission Bay to see about the suspect, Choi finished reinforcing the security of the Interceptor's control modules, then drove over to Guardian to reinstall them. He was so enthused about the modifications being made to the Interceptor that he found himself whistling on the way back to the Hall of Justice, which is the building that houses the DA's office, among other organizations, all generally related to law enforcement and the justice system. The pursuit-rated SUV would now be able to reach a much higher top speed—despite the weight of its new armor plating—and its glass windows were being replaced with level-eight bullet-resistant polycarbonate, in addition to a few other surprises for anyone with malicious intent.

Before leaving the garage, Choi had placed a call to Taylor to see how he was progressing, whether he needed any assistance, and also to share the happy news. But Taylor hadn't answered, so now, as Choi strode into their office to see Taylor's desk still vacant and the coffee pot still full, he was hit by an icy sense of dread. *It was too easy*, he realized. *The hacker wanted me to find him!*

He pounded a cup of coffee, ran back to his car, squealed out of the parking garage with the gas pedal down, and called Taylor the whole way there. *Practically* the whole way there, to be precise; as Choi neared his destination, his mouth went numb, and then his arms and legs. Worse yet, he felt as if his throat and stomach were being consumed by fire. And as he braked to a jerky stop near an actual blaze, he vomited all over his lap and the car's interior.

Unbearably dizzy, Choi staggered past firefighters and police officers toward a team of EMTs treating Taylor, who appeared to be horribly injured. "Help!" Choi called out, but his strangled voice couldn't be heard. By then he was sweating profusely, with an alarmingly fast heart rate and the most terrible pain he'd ever had in his bowels. He dropped to his hands and knees. "Help," he croaked once more, and then he fell unconscious.

***

Sitting close to her colleagues in the hospital waiting area, Lynn Peters hung her head, and the red-haired Dea Bladet put an arm around Cammie O'Mara. "It could have been a lot worse," Bladet whispered.

"I know," said Cammie miserably.

According to a doctor who had just come out to speak with them, if Choi had been treated any later, he'd have died for sure, and Taylor's injuries would have killed a weaker man. As it was, the latter was still in a coma with many bones to be reset and a variety of other surgeries to undergo.

"We broke up last night," Cammie said, brushing her black bangs aside.

Bladet nodded slowly, encouragingly.

"I think we did, anyway. I was hoping we could work it out, but—"

That was far as Cammie got before a sob swelled up and burst out from between her lips. The grief was overwhelming. Bladet pulled her close and rocked her like a mother as she wept.

Later, with visitation still impossible, the trio headed for the cafeteria, ordered tea, and settled around a table. They spoke in soft tones about recovery times, prognoses, and possible outcomes, but when Cammie and Lynn connected on the topic of their separate relationships with Taylor, Bladet rose and left them to it.

"I owe you an apology," Cammie began. An uncomfortable silence ensued as she wondered how to keep from losing a friend. A *good* friend, and it wouldn't be the first time. Ultimately, she knew, there was nothing to say; the facts were clear enough.

"No you don't. Dom and I had already broken up," said the blonde chief prosecutor, catching Cammie's eye. "Hadn't we?"

After a second uneasy pause Cammie said, "Well...more or less."

"I know. I saw you flirting when we were still together, and that's what got me so upset. But the truth is, he and I had been having trouble for a long time."

"I know. And for what it's worth, he and I are done. At least I think we are."

Then came the longest silence of all, as they both drew a conclusion that neither one could bring herself to say out loud: *You are definitely done if he doesn't wake up.*

"I don't know how to tell you...how terrible I feel," Cammie stammered, on the verge of tears again. "After all you've done for me."

"Oh, honey. You earned *that* on your own." Peters scooted back her chair and stood, reaching out her arms, wrapping them around her friend in a long, loving embrace.

Once they'd sat back down to face each other, Cammie made an attempt at humor. "I guess I forgot the golden rule."

"What's that?"

"Chicks before dicks."

This caused a badly needed round of giggles.

"Seriously," Cammie went on, wiping mixed emotions from her cheeks, "I'll never let you down again."

"I know. It's okay, really. I'm not the easiest person to work with, either."

As they reached for each other's hands and traded weak smiles, Dea Bladet strode back into the cafeteria. "Happy to see you two are getting along," she said, "'cause we've got work to do."

5

A CREEPING SUSPICION

The night before the explosion that sent Dom Taylor to the hospital, Vincent Tyson had put down his knife and fork, pausing to savor his meal: a large, juicy rib-eye cooked medium-rare, exactly how he'd always preferred it. He leaned back in his chair to listen to the waves sloshing repeatedly below him, and reveled in the fresh salty breeze. Then, declaring himself satisfied, he pushed his half-eaten plate away.

He wasn't angry over Asher's failure to stop Taylor and Choi from digging into the Southern Trust matter. To the contrary, Tyson was grateful for the digital mercenary's broad array of skills. With a deep drink of an old Cabernet, he concluded that one of the keys to his long-standing dominance was humility. The ability to admit where his operations were weak and not being too proud to enlist the assistance of people who were stronger, faster, or more specialized in a certain area than he was. Take Igmar, for instance, the first of these recruits. Tyson had adopted him out of foster care when Igmar was just a boy, then brought him to the United States and raised him more or less as if Igmar had been his actual offspring. Now, as a result, Tyson could count on the hulking blond to defend him. To care for him in case of illness. And this rescue had been effected with exactly that goal in mind, when such protection hadn't been remotely necessary. *Humility and foresight then,* Tyson corrected himself, nodding appreciatively to that same faithful attendant, who topped up his glass of wine.

"Not hungry tonight, sir?" Igmar asked, lifting the plate from the table.

"I thought you might like to have it," said Tyson kindly.

Igmar nodded and took it away.

Asher had just left the premises, having helped Tyson map out a response to the latest developments in his affairs. It was a solid plan, Tyson thought, despite the inherent risk, which he'd minimized by contracting the best in the business: Voss, the firearms and demolitions expert who at the moment was laying an explosive trap for Choi and Taylor. And Morgan, the master of disguise and impersonation whose skills had proven more useful than those of any other member of the team. Recently, though, Morgan's work had been inconsistent, which Tyson made a mental note to check on.

He glanced at his watch. Speaking of Morgan, in five hours the man would be leading Millie Haukea and Asher into the Hall of Justice on a critical mission that would either fortify Tyson's position or cause it to become even more precarious than it already was. *Well,* Tyson told himself, swallowing the last of his wine, *when you've done all you can, all you can do is try to relax.* So that's what he did: Tyson rose from his chair and strode inside to relax, with Kang, the martial artist, whose acrobatics were a major factor in her deadly set of skills, and also in his decision to ask her to move in with him.

***

Later that night, or early the next day, mere hours before Choi would nearly die due to some type of poison, Millie Haukea took note of her pulse. It was slow and steady. But if she hadn't extracted several key alkaloids into a tincture and applied a few drops under her tongue before stepping into the Hall of Justice, her anxiety might very well have pushed her heart rate up to dangerous levels.

As she and her comrades neared the elevator, her on-again, off-again boyfriend, Morgan (a significant source of that anxiety), inserted a cloned keycard into a slot on the wall. Like her and Asher, he was wearing the uniform of an IT technician.

Morgan gave Millie a self-sure wink as the three of them entered the lift and turned around to face the doors. At the security station they'd just passed, the guards had actually spoken with him as though they'd known him well, as his bearing, body shape, eye color, voice, and facial features exactly matched those of the regular on-call IT supervisor. It was a science, Millie knew, of which her grasp was elementary, but better than that of the others. Particularly better than that of the real IT specialist standing to her left. Asher had never been able to change his voice without sounding ridiculous, and his body awareness was nonexistent. Fortunately, the digital mercenary was playing a role he didn't need to fake.

Supposedly in response to an urgent cybersecurity threat, they rode up to the thirteenth floor in silence. Millie glanced up at Morgan, who was tall and strong, confident again after months of ups and downs. *It's about time*, she thought.

When the doors slid open, they marched along the hallway to a heavy door where the keycard did its job again. Once inside, they navigated to the target suite, where they followed certain routes and held specific positions for the security cameras to record before Asher put that footage on a loop. As she performed this well-rehearsed routine, Millie recalled how Morgan's recent instability had nearly led to disaster. *And it still could,* she feared.

The first job had gone without a hitch. Morgan had helped her design the fat suit and gotten her fake ID, and Millie had done the rest—purchased a blond wig, lightened her skin, prepared and brought to the Convention Center a bottle of tasteless powder, which, mixed into the steak tartare she delivered to table twelve, proved fatal to the target, one of the two Southern Trust executives they'd been hired to kill.

For the next job, she'd done some of her best work ever, doctoring a pack of cigarettes so that only a puff or two would silence the second witness, but Morgan had made two boneheaded mistakes: First, when he'd shown up in disguise to scout out Southern Trust, he'd taken too long and ventured into areas he shouldn't have, forcing Asher to find a way to delete the camera footage. To Morgan's credit, in that incursion he *had* managed to learn which brand of cigarettes Michael Schmidt preferred.

Later, when Morgan had pulled up to Southern Trust in a van, posing as a deliveryman who needed Schmidt's signature before he could unload the cargo, his appearance had been too similar to the first disguise. He *did* pull off a tricky bit of sleight-of-hand after asking Schmidt for a cigarette, by switching out the packs, but when Morgan had gone upstairs to lure Schmidt outside, he'd spoken to the same receptionist as before, leaving a loose end that could potentially result in disaster.

With the camera feed now on a loop, Millie sprang into action, taking a bag of powder made from wolfsbane root out of her toolbox. To her surprise, the coffee maker in Taylor's and Choi's office had already been loaded and set on a timer, so all she had to do was mix it into the grounds. It was too easy. That done, she and Morgan watched as Asher finished his work: deleting some computer files from Taylor's computer, copying others, then disappearing into the server room to cover his tracks. As she stood there beside him, Millie wanted to believe that the old Morgan was back for good, but she had a creeping suspicion that his drug addiction might come back to haunt him—and her—in the end.

***

"I'm glad you finally agreed to come out of your cave," said Dea Bladet two days later, standing second in line to order lunch at a busy deli downtown.

Third in line and still upset by Taylor's unchanged condition, Cammie O'Mara tore her gaze away from the floor. "Thanks for inviting me," she replied.

Bladet smiled as she readied her wallet.

Now it was Johnny Roche who stood third in line since Bladet was up at the counter; he'd insisted on joining them. "How's Taylor doing?" he asked.

"Still in a coma," Cammie replied dejectedly. "The neurologist said he might never come out of it." At that, her eyes clouded over with tears.

Roche took a step closer, as if he'd wanted to put a hand on her shoulder but didn't know her well enough to complete the gesture.

Finished with her business at the counter, Bladet did reach out with a comforting touch. Then she said softly, "I already paid. Let's grab a seat."

As they moved through the crowded eatery, Bladet turned to Roche. "I appreciate you coming, even though nothing's gonna happen."

"I agree it's unlikely," Roche said, nodding at an empty table. "I just feel better this way."

Cammie and Roche chose their spots, making easy conversation, while Bladet paused to watch them very closely. Then she dropped into a chair as well.

"What about Choi?" asked Roche, once they'd gotten their food. "He's okay, isn't he?"

"Yes," said both women in unison, but the younger deferred to the senior.

"He's stable now," Bladet explained. "Should be back to work this week."

After they'd finished their meal, they crumpled up their wrappers, tossed them into the hole over the trash bin, filed out through the door, and marched six blocks under the "winter" sun of San Diego to Grimes Pharmacy.

A bell over the door jingled to announce their arrival and a jaded-looking cashier directed them to the pickup counter at the rear. There stood Dr. Millie Haukea, the head pharmacist, waiting with a delighted smile. Cammie reckoned she was about her own age. Fairly tall, maybe five foot nine. Remarkably pretty. Unfortunately, with that strong, athletic body and brown skin and hair, the pharmacist bore no resemblance to the suspect caught on camera at the Convention Center, nor did she have any criminal record according to the reports received from law enforcement.

"How can I help you folks?" asked Dr. Haukea, whose quick amber eyes studied the three of them.

Bladet flashed her ID card. "We're from the district attorney's office. Just want to ask you a few questions, if you don't mind."

"Of course not," Dr. Haukea said, still smiling.

"What can you tell us about the death of Connie Riker?"

"It was an accident. The manufacturer supplied us with an incorrectly labeled product. The tablets closely resembled the actual medication, so they passed our verification checks."

Bladet nodded. "A high-dose barbiturate instead of a mild sedative."

"That's right."

Cammie had an idea. She glanced at Bladet, who gave her the go-ahead. "You had to go down to the police station and give a statement, right?"

"Yes, I did," said Haukea, whose cheerfulness began to wane.

"Did you invoke counsel? I mean did you have an attorney with you at the time?"

Coldly now, Haukea replied, "Ms. O'Mara, wasn't it? I was out of town when that prescription was filled, and all of our employees were discharged of any liability."

Cammie met the woman's gaze evenly. "It just struck me as odd that there was no name given in the police report, but if it were *my* career in jeopardy, I would definitely have hired a lawyer—and I *am* one."

"All right. I have nothing to hide. So yes, I did *invoke counsel*."

"Do you mind giving us the name?" asked Bladet.

"Vincent Tyson."

The three attorneys stared at her with the same incredulous look.

"He's an old family friend."

6

LEGENDS

Southern Trust was the next stop on the train comprising Cammie, Roche, and Bladet, who walked there with renewed vigor after learning that Millie Haukea was connected to that finance company through Vincent Tyson.

"Taylor and Choi were here last Thursday," Bladet said as they stepped into the building, with Roche holding the door. Then, before speaking again, she paused to give Cammie a look. "I think you know this already, but on their way back, Taylor lost control of his SUV. And *that* was the day before—" Bladet's voice trailed off.

"It's okay," said Cammie. "You can say it. That was the day before the explosion."

"Right," said Bladet, stopping at the elevator. "Interestingly, Taylor told the office manager to have Tyson give him a call, but that never happened."

"Interestingly but not surprisingly," said Roche, hitting the button for floor three. As the doors slid closed, he blew out a breath. "I know that guy, and I can't say I care for him."

"Who, Tyson or the office manager?" asked Cammie on the way up.

"Both. As the lead prosecutor on the financial case, I've run into them several times. That was before the judge ordered a mistrial. But I meant Tyson."

"What do you think of Tyson professionally?" asked Bladet.

The doors glided open and Roche stepped out first. "He's a hell of a trial lawyer. Hard to track down, though. Maybe *this* guy can tell us how." Pointing with his solid jaw, Roche had indicated the receptionist, an overdressed individual ten years his junior.

"Jonathan Lee," said the young man as he shook Cammie's hand. "Good to see you again, Mr. Roche."

"Likewise, Mr. Lee."

"I'm not sure what I can do for you, though. As you can see, no one's here."

Cammie glanced around at empty offices. They were completely vacant, as in no desks, no chairs, and nothing on the walls but nail holes. This, she concluded, was a fly-by-night operation if there'd ever been one.

Roche said, "We were hoping to run into Vincent Tyson. He's not answering our calls."

"Oh, he does the same thing to me. Just keep trying."

Roche ran his gaze over the same deserted scene as Cammie had. "Looks like you've closed up shop."

The office manager nodded. "Yeah, I'm just here to take delivery of a few packages and answer the phone for a week or so. Then it's off to Bali."

"That sounds lovely," said Bladet dryly, tossing her long and curly red hair. "Can we ask you a few questions?"

Lee's enthusiasm fell flat. "Sure," he groaned.

"Did you have any visitors around the time of Michael Schmidt's death?"

"Not that I recall."

"Did you know, Mr. Lee," Roche inquired, "that if we put you on the stand and you say something false or misleading, you could spend up to four years in state prison?"

Lee pursed his lips thoughtfully and then shook his head. "No visitors. It was business as usual, just normal service providers and deliverymen."

"I see," said Roche, whose gaze was unwavering, the threat of incarceration still clearly implied.

Lee cleared his throat uncomfortably. "You know, I didn't think of this before, but there *was* this maintenance technician who came in about a week before Mr. Schmidt died. The guy took so long working on the AC that I had to go back to check on him. Found him wandering around like he was drunk or high."

"And there's no security footage from that day?" Cammie asked Bladet, who shook her head no.

"Mr. Lee," Roche pressed, "is there anything else you'd like to tell us?"

Lee flitted his nervous gaze from Roche to Bladet to Cammie and back again, saying nothing. Then he finally cracked. "Okay. On the day of Schmidt's death, a deliveryman came in asking for a signature. I said it was my job to receive things, hence the word reception, you know?"

No one found that funny.

"But he insisted that Mr. Schmidt had to come down to the street and sign. And boy did he look like the maintenance worker who'd come in the week before; they could have been brothers."

"You didn't 'think of this' before?" Bladet parroted angrily.

"My manager strongly suggested we keep any irrelevant details to ourselves."

"How strongly?" Bladet said sharply.

Once more Lee hesitated, so Roche gave him another look of warning.

Now totally defeated, Lee frowned resignedly and let his shoulders slump. "He said we'd all get a month's vacation if everything went smoothly with the trial."

"Let's get you down to SDPD to meet with a forensic artist," said Roche, putting his hand on Lee's shoulder as they all strode toward the door. "It's either that or a totally different kind of vacation."

***

Johnny Roche drove home after work, where he ate a typically efficient bachelor's dinner of reheated leftovers. Then he pulled the dusty cover off his Honda 650, hit the ignition, and smiled at the bike's throaty purr.

It would be a sorely needed outing, since neither man nor motorcycle had gone out on the town in what seemed like a lifetime, but back in Johnny Roche's heyday—all through law school and several years thereafter—he had achieved legendary status among the college bar crowd as the luckiest man alive.

But it wasn't luck, he rued as he rolled down his driveway and onto the street, hitting the throttle and roaring away. *Just a bunch of broken promises and wasted time. And what have I got to show for it now? An empty house with no one to come home to. Not even a dog.*

He and his old two-wheeled friend rumbled through Ocean Beach, or OB, the seaside community in which he lived, and when he came to the freeway, he thought of heading over to one of his old haunts—just for old times' sake—but instead he steered toward downtown.

Before long he'd set up camp at a corner table in a lounge with dim lighting and dark leather furniture. Having ordered a drink, he pulled out his phone, found a text message, and thumbed in a cautious reply. Then, when his cold vodka martini was delivered and after a magnificently refreshing sip of it, he turned his mind to Vincent Tyson, whom he considered a proper legend, despite the man's bad reputation. At the time, Roche had been relieved at the occurrence of a mistrial because it meant he wouldn't have to face Tyson in court. But now, after another delicious pull of that icy liquor, he concluded that such a showdown might be both inevitable and the right thing to do. *After all,* he thought, *whatever doesn't kill me can only make me stronger.* Then again, the Southern Trust case had already involved quite a lot of killing, and he was beginning to suspect that matters were only going to get worse.

*****

How in the <u>hell</u> can it be that if a man walks into a bar and comes out with a sexy undergrad hanging on both of his shoulders, he's considered a legend; and yet, fumed Dea Bladet while brushing her hair in the mirror, *if a woman does the same thing, suddenly she's—how did someone put it?—known for her passion for justice, among other pursuits?!*

It's not that Johnny Roche was a bad guy—far from it. It was the general lack of respect shown to women that had always irked her. Snatching up her purse and keys, and with one last look at her reflection (*I've still got it!*), she wondered how her encounter with Roche would turn out. It would be the first time in years that they'd met after hours without the express intention to commit a major violation, as they'd often said in jest.

While riding in the Uber that took her downtown, Bladet felt proud of herself for turning her life around, and she knew Johnny felt the same way about his own transformation. Which is not to say she wasn't tempted when she saw him there in the corner and looked into those blue-green eyes of his. Discipline prevailed, however, as he stood to greet her with a handshake and she took a seat with a friendly air.

"Roche. John Roche. Shaken not *shturred*," she intoned in her best attempt at Sean Connery's voice. "Is that a Vesper?"

"No, just vodka with a drop of vermouth. What can I get you?"

For Dea Bladet it was soda water with plenty of ice, for which she insisted on paying, and over which they delved into one of the most perplexing aspects of the case at hand.

"You handled yourself well at the pharmacy," he told her.

"Cammie did too," she returned.

"So do you think Haukea did it?"

He had great hair. Sandy blond, cut shorter than before. Bladet's nostalgia carried her back to one time when she'd run her fingers through it after they'd just—

"Are you with me? I asked if you thought she did it."

"Did what? Killed her co-worker? She was out of town."

"There's always a way." Roche signaled for the same again. "One thing seems clear, though. She's an expert in poisons—"

"Pharmacology."

"Okay. In pharmacology," Roche conceded, "and in medicinal chemistry, toxicology, and drug formulation. I looked it up. Either way, if someone like that is connected to the Southern Trust poisonings through Vincent Tyson, she definitely warrants further investigation."

"I agree. So how did you and Mr. Lee do at SDPD?"

"Fine. We got the sketch done, then converted it to a synthetic photograph using AI."

"Cool!" she said. "I've heard about that. So now they can run it through facial recognition."

"Exshactly," was Roche's own impression of the famous actor. As he lifted his glass in a toast to her, Bladet wondered if he might be a little drunk. She got her answer later, down on the street by his bike.

"Looks like we're gonna be working together again," he observed. "We always *did* make a great team."

"Yes, we did," she said. *And here it comes.*

"Sure you don't want to go for a ride?" He grinned. "A major breakthrough might emerge if we take this back to Ocean Beach."

"No, I'm good. And so are *you*," she reminded him. "See you bright and early."

7

WITCHES' BREW

"Gotcha!" said Sean Choi to the hacker he saw on a computer screen while sitting in a hospital bed. The room was dark, so his laptop's backlighting danced in his eyes as he grinned. He'd caught on camera the crook responsible for his best friend's present condition—which, Choi thought with violence on his mind, might very well turn out to be permanent. Also appearing in the video footage was the poisoner who'd spiked his and Taylor's coffee and a third suspect Choi had yet to identify. The woman had somehow managed to keep her face away from his backup camera, and the third guy looked just like the actual IT supervisor, but Choi figured he was much more likely to be a criminal in disguise. It wouldn't take long to find out.

He only wished he had installed a motion detector in his backup system. If he had, he would have been alerted to the break-in earlier and thus wouldn't have drunk that witch's brew. Another serious problem was the likelihood that Asher had copied the contents of Taylor's hard disk. If used for malicious purposes, that information could do a great deal of damage.

One source of consolation, however, was that the data in the server room, the most sensitive of all, could not have been compromised. Of that Choi was sure, since the entire twenty minutes the intruders had spent in the office wouldn't have been sufficient to breach the cyber defenses that he himself had installed.

At any rate, he was beyond glad to have identified the hacker known only as Asher. When he'd seen the guy inadvertently turning to face the hidden camera, with that straight brown hair cut like an upside-down bowl and clean shaven underneath, with his thin, deathly pale face, and those hard brown eyes, it brought Choi back to their younger days. The two digital whiz kids had first butted heads at the DEF CON hacking competition, and crossed paths in cyberspace several times since then. Unfortunately, DEF CON wouldn't be able to supply Asher's real name, not even under subpoena, because they didn't collect that kind of information.

He kicked off his covers to start unplugging hardware and winding up cords. Only minutes from being discharged from Scripps Mercy Hospital, Choi would be heading straight to work, but not before visiting the neuroICU to see his buddy.

When he saw Taylor stretched out in bed, totally unresponsive as though he were a corpse, with a tube down his throat pushing air in and letting it out with a rhythmic hissing sound, Choi's eyes clouded over with stinging tears. He wished he could go back in time to the day of the explosion, that he hadn't taken "no" for an answer, that he'd insisted on riding along. Then he could have scanned the condo for suspicious signals. Was it fear that had prevented him from doing so? Laziness? It didn't matter. *Should've, could've, would've,* Taylor would say, if he hadn't been lying there helpless.

Choi hung his head and wept. Sobbing, with tears streaming down his cheeks, he would have given anything to hop into the new and improved Interceptor with the man who'd shown him how to be a man and chase the crooks. That was his favorite thing in the world to do, and now he might never have that chance again. Worst of all, it was his fault!

He wiped his eyes with his sleeve and walked closer to the bed; with each step his heart broke a little more. Placing his hand on Taylor's shoulder, he said, "I'll get 'em Dom. You can count on me."

***

An hour later, Choi strode into the Hall of Justice with renewed determination, meeting Dea Bladet and Cammie O'Mara in his office suite by prearrangement.

"In a *limited* capacity, Sean," Cammie said as soon as she laid eyes on him. "Do doctor's orders mean nothing to you?"

"Are you sure your name's not Cammie O'Mother?" he replied as he fell into his chair and woke up his computer by moving the mouse. "Wait till you see this."

Shaking their heads and trading smiles, Bladet and Cammie stood behind his shoulders to watch. But before he pressed play, Choi pointed to the corner of the room. "See that potted plant over there? A couple days ago I put a pinhole camera in it with separate storage and power buried in the soil." Then he proceeded to show them the footage captured on the night of the intrusion and provided narration, explaining certain details such as his knowing Asher.

Bladet asked, "What was he doing on Dom's computer?"

"I'm not sure," said Choi. "There's no way to tell."

The recording showed the female intruder tampering with the coffee grounds, but her face could never be seen. When she'd finished with that act of sabotage, she joined the larger of the two male suspects while Asher hurried offscreen to the server room.

"How did she know where your camera was?" Cammie asked.

"She didn't," said Choi, keeping his eyes on the screen. "Otherwise they would have disabled it. She just got lucky."

"What about the bigger guy?" asked Bladet. She was so close Choi could smell her perfume.

"Impossible to identify since he's wearing a disguise. Unlike Asher," Choi scoffed. "So bright and yet so dim. But I just sent this recording to SDPD, so hopefully they'll be able to do something with it."

"It's possible," came Roche's voice from behind them, and they turned in his direction. "He looks a little like the service provider who came to Southern Trust twice. You know, the guy Jonathan Lee described to the forensic sketch artist? Even in disguise, SDPD might still be able to confirm the match."

"So the police used AI to turn the sketch into a photograph," Choi concluded. "Then they'll use multimodal identification to process it. But that technology's new enough that it might be thrown out in court." Then his discouraged expression brightened. "Hang on." Choi's fingers flew over the keys, entering commands with blazing agility.

Bladet, Roche, and Cammie watched over Choi's shoulder as he searched for and found video footage from police traffic cams, Petco Park's security system, and a bank ATM captured just minutes before Michael Schmidt died, all showing the outside of the Southern Trust building from a slightly different angle. Spellbound, the foursome watched a van pull up to the curb and its driver get out, enter the building, and return with Schmidt, who popped his head into the delivery van and then signed something on a clipboard handed him by the delivery driver, whose size didn't rule him out as the intruder at the Hall of Justice.

The driver said something to Schmidt, who reached into his coat for a pack of cigarettes. Meanwhile, the driver subtly produced a second pack and swapped it for the other in a practiced display of misdirection and manual dexterity. The two men lit up and laughed about something, and a few puffs later Schmidt suffered a coughing fit and hurried back into the Southern Trust building.

"This is incredible, Sean," said Cammie, straightening now along with her colleagues. "But since you got it by hacking into private systems, it can't be used as evidence."

Choi nodded. "You're right. But this was just to see if the footage existed somewhere. Now we can call SDPD and ask them to pull the traffic cam feeds."

"Just in case they find something," Roche said wryly.

"Exactly." Choi smiled. "And we can issue emergency subpoenas to the bank and the stadium owners. That'll be enough for a warrant. Now, the real problem is—"

Choi spun his swivel chair to explain the final piece of the puzzle, but no one was standing behind him. Chuckling, he turned back to the monitors and got to work, just as his colleagues had already done.

***

One last plant sailed through the air and landed atop what had become a tall pile of uprooted growth forms—castor bean, henbane, wolfsbane, mandrake, belladonna, tobacco, and several others. Dr. Millie Haukea felt deeply indignant, as it had taken her an entire year to cultivate this garden after moving to San Diego from Ventura, where she'd also had to destroy what she'd grown. Both times, as a precaution against a police raid, she and Morgan had been ordered by Vincent Tyson to pull out and dispose of all these witches' weeds in addition to the lab equipment she'd been using to concentrate the active ingredients into a more potent form.

"Smoke break," Morgan announced, which didn't sound bad to Millie, so they pulled off their gloves and settled into patio chairs, each removing from their pockets a different kind of pouch. He, cannabis flowers, and she, just plain tobacco, but it was a special blend she'd harvested last fall.

"I always liked *your* flowers better," he told her, looking intently at a pile of crumbled weed he was making in his lap on a little piece of rolling paper.

"You sure did," Millie replied, busying herself with a similar task. Then she fired up her own hand-rolled smoke, blew out a cloud, and watched as it drifted over her ruined garden.

Morgan did likewise and leaned back in his seat. He used to sit there tall and strong with a neatly trimmed military mustache and stern, focused features, but now he was slouching, soft around the middle, stubble-faced, and grinning like a fool. This was exactly why Millie no longer grew cannabis, peyote, datura, opium poppy, or several other psychoactive plants—because of his insatiable desire to consume them. Just yesterday she'd issued an ultimatum, and he'd made his choice, so now they were only friends. Off again.

"I'm done after this job," he told her.

"Why?"

"It doesn't feel right anymore."

"You think Tyson'll let you out?"

"Do *you* think he'll be able to locate me?"

"In your present state? Yes I do. *You're* the reason we had to rip out the garden, dammit! And *I'm* driving."

He nodded absently, but Millie was sure he hadn't heard what she'd said. Instead of listening, he'd more likely been entertaining thoughts of a stronger drug than pot and where he could get it, if he hadn't done so already.

Years ago, while studying for her doctor of pharmacy degree, Millie had been trained in a more traditional kind of pharmacology. By a *bruja*, or witch, an Indigenous American expert in poisonous and psychoactive plants. Over the years that followed, she had ingested these plants before her kill missions, believing that their consumption—of datura and peyote in particular—made her more in tune with the universe. And it did, sometimes. On again, off again. Until they failed her completely in yet another betrayal, one of so many in her life.

Then, through force of will, Millie had dug herself out of that hole, but Morgan hadn't been willing or able to do the same. And she felt guilty for that. Before they'd started consuming power plants together, Morgan had achieved dizzying heights. Having served in military intelligence, he was highly skilled in the art of deception, and his IQ was completely off the charts. They'd been lovers, but with a mentor-mentee dynamic. Same as with Victor Lager in Hawaii, where Mille had lost control of herself, like Morgan had done but in a different way.

As she turned her gaze on a shell of the man he'd once been, Millie realized that their roles were now reversed. She was playing a maternal role, and this brought to mind her junkie mother, a separate topic she didn't want to get started on. So she stubbed out her smoke and said, "Let's do it."

Morgan sucked in one last lungful before hopping to his feet. Then they loaded the evidence into the car and drove to a secluded location to dispose of it.

***

"We got the warrants," announced Chief Deputy DA Lynn Peters. "I'm driving."

"Shotgun," said Choi.

"You're not going. You need to go home and get some rest."

"Doctor's orders," gloated Cammie as Choi marched glumly off. Then she, Peters, Roche, and Bladet headed down to Peters' government-issued sedan.

Twenty minutes later, as they trooped through the inner corridors of SDPD headquarters, Lynn Peters was stopped by several high-ranking police officers and everyone seemed eager to speak with her.

"I wouldn't be surprised if she were elected mayor one of these days," said Bladet.

Roche agreed while Cammie looked on admiringly.

When Peters finally managed to disentangle herself from her law enforcement colleagues, the group continued through the halls to Special Operations, where Peters introduced them to a stocky Filipino man wearing tactical gear. "This is Lieutenant Ron Ragasa," she said. "SDPD SWAT team leader."

Ragasa greeted them with a quick handshake and a vanishing smile, which Bladet figured might have reflected his concern for their safety. If not that, then certainly his single focus on the mission. She and Roche would be riding along to oversee the lawful service of the warrants and any resulting arrests. To make sure everything was done by the book.

"Good luck y'all," said Peters, who then departed with Cammie to take Jonathan Lee's statement and that of Schmidt's secretary.

Roche and Bladet followed Ragasa to the police vehicle area, where they met three more SWAT team members, and everyone piled into the back of a BearCat, an armored vehicle designed for high-risk operations. On their way to the target residence, the two attorneys sat facing each other on parallel bench seats, exchanging uncertain looks while the tactical team double-checked their gear.

Then Roche caught Ragasa's eye and had to shout over the big diesel engine to draw his attention. "How'd you locate the suspect?"

Lieutenant Ragasa bellowed back, "We were searching for any residence connected to Vincent Tyson, and we found one rented by a shell company that his law firm set up. So we conducted surveillance and were able to identify the suspect based on the forensic sketch and the video feeds. His name is Morrison Grant, formerly a master sergeant in U.S. Army human intelligence. An expert in disguise and impersonation."

Then the BearCat ground to a halt and Ragasa handed Roche a portable radio. "We'll let you know when it's safe to enter." Then he turned to his team. "Listen up! As you know, our target is highly trained and most likely armed, so we're assuming a hostile response. Stick to your training, trust each other, and we all go home."

After the tactical team poured out of the vehicle and Ragasa closed the rear door with an ominous clunk, Bladet and Roche were left to their private thoughts. As the minutes dragged by, Bladet grew unbearably nervous. *What if this is a trap like the one that put Taylor in a coma? What if the crooks kill the SWAT team and come outside for us?*

She turned to Roche, who met her gaze with those blue-green eyes and smiled reassuringly, then reached for her hand and took it in his.

"We'll be fine," he said.

8

THE WORST PUNISHMENT OF ALL

For Morgan it was a magic carpet ride out to East County where they burned and buried the evidence, but the same wasn't true for Millie. Not at all. It was bad enough that her lovingly tended and professionally valuable witch's garden was now just a bed of dirt, but worse was that she had to dispose of her laboratory equipment and supplies—again.

On the drive back, the shell of a man in the passenger seat busied himself with a video game, of all things. Millie reminded herself that this was the leader's curse, that followers often feel like dead weight. And she couldn't blame him for doing the same thing that she had done ten years earlier. On the North Shore of Oahu, in Hawaii, she'd lost control, but not to drugs; Millie had been a slave to murder. Addicted to mounting stout young men, wrapping her hands around their throats, and watching the life drain out of their eyes. This act had given her sexual pleasure to such an extent that, like Morgan, she had found herself unable or unwilling to stop. And it would have cost her a lifetime in prison if it hadn't been for Vincent Tyson's brilliant intervention.

Aside from her confession and the DNA she'd left at the crime scenes, another piece of evidence that Tyson had had to discredit were the statements made by Jeff Walker and Tony Park, then a pair of lifeguards visiting Oahu, but whose permanent residence was San Diego, where they still lived. And now that Park and Walker were police officers, they represented a major threat to Millie's freedom and future plans. Fortunately, they didn't know she lived in town.

As she zipped down the foothills on her way to the coast, Millie thought back to when Tyson had visited her in Ventura to discuss the San Diego job. She'd objected, citing the risk posed by Park and Walker.

"You'll be fine," Tyson had assured her. "It's a couple years at most, and we'll have your nose done and your hair cut and dyed."

"Absolutely not," she'd said.

"It comes with a life-changing payday," Tyson persisted. "But you'll have to use your real name since you'll be working at a pharmacy."

"What if Park or Walker see me somewhere I can't get away, like at work?"

"If that happens, then I'll make sure you're acquitted. You have my word on that. And we can always terminate them if we need to."

"What if I refuse?" Millie protested again, weakly this time, since she knew what he would say.

"You'd be within your rights to do so," Tyson conceded, "just as I would be entitled to leak certain details about your mishap in Hawaii to the police. Remember, there's no statute of limitations on murder."

So they'd settled on compensation sufficient to ensure Millie's early retirement—more than enough for her and Morgan to run away together, which had been an exciting prospect at the time. Now, however, as she braked to a stop outside her house in San Diego, she felt as if the earth were crumbling beneath her.

Then, once she'd gone inside, her world actually did fall in on itself, plunging her into an icy abyss of fear as a fist pounded on the door and a male voice barked, "It's SDPD with a warrant. Open up!"

***

"We're all clear," came Lieutenant Ragasa's voice on the handheld radio, prompting Bladet and Roche to let themselves out of the BearCat and stride up to the target residence. Bladet was wary at first, thinking Ragasa might have been forced to give her and Roche the green light, but when she saw two SWAT team operators standing just inside the door looking confident and relaxed, she breathed a great deal easier.

The suspect named on the warrant, Morrison Grant, was just being flex-cuffed and informed of his rights. He looked to Bladet like a strung-out Johnny Roche. She turned her attention from him to the only other person present who didn't work for the justice system: Millie Haukea, whom she recognized from her visit to Grimes Pharmacy.

"Am I under arrest?" Dr. Haukea demanded to know. Her flowing brown hair was radiant, her features noble, her body strong, but her eyes were frightened like those of a cornered animal.

"No, you're not," said Lieutenant Ragasa, reaching into a pouch on his belt for a second pair of flex cuffs. "But you *are* being detained while we search the premises."

"Whose house is this?" asked Roche.

Now seated on the floor in the living room with their hands behind their backs, Morrison Grant and Millie Haukea exercised their right to remain silent, both visibly upset as an initial inspection revealed nothing more than vacuumed carpets, wiped-down surfaces, large planter boxes in the back yard containing only soil, and an empty room, in the center of which stood a table bolted to the floor.

"We're gonna have to let her go," said Roche to Bladet in that empty room, peering quizzically down at the table. Its glossy black surface made it look like a kitchen island, but the space was more like a study with no books on the shelves.

"At least we got one of them," said Bladet.

"No, we got 'em both," said a triumphant Ragasa as he joined them. "What do y'all think this room was being used for?"

"Well," said Bladet, "she's a pharmacist, right?"

"So this is a lab table," said Roche with new understanding. "But where's the equipment?"

"Exactly," said Ragasa, whose grin now lit up his eyes. "We just received an anonymous tip about some buried laboratory supplies out in East County."

"And that's probable cause," concluded Roche with a tight-lipped smile.

The SWAT team led the suspects to a police car parked behind the BearCat, and this filled Bladet with a warm sense of relief. Roche offered her a celebratory fist bump, and as she watched the cruiser pull away, Bladet believed the case was closed.

***

"Good afternoon, Mr. Tyson," came a deep and cultured male voice on the other end of the line.

"Same to you, but you're not the Chancellor."

"That's correct. He is no longer part of our organization. I'll be your point of contact from now on."

"You have me at a disadvantage. What's your code name or how should I refer to you?"

"I recommend that you never refer to me."

"Understood."

"What can I do for you, Mr. Tyson?"

"I need to disappear. Soon, maybe in a month."

"That can be arranged, of course, but first you need to take care of Southern Trust. Then we'll talk."

As Tyson ended the conversation with every bit of false gratitude he could muster, he strode across his bedroom toward a large framed painting of a courtroom scene. He took it off the wall to reveal a safe, in which he stored the military-grade encrypted smartphone he'd been given for the sole purpose of calling the organization. Then, with no time or desire to appreciate the spectacular sunset on the far side of his third-floor window, he clomped downstairs to rejoin a meeting in progress.

Igmar opened the door for Tyson's reappearance onto the terrace, where Asher, Kang, Voss, and Dane were gathered around a long glass dinner table, all with a beverage within reach. "Where were we?" Tyson asked, lowering himself into the seat of command. All eyes were on him.

"Morgan's arraignment," growled Voss, the bald-headed sniper with a bushy mustache.

"Right," said Tyson. "I want you in position by ten thirty."

"Yes sir."

"What about Millie?" asked Kang, the expert in martial arts. She was dressed in black as usual and wearing her dark hair down.

"We'll have to see," Tyson replied. "I'd like to keep her alive if I can."

A murmur of agreement arose from everyone but Kang, which was understandable—but not justified, Tyson felt, since he'd never once looked at Millie Haukea as anything other than a contractor, while he'd been exceedingly generous to his live-in lover and masseuse.

"Now," he proceeded, "there's something I need to say. After this job, you will never see me again. Besides your new identities, you'll be getting a substantial bonus, above and beyond what we agreed. But *only* if we pull it off."

"So what's the plan?" This question came from Dane, the muscular specialist in staged accidents and suicides.

Tyson paused to consider his answer and also for dramatic effect. Then he spoke. "You and Asher will deal with Bladet and Roche, regardless of whether Millie's case goes to trial." Then he turned to Kang. "*You've* got Lynn Peters and Cammie O'Mara."

"What about Dominick Taylor?" This from Asher, the pale-faced hacker with the bowl haircut. "If he wakes up, he's likely to talk to Park and Walker, and that would destroy Millie's case."

Tyson nodded in agreement. "So make sure he doesn't wake up."

***

"Where's my lawyer?" asked Morrison Grant, also known as Morgan.

"I don't know," replied Lieutenant Ragasa. "But I'd like to get started without him."

"That's not gonna happen." Morgan eyed the upper corner of the interview room, where a small white camera eyed him back, no doubt recording everything done or said since he'd been seated an hour before.

Ragasa leaned forward over the table between them. He seemed like a decent guy. Maybe Mexican or Filipino. He had brown skin, Asian eyes, and a thin mustache on his upper lip.

"Look," said Ragasa. "We've got you on video—on ten different recordings. Plus two witnesses ready to testify that it was you at Southern Trust. Now, Vincent Tyson being here isn't going to change any of that, and the DA will be more likely to cut you a break if you cooperate."

Morgan's head was clear enough for him to know that it wouldn't make much of a difference either way because Tyson was probably going to have him killed. The attorney's absence practically confirmed it. *Should I make a deal?* he wondered. *Or try to escape?* Neither course of action was appealing, so Morgan studied the floor, enduring Ragasa's stare until the lawman got fed up and left the room.

Later, Ragasa returned, this time with Millie Haukea. "She wanted to talk to you," he said. "No touching or the conversation's over."

Once the SWAT team leader had left them alone, Millie surprised Morgan with a kiss on the lips, then dropped into the chair across from him. "How are you?" she asked, with real concern in her voice. She'd pulled back her hair in a tight brown ponytail.

"What'd you do that for?!" he cried out. "Now they're gonna drag you outta here."

"No they won't," she said with a sad little smile. Then she looked up at the camera in the corner. "They've got us exactly where they want us. Be careful what you say."

"I'm not an idiot."

"You've been acting like one."

"I know."

Morgan was sorry now, but now was far too late. Not only had his refusal to stay off drugs landed him in police custody and put the whole of Tyson's team at risk, for which he would probably die, but now, it seemed, the love of his life might also be killed.

"I'm gonna make it up to you," he told her.

Millie nodded, but her eyes were hard and her lips pressed together in disgust. That, Morgan felt, was the worst punishment of all. Nothing could hurt him more than that.

They spoke for ten more minutes, sometimes in code, but there wasn't much they could say or do with the camera constantly watching.

You idiot! Morgan berated himself as the door popped open again. When Millie rose to go, he caught her deep amber eyes for the last time. She loved him, he knew, so much that she'd followed him to her death.

9

HONOR AMONG THIEVES

Vincent Tyson had deliberately failed to appear at Morgan's interview with the police, having made that choice in order to send his disappointment of a disguise artist a terrifying message. But he did show up to the courthouse the next day, shortly before Morgan's arraignment hearing.

At precisely ten thirty in the morning, Tyson stepped out of the rear entrance and onto the sidewalk, dressed as usual in a silk-linen suit. It was black, matching his hair, which was dyed to hide the gray. He slipped on his sunglasses to conceal the direction of his gaze as he verified that Voss was in position.

And Voss *was* in position, facing Tyson on the roof of a high-rise building. The criminal defender would never have spotted the sniper, what with the man's camouflage, his careful positioning, and the considerable distance between them, but each man had been watching for the other. Tyson gave no signal, with which Voss knew he was to proceed according to plan. Then the expert marksman melted back into his surroundings.

***

Voss rolled over, face up, and pulled a plastic sheet painted the same off-white color as the roof over his body. With only time to kill at the moment, he thought back to the most recent job he and Morgan had worked together, the day they'd set an explosive trap for Taylor and Choi.

While Morgan had been installing the pressure plate at the front door, rigging the entryway to sense the weight of a visitor, he had made two rookie mistakes that had taken Voss a long time to correct and caused him great irritation. That was when Voss had begun to suspect he might be ordered to do exactly what he was preparing to do now. It was standard policy and everyone knew it. If you were working for Vincent Tyson and blew a job for the rest of the team, especially if you were captured, you were likely to be executed. Morgan had been taking an enormous risk by using drugs on the job, and now it had come back to bite him in the ass. *In the head is more like it*, Voss joked to himself while rolling back into the prone and peering through his scope. The problem was, he reckoned while adjusting for wind and distance, Morgan hadn't always been a failure. For years the man had served as Tyson's second-in-command, been a model operative for the team, and, most significantly, saved Voss's life on more than one occasion.

So Voss was torn. Should he do what he'd been ordered to do or do what was right, thus risking the same punishment for himself and losing his life-changing payday?

In the end, when he saw the transport vehicle pulling to a stop at the rear entrance to the courthouse, he settled on loyalty over safety and money. So as Morgan stepped out of the vehicle and into the crosshairs, Voss aimed slightly right and blew off the top of his teammate's ear.

***

Morgan could barely contain his terror while riding to the courthouse. Finally the police cruiser pulled to a stop. His door came open. And there stood the transport officer, ordering him to get out. Before complying, Morgan relived a lifetime of ups and downs in only seconds. From dizzying heights to soul-crushing lows. *It was a good run*, he decided. *Well, good and bad. But no regrets, right?* Then he scooted toward the officer ever so slowly, swung his legs out, stood, and turned his face to the sun for what he imagined was the last time.

As expected, there came a distant CRACK, but then a sudden pain blooming hot on his ear. *Voss missed*, Morgan thought at first. But as the officer started pushing him into the courthouse, he realized that couldn't be true. So he held up his handcuffed wrists.

CRACK! Morgan's hands were free, and in an instant he was sprinting down the block. The last thing he saw before rounding the corner was Vincent Tyson standing nearby, glaring at him with hate.

***

"Sorry," said a breathless Tyson from outside Millie Haukea's jail cell. For once, the man's suit was misaligned, his tie loosened and off-center. "I had to file a motion to withdraw as Morgan's counsel."

"Okay," Millie said slowly as she rose from her bunk to approach the bars. "What happened?"

"Well," said Tyson, "you won't believe this, but a sniper tried to shoot him on his way into the courthouse, but Morgan escaped."

Neither one spoke for a time as they stood facing each other from opposite sides of the bars.

"So why are you here?" she finally asked, meaning *If you ordered Voss to kill Morgan, why not get rid of me as well?*

"I gave you my word. Remember?"

She nodded slowly, unsure whether or not to trust him, even after all these years.

"We don't have much time," he told her, briskly now, straightening his tie. "You're about to be questioned by the police."

"Why should I even talk to them?"

"Two reasons—so we can gauge their case against you and so we can control the narrative. That second part is gonna be tough, since we don't know what new evidence they have against you."

"It's gotta be something big," she replied. "Just the other day, they had probable cause for Morgan, but nothing on me."

"Right. So you'll have to change your story on the spot, depending on how the meeting goes. Try to piss them off, get them to tell you what they know, and then act accordingly. When in doubt, let *me* take the lead."

Fifteen minutes later, Millie and Tyson were sitting at a table in an interview room across from two men in dark slacks and sport coats with white shirts underneath. "My name's Detective Chase," said one of them. He was large and sported a brown goatee.

"And I'm Rapoza," said the other, who was better looking and ten years younger. "We're homicide detectives with SDPD. Do you remember your rights?"

Millie looked not at them, but up at the camera in the corner. "Yes," she said. "I don't have to talk to you."

"That's right," growled Detective Chase. "But you *should* talk to us. We've got you on two counts of murder one, plus burglary, data theft, and attempted murder. That's just for starters."

"The good news," said Rapoza more softly than his partner, "is that the DA's here right now, watching us." He nodded up at the camera. "Let's say you help us locate Morrison Grant. Then you might only get ten years."

"Or you could die in prison," said Chase, shooting her a hard look. "Your choice."

Millie turned to Tyson, who was locking eyes with Chase. "Your line of questioning is improper, Detective. For one thing, it's coercive. For another, you're harassing my client, fishing for clues when there's no real evidence against her. So you must be lying about those charges, and if you keep this up, I'll have this entire interview suppressed and file a formal complaint against you both."

Chase ignored him. "How do you know Morrison Grant, Doctor Haukea?"

"We met at a party a few weeks ago," she said.

"What was he doing at your house the other day? Or is it *your* house, Mr. Tyson?"

Tyson's reply was a fleeting glance that only Millie knew was actually a death threat.

"He came over to smoke," she said.

"Oh yes," Chase sneered. "We found some stubbed-out joints and cigarettes. They don't test you for drugs at your job?"

"Don't answer that!" Tyson snapped, but he'd raised his voice and was flitting his eyes toward the cops pointedly, telling her just the opposite, that it was time to rile them up.

"Why shouldn't I?" she fired back, as though Tyson had upset her. Then she turned to Chase. "It's not a crime to smoke pot in California. Maybe I *did* give him some. But I don't use drugs, and yes, I *am* subject to random testing."

"It's still a crime under federal law," Chase retorted weakly.

Millie rolled her eyes at him.

Now the younger detective stepped in. "Let's talk about your garden," he said. "We had your soil analyzed, so we have a good idea as to what was growing there. Clearly you got rid of all your plants, and recently. But why? Since you claim they were for medicinal use, why didn't you just toss 'em in the trash?"

"Officer Rapoza," she answered, as if she were speaking to a child. "I am a doctor of pharmacy—a highly trained professional.

I spent six years studying biochemistry, pharmacokinetics, and clinical medicine. What about you? What did it take—six months at the academy to learn how to throw a punch and fill out paperwork?"

A tense silence gripped the room as the detective's eyes grew wide with fury. He gritted his teeth and leaned forward, looking mad enough to slap her in the face, but Chase broke in at that point.

"It's *Detective* Rapoza, Miss Haukea," he informed her. "Answer me this: Did you drive out to the Cleveland National Forest with Morrison Grant on the day you two were arrested? Maybe stopping just off Sunrise Highway where you broke your laboratory gear, burned the plants, and buried it all? And was that the same equipment you used to purify the toxins that killed the two Southern Trust executives?"

"It's *Doctor* Haukea," she returned, feigning coolness as her mind spun at maximum speed. *Should I confirm the drive but deny the disposal of evidence? What good would that do? Maybe just deny everything.* SDPD had obviously found the laboratory equipment, so there was no good answer.

Millie looked up at the camera again; its blinking red light seemed to be mocking her. Then she turned back to the detectives, whose eyes were gleaming in triumph. And she didn't even look at Tyson; there was nothing to say. But she did know what he was thinking—that someone on their team had betrayed her.

***

A few days earlier, Kang had been waiting in silence at the top of a dark and filthy staircase. *I didn't betray Millie*, the master of martial arts thought. *I gave her what she deserved. What if I were to commit a series of murders just for the thrill of it? Would Vince take my case for free? Would he pay for my PhD and buy me a car and a house?* Kang was filled with envy and then she felt disgusted, by Tyson and all the "full-release" massages she'd given him, both before and after moving in to his beachfront house.

Her phone buzzed once in her pocket. This meant Morgan's transport vehicle had arrived at the courthouse, so she pushed open the door at the top of the staircase, just a hair. The hinges made no sound because she'd oiled them the night before. Through the crack she saw Voss, lying in the prone with a white plastic sheet on his back. He was facing away from her, aiming his rifle down at the courthouse. So Kang unfolded her stiletto, slipped quietly outside, and positioned herself within striking distance.

She was fairly well acquainted with the former Army sniper. Well enough to correctly suppose that he was wavering between taking the shot and leaving Tyson's employ. If he did execute Morgan, she would simply slip the knife back into her pocket and tell Voss the truth about why she was there. But if he failed to pull the trigger, as Tyson had suspected he might, then she would be the one taking a life that day.

Over Voss's shoulder she watched as the driver got out of the police car and opened the rear door for Morgan, who climbed out reluctantly, giving Voss a perfect shot at his head. Voss fired, but Morgan remained on his feet.

Kang froze. Two long seconds dragged by as she stood poised over Voss with the stiletto ready.

Voss fired again, freeing Morgan's wrists, so Kang stepped immediately forward and plunged her long knife into Voss's upper neck, severing his spinal cord.

What a fool, she thought, smiling as she twisted the blade. *With him out of the way, Morgan on the run, Haukea on trial, and Asher suspected for leading the police to the laboratory equipment, there'll be a lot more money to go around, and if Vince doesn't give it to me—*

No, Kang decided, waving to Dane as he brought a helicopter down on the roof. *Vince <u>will</u> give it to me. All of it, one way or another. And if he thinks I'm happy in that house, then he's in for a rude awakening.*

As the chopper lifted off and banked northward, she was sitting in the aft cabin holding on to a heavy body bag so that it wouldn't slide around on the floor. She glanced up at Dane in the cockpit. He wasn't a friend, but certainly more reliable than the others. He swiveled in the pilot's seat to give her a thumbs up and a good-looking grin. She nodded. Maybe she'd spare him. Maybe not, but she certainly wasn't going to let Asher live. Kang hated that smug little know-it-all, which is why she'd set him up. And when Vince drew the mistaken conclusion that Asher was the only member of the team who could have known where the evidence was buried, he might even take care of the hacker himself.

With the chopper now stable, she let go of Voss's corpse, sat back, and tried to enjoy the aerial view. Yet her mind was so distracted, swept into frenzy by all the scheming and lying, the fear of being found out, and her plans to prevent that from happening that the next thing she knew, the trip was over and she was stepping out of the aircraft.

And there stood Vincent Tyson. "Hey babe," he said. "I could really use a massage."

Ugh.

10

DARKNESS PREVAILS

"Three people asked me how to say my last name today," remarked Johnny Roche.

"Is that good or bad?" asked Dea Bladet as they strolled along.

"It's bad if I've already told them ten times," he answered, stopping to raise his eyes to the star-filled sky and his voice to the entire world. "Come on, it's not that hard! Roche rhymes with John!"

Bladet also halted, took his hands in hers, gazed into his sea-green eyes, and favored him with a tender smile. She knew Johnny wasn't mad about people's pronunciation; he was upset by the case. So she stepped closer to lay a sweet little kiss on his cheek—their first show of affection in years—then pulled back to see the shock that she'd known would be on his chiseled features. And she'd been right—Johnny Roche was indeed struck dumb, but his eyes were shining with delight.

It's meant to be, she reckoned, holding one of his hands as they continued on toward their destination. *So what if we got in trouble at work when we were younger? Now we're more mature. And the chemistry's undeniable.*

Minutes later, Roche was standing behind her chair and scooting it in for her in a softly lit dining room that smelled of fried cheese, garlic sauce, and fresh-baked bread. When he settled down opposite her, it was with his back to the wall and a clear view of the room. She'd forgotten about that; he'd always insisted on corner tables and their being seated in this configuration, so he could keep an eye on the door in case of emergencies. One had never occurred, but it was the thought that counted.

With a clink of their glasses, she took a rich swig of cabernet sauvignon and he of an ice-cold martini. Their gazes caught and held, and their smiles grew wide together, and soon they fell into the Sean Connery routine. After ordering their food, the conversation naturally came around to the impending trial.

"It was weird, don't you think?" Roche asked, *it* meaning the meeting they'd just come from, which had taken place in Lynn Peters' corner office. "We had a view of San Diego Bay to die for."

"With calm and sparkling waters," she continued, knowing where he was headed and playing along.

"On which a smattering of sailboats cruised freely about the island," Roche went on in a slow, dramatic tone.

Grinning, she matched his vocal style. "Down below, throngs of smiling sun-drunk tourists strolled along the Embarcadero snapping pictures."

"And yet," said Roche, pausing at the punch line, "as Lynn Peters, Cammie O'Mara, and Bladet and Roche reviewed the facts of the case, their weighty concerns seemed to swirl up into the air, forming thick black clouds of worry that filled the high-rise workroom..."

"Which billowed out the window, casting a shadow over the whole seaside community," Bladet concluded, calling for another drink. *One more and I'll switch to water.*

This spontaneous composition lightened the mood even more; she giggled, he chortled, and they eyed each other with a hunger that Bladet felt was sure to culminate in lustful whimpers and moans of ecstasy.

But it would merely be a reprieve from that cloud of alarm cast over Lynn Peters' office, which would likely continue to keep all four attorneys on edge for quite a while. Having successfully escaped at the courthouse, Morrison Grant remained at large, so his trial had been put on hold. This was terrible news for the Major Violators Unit because the case against him was airtight. As for Millie Haukea, her arraignment was scheduled for the following day, in only twelve hours' time. At that hearing, the charges against her would be read and Bladet would argue against the granting of bail in any amount.

On only three hours of sleep, she thought with a little smile.

"If that," said Roche.

"What?" she blurted out, thinking for a second that he'd read her mind, but then she realized it was impossible.

"Sorry," he said, sipping at a glass of water. "I got something caught in my throat. I was about to say, *if that* waiter takes any longer to bring our food, he can kiss his tip goodbye."

"That'd be a good thing, though, right?"

He placed his cloth napkin on the table and looked her in the eye as he stood. "Yes, it would. You're such a positive person, Dea. That's one of the many things I love about you." He came around the table, leaned close while setting a warm, strong hand on her back, and took her by surprise with a soft lip-lock that promised more. It was a taste of heaven. "Be right back," he murmured.

"Don't say it," she replied as he started for the men's room, certain he'd been about to deliver that well-worn line about having to shake hands with an old friend.

He gave a deep and honest belly laugh, then turned to flash her a handsome grin.

"It's on the house," someone said as Bladet's second glass of wine materialized. She looked up to see their waiter, who'd caught her staring after Roche. He smiled knowingly. "With our apologies for the delay."

At that instant the lights cut out, plunging the room into total darkness, since even the streetlamps outside had lost their power. Nervous utterances rippled through the restaurant as Bladet rooted around in her purse for her phone. Telling herself not to worry, she found the familiar shape of her cell phone, powered it on, swiped the screen, and tapped it to activate the flashlight.

Calmer now, she shined it on her drink, reached for it, and knocked back a comforting swallow. Soon she and Johnny would be eating well, then sleeping poorly. But would it be at his place or hers?

Mine, she decided, just as a gunman strode silently up behind her, aimed his weapon at her head, and fired.

***

Dane flew out of the Italian restaurant, sprinted along the sidewalk to the corner, cut left, and there waited Asher on a rented motorcycle, with another bike parked right next to his.

Asher held open a backpack, into which Dane put his pistol, but not before racking the slide to clear the chamber, catching the ejected round in midair, and then engaging the safety. He stuffed his night vision device in there as well, but not his full-face balaclava mask. He kept that garment on as he donned a helmet and raced off with his partner to complete the second phase of their job.

"Any problems?" came Asher's voice in his helmet as they zipped along in single file.

"I got Bladet but Roche wasn't at the table," said Dane into his mic.

They both leaned to turn left, and hit the gas again as they straightened out, gaining speed. Up ahead, Asher was busy with his handlebar-mounted tablet, so Dane said nothing else. He felt the urge to crack a joke about texting and driving, but this was not the time. Most likely the hacker was restoring power to the city block he'd darkened and covering his digital tracks.

Soon they braked to a stop on the open-air top level of a parking structure. Across the street loomed the night-lit facade of Scripps Mercy Hospital with its grand entrance below. Now Dane did remove his balaclava as Asher stepped away to take a call. When Asher returned, he didn't identify the caller, and Dane didn't ask. Then, in tandem, they fitted surgical masks over their mouths and noses, covered their heads with ball caps, and Dane slipped on a pair of thick-framed eyeglasses to further hinder facial recognition.

Having studied maps and building plans, they were familiar with the hospital's layout, but now they needed to walk the halls. After entering through the automatic sliding glass doors, they wandered the halls as if they were lost while Asher studied the electrical and security systems and Dane took note of staff procedures and routines.

Then they took the elevator to the tenth floor, where they talked their way into the neuroICU by telling the nurse at the counter they were there to visit a real patient being treated there. As expected, when they came to Taylor's room, the door was closed and guarded by two stern men in slacks and sport coats with bulges under their jackets, so Dane and Asher just walked by. Then they stopped for coffee on the next floor down.

A window near the vending machine offered a clear view of the parking structure across the street. Asher peered through it absently.

Dane wondered what was going on in Asher's complex mind; one could never tell. But he didn't look out the window. Still jumpy after shooting Bladet, Dane was more focused on his hot liquid refreshment. *It's terrible*, he thought. *But even bad coffee is good. Just like pizza and sex.*

***

Four hours earlier, at the end of the dismally serious meeting in Lynn Peters' corner office, Bladet and Roche had set off for dinner at a local Italian restaurant, leaving Cammie and Peters on their own for the evening meal.

"Do you feel like Thai food?" asked Cammie, looking to her blond-haired boss, who was still shuffling papers on her desk. "I can go down and grab it if you've got work to do."

"No, I'm done," said Peters, standing to grab her purse. "Let's go."

The farther they got from the thirteenth floor, the freer and more relaxed Cammie started to feel, so by the time the elevator doors slid open and she and Peters strode through the lobby, she was almost back to her normal self. Then, when she stepped out into the night, enveloped by the cool bayside air, she broke into a carefree smile.

"Must be nice to be young," groused Peters as they proceeded down the block. "Did you get the test results back?"

"No, not yet, but tomorrow's just the arraignment."

"That's true."

At the next day's hearing, it wouldn't be important to know what types of residue were contained in the lab equipment that had been broken, buried, and located through an anonymous tip. The mere discovery of it, plus what they'd had already, had been plenty of evidence against Millie Haukea for the purpose of filing charges, and it would probably suffice to support the district attorney's argument against the granting of bail. As Cammie walked under the streetlamps with her boss, she felt reassured, believing that Dr. Haukea would be locked up for the duration of the trial and for many years thereafter, since Dea Bladet was a top-notch trial lawyer.

"What else was found at the site?" Peters wanted to know.

"Melted plastic containers, rubber tubing. A lot of ashes with some unburned plant matter, which we also sent in for testing."

"Of course. What was Sean saying about a mockup?"

"He's at home working on it," said Cammie, "which is why he didn't come in today."

"No, but what is it?"

"Ah, okay. It's a new idea he came up with to place Haukea at the crime scenes. You know how the pictures of the food server at the Convention Center don't look like the female suspect on the Hall of Justice recording, and neither of those match Haukea's mugshot?"

"Yes."

"Well, our theory is that it was her both times, but in different disguises. So Sean's working on a new computer program based on facial recognition, body shape, posture, and a bunch of other variables I can't remember right now."

"That sounds promising."

The Thai place was just past the next intersection. As they crossed the street, Cammie was starting to consider her menu options when something slammed into the back of her head and knocked her down. Dizzy, disoriented, with a shooting pain in her head and a sharp ringing in her ears, she tried to push herself to her feet but failed. So Cammie could only watch, astonished, as Lynn Peters drew a pistol from her purse and leveled it at their attacker.

It was a woman. That much was clear, even in the feeble glow of the streetlamps. She was strong and lean. Asian, probably, but her face was covered with a black mask that made her look like a ninja. With a knife in one hand, the woman squared off with Peters, dropping into a fighting stance.

"Don't move!" Peters screamed at Cammie's attacker from a two-handed firing position. "I'm placing you under citizen's arrest for aggravated assault. Drop your weapon and—"

But the woman stopped her in mid-sentence with a flick of the wrist, then slipped into the shadows as Peters fired, missed, and fell to her knees with a shocked expression and a knife in her gut.

11

DOG EAT DOG

Kang threw the knife—precisely on target—while dodging the bullet fired by Peters. As she melted back into the shadows and sprinted away, she cursed herself for failing to prepare for the possibility that one of her targets might be carrying a concealed firearm. *Isn't that illegal? Certainly unlikely*, she thought, *but in any case I should have brought one myself*. Not winded in the least as she came to her car, Kang jumped behind the wheel, fired up the engine, and drove to Scripps Mercy Hospital at a moderate rate of speed.

Along the way, she called Asher, whom she had framed for giving the police the anonymous tip that led to the buried evidence. Her mobile phone, like those of everyone else on Tyson's team, had been built with hardware that rendered their calls practically undetectable.

"Where are you?" she asked.

"Why? Wanna give me a happy ending?"

"If you say that again I will give you an unbearably painful ending."

Asher did not say it again.

"I need to talk to you," she went on.

"No thanks. I think it was you who set me up. The only place I'll meet you is at Tyson's. Otherwise I'll probably end up with a knife in my back, like Voss did."

"I was ordered to execute him."

Again Asher gave no reply and even ended the call, but this didn't trouble Kang. Dane had already told her that he and Asher would be scoping out the hospital that night, so she was fairly sure she knew where to find the scrawny typist.

Kang paid for parking and drove up the ramps past the rows of taken spots, and as she came to the top of the structure, she spotted two nondescript motorcycles parked side by side. Pulling in to an adjacent slot, she saw that one of the bikes was fitted with Asher's tablet mounting rack. Certain now that she was in the right place, she knelt beside her car to remove the tracking device from under it, tossed the tracker aside, then drove to a dark distant corner of the parking area to wait for Asher to return.

As she sat there in the shadows, Kang felt more than a little disappointed. She'd been looking forward to Tyson's reaction when he determined—mistakenly—that Asher had tipped off the police as to the location of the buried lab equipment. Yet this was a cleaner course of action. Things were getting hot, and quickly, so her new plan was to remain on good terms with Tyson for now, with Dane as well—since she'd need an ally—and eliminate the rest of the competition, meaning Asher, and Morgan, too, if she could find him.

It was such a good plan, she rued. Since Tyson always kept an eye on his team by tracking their vehicles, and since the only two people who had access to the software that showed the location of those vehicles were Tyson and Asher, only they could have known exactly where Millie had gone to bury the evidence. And it hadn't been Asher who'd ratted on Millie, nor Tyson, obviously, but Kang. She'd followed Millie out to East County for the express purpose of setting her up to be convicted. Naturally, Tyson would then suspect Asher. In fact, as she waited in her car, Kang remembered hearing Tyson say something about a meeting that night with Asher, so she figured the scrawny typist might even be heading to Tyson's house after his recon run at the hospital.

But he won't make it there.

***

While Dane was drinking his coffee—*which he'd had to have, the idiot*—jeopardizing the mission by staying at the hospital when it was no longer necessary, Asher stood at the ninth-floor window, peering down at their rented bikes across the street. They were fast machines, but nothing like his own, or Dane's, both of which he'd modified and maintained at a professional level. Then he spotted a brown sedan emerging onto the top level of the parking structure. It was Kang's car! Dressed all in black, she popped out to inspect the bikes and unstuck the tracking device from the underside of her sedan. Asher nearly laughed out loud as she got back in and headed for a far corner of the parking lot. *Waiting for me to leave, no doubt, so she can run me off the road, or shoot me or my fuel tank. But why? It has to be the money*, he reckoned. *Why else would she move in with an old man like Vincent Tyson? She wants all his cash and is now planning to kill everyone he owes, starting with yours truly. She always hated me, and the feeling's mutual.*

So before Dane swallowed the last of his hot liquid refreshment, Asher said he'd see him later, headed out to his bike, clipped his tablet into the handlebar rack, and sped away as though he had no idea what was about to happen.

She'd been smart to get rid of the monitoring device. Now he wouldn't be able to track her in any way other than by his rear-view mirrors. That fact made what he was preparing to do more difficult, but Asher liked a challenge. He always had.

This will be fun, he predicted, stopping at a light in a left-turn lane. She was four cars behind him. There weren't many vehicles cruising the downtown streets, which was normal for that time of night. But straight ahead, there was an oncoming bus lane, the path of which he'd have to cross as he made the left turn. And a bus in the distance, so now was the time. He set to work, his fingers flying, tapping expertly so as to enter every needed command before the light went green. *Got it!* Asher rolled the throttle back, picked his feet up as he started to roll, gave it more gas, leaned into the left turn, and timed his last line of code—entered with only one hand—so that the approaching bus would collide with Kang's car as it barreled through the intersection. And that's exactly what happened. Even at an estimated forty miles per hour, the twenty-ton monster tore that brown sedan apart.

***

Sean Choi had just left the neuroICU after checking on Taylor. He hadn't passed Asher and Dane in the hallway, nor seen their bikes on the top floor of the parking structure because he'd left Taylor's newly repaired, repainted, and upgraded Interceptor on a different level, but when he climbed back into the pursuit-rated SUV to resume his surveillance of the hospital's wireless signals, he saw one of them step out of the medical center and walk across the street.

Despite the disposable face mask Asher wore and the ball cap pulled down over his eyes, Choi had no trouble recognizing his rival. Curiously, once Asher rode down to Choi's level on a bike, passing him, a mid-size brown sedan came rolling by only seconds later. So Choi brought the big engine to life and fell in line, making sure to leave a conservative distance between his vehicle and the middle one.

Not far from the hospital, Choi was stopped at a light. When it turned green, he started forward and was about to turn left when suddenly he slammed on the brakes to narrowly avoid a collision. Then he watched in horror as a city bus slammed into the brown sedan. Immediately afterward, Asher came sprinting onto the scene, still in his disguise, apparently providing aid to the driver of the car that had been following him.

Choi concluded that the aid provided was just a pretense, since the only way the bus wouldn't have stopped at the light was if Asher had manipulated the traffic signals; therefore, he further deduced, the only reason for Asher to be at the crash site was to make sure that his victim was dead.

Choi popped open the glove box, grabbed Taylor's brass knuckles, leapt out of the Interceptor, and ran over to confront the crook, but Asher was already on his bike and speeding away. So Choi took a picture of the victim before hustling back to the SUV and starting it up with a roar. Thrilled by its new capacity for acceleration, he tore through the streets, fishtailing at the turns, then gunning the engine in high-speed pursuit. At the freeway on-ramp he spotted Asher, and followed him north up the coast.

***

Judge Andrew Toles lived just north of Vincent Tyson, which meant a ten-minute drive down the moonlit coast to make it to an illegal meeting. Neither friend nor foe of the criminal defender, Toles made sure to bring his pipe and tobacco, as their conversations always went long and never were pleasant.

After cruising through the security checkpoint in his well-maintained but aging blue Jaguar, Judge Toles eased to a stop on the driveway outside, limped to the front door, and was shown in by Igmar, Tyson's giant Scandinavian assistant.

"Why don't you get that fixed?" Tyson called out from the back yard, jutting his chin toward Toles' knee as the judge hobbled outside. "Hell, if the jury finds for Haukea, I'll pay for the operation myself. Drink?"

With Tyson there's always an 'if,' Judge Toles knew, dropping into a seat at the table opposite the criminal defender. "Bourbon, neat," he said, offering no comment on the matter of the knee.

"So, did you get it?" asked Tyson. His strong jaw was clean shaven and showed his age, but for sixty, the famous attorney was in fairly good shape. He did have a paunch, but it was much smaller than that of his visitor, an enormous Black man about his same age. The two of them would occasionally cross paths down on the beach, as it connected their respective dwellings. Tyson's home was much larger than Toles', a fact that the former never let the latter forget. Down on the sand, Tyson would be jogging, sometimes with a much younger Asian woman, while Toles was relegated to a slow lame gait due to an old sports injury.

As he eyed his longtime collaborator, Judge Toles longed to put the man in his place. *Maybe this will be the year*, he thought. *Maybe I will take Tyson up on his offer to pay for the surgery. Then I'll get back in shape and sprint past him on the beach, running like I used to in the football games.*

Judge Toles was brought out of these musings by Igmar, who lumbered up to set a drink on the table before him. Toles suddenly wished it were four fingers instead of two, so he knocked back the liquid fire and handed the tumbler back to the giant blond. "Same again, please," he said.

Tyson merely sipped from his own glass, radiating superiority as usual. "Well?" he insisted.

"Yes, I got it," Judge Toles replied, meaning he'd been assigned to Millie Haukea's trial. Then he pulled out his pipe and started to fill its bowl.

"Do I need to tell you how I need it to go?" Tyson asked.

"Do *I* need to tell *you* what we're risking by continuing to meet like this?"

"Watch your tone," said Tyson, staring hard.

Judge Toles looked away and puffed on his pipe as his sense of ethics waged war with his concern for the safety of his family. Then he reluctantly turned to Tyson again. "Are we letting her walk for now?"

"No need. You can set her bail high, or deny it altogether. Either way."

Silence passed between the men but for the waves breaking on the nearby shore. With each periodic crash, after every pull on his pipe, and with a hot spreading sensation in his belly as the liquor was absorbed, Judge Toles fell deeper into a hypnotic state of relaxation. He gazed out at the vast, seemingly endless expanse of rippling black water to the west. Partially obscured by passing gray clouds, the moon cast its pale glow on the rolling whitecaps. It was the same view he often enjoyed at home, but only from his balcony, since Toles' house stood a block away from the beach.

"Your account details haven't changed?" Tyson asked.

"They have, actually." Toles handed over a folded slip of paper.

Tyson's phone then rattled on the table and he answered the call; after listening for a moment with a look of great surprise, the attorney leapt to his feet and strode off with the phone to his ear. A few minutes later he returned. "I need to take care of something," Tyson growled, shooting the judge a look that told him to leave immediately and promised the gravest of consequences should it even occur to him to conduct the trial in any manner other than as agreed.

So the Honorable Andrew Toles knocked his pipe against the leg of his chair, emptying its contents onto the grass, and headed home early for some much-needed rest. It was going to be a hell of a trial.

12

PRETRIAL MEETINGS

Soon after Judge Toles had gone home to rest, Asher came grumbling up Tyson's driveway in his rented motorcycle. Still in the grip of an intense adrenaline rush after murdering Kang, he hopped off the steel horse, removed his helmet to expose a second one, that of his straight brown hair, and strode up to the door. Before he knocked it came swinging open, attended by the same giant blond as always.

Igmar held the door without stepping aside, gazing down at Asher with some uncertainty.

"You're blocking my path," said Asher dryly.

"My apologies," said Igmar, moving out of the way deferentially, which caused a cold chill of dread to travel up Asher's spine. *No insulting first shot? Not even a sarcastic reply?*

As he passed through the grand residence alone, Asher rehearsed his story in his mind, searching for weak points or inconsistencies, finding none. Then, when he emerged onto the backyard terrace, he forced himself to take slow breaths, slow steps, and to assume an air of indifference.

"Asher, my boy!" said Tyson, standing to receive him with a broad, welcoming grin for once. "I ordered you a bourbon. Please." This unusually warm reception continued as he waved his visitor into the chair opposite him. "I thought you might need it after your ordeal."

Now Asher was terrified. *What did Tyson mean by 'ordeal'? Does he know about Kang's death and my role in it?*

"How was the hospital run?" Tyson inquired affably.

"No problems." Asher reached for the tumbler and took a pull. It was the good stuff, another distressing sign.

"Good. Listen, I called you here to talk about the trial, which starts tomorrow, as you know. I'll be needing your assistance throughout, but especially for voir dire," said Tyson, pronouncing it *vwar deer*.

"That's fine," said Asher, before downing his liquor in a single swig. "But I thought you wanted to talk about the anonymous tip."

Tyson shook his head dismissively. "I already know who it was. What we need to discuss is how that person met her demise."

A crushing silence fell over the table like a truckload of bricks, the only sound being the raging surf down on the beach as Tyson glared at Asher with hard and violent eyes. Every fiber of Asher's being screamed at him to leap to his feet and flee.

Without averting his gaze, Tyson said coldly, "Kang called me just after the crash. She said you were coming to kill her and left the phone line open. I heard her die."

There was no good answer. "She set me up," was the best Asher could do.

"I know," said Tyson, still staring.

If he needs me for jury selection and all the rest of the proceedings, Asher thought, *then he can't kill me or even hurt me badly.* Then it dawned on him what the consequence would have to be, and the thought of it was nauseating. Igmar came to set down his refill but Asher couldn't touch it, sure that he'd throw it up.

"Please," said the criminal defender with a creeping smile. "Go on."

"I—I knew she'd framed me for calling the police, which meant she wanted me dead. Then I saw her following me, so I had to take her out. It was me or her, Boss."

Further silence. More pounding waves, one heavy thump after another. Tyson hadn't stopped glaring.

"She was after your money," Asher finally blurted out. "I did you a favor."

"Of *course* she was after my money. But you didn't think I could handle my own girlfriend. Either that or you did it for the thrill. Maybe both."

"She *wasn't* your girlfriend."

"What's your father's address?"

"I won't tell you."

"Igmar!" Tyson barked, at which his loyal assistant reappeared, looming eagerly over the table like an attack dog waiting for the command. "If you tell me where he is," Tyson continued, "he'll only suffer a beating. But if you don't, I'll still find out and it'll be a different kind of visit."

Asher had always known of Tyson's heartlessness, always feared that it might someday find its way to him, and now it had. "I'm not sure," he finally said, defeated. "I need to use your computer."

Tyson nodded to his gargantuan enforcer, who motioned toward the house and followed Asher inside. Now left to himself in the cool seaside breeze, he picked up Asher's untouched refill and blew out a long end-of-the-day sigh.

Asher was absolutely right. Kang wasn't my girlfriend, and the kid actually did do me a favor. A five-figure favor, he thought, since Tyson had been seriously considering having her terminated anyway, and maybe by Asher himself. Still, it had been necessary to impose such a consequence; what was left of Tyson's team couldn't be making unilateral decisions, not important ones like that, and especially not during this crucial trial.

The Chancellor had told Tyson that if all went well in terms of the Southern Trust matter, Tyson might be introduced to the organization, the members of which could certainly benefit from his vast knowledge and experience, and they could absolutely afford any fee he might see fit to charge. These people weren't wealthy in the beachside terrace sort of way, Tyson knew. They bought governments, and industries, and often funded wars. Theirs was a world unlike anything he could possibly imagine.

This prospect was beyond exciting, but now it was time to get to work. Tomorrow would be a big day, the first of many, and the DA's office, crippled as it was, would not go down without a fight. But they *would* go down.

***

After witnessing the bus crash and snapping a photo of the victim, Sean Choi had followed Asher's motorcycle north to Solana Beach, where he took the off-ramp, drove over the freeway and back down to the ocean side. Ever careful to stay away from the bike, he had trailed Asher to a security checkpoint, which he was sure he wouldn't be allowed to pass, so he had driven on, parked some distance away, and infiltrated the gated complex under the cover of darkness using a variety of techniques his law enforcement friends had shown him over the years. Currently he sat astride a sturdy tree branch that afforded him a fairly good view of Asher's and Tyson's meeting.

At the end of that meeting, when Igmar followed a deflated Asher into Tyson's house to locate the hacker's father, Choi packed up his audio and video recording equipment, then climbed silently down and stole away. Following the same stealthy route to the Interceptor as he'd taken on the way in, he knew he hadn't obtained any admissible evidence, but he did now possess some valuable information—namely, that Asher would be illegally assisting Tyson with jury selection. And Igmar the butler warranted further investigation.

***

"Oh, all right," said the nurse, despite the rules, having been accosted by a persuasive pair of attorneys. "Five minutes."

Cammie nodded, as did Roche, and they eased into the private room where Lynn Peters lay in bed. Their chief deputy didn't sit up or even stir as they approached.

"Hey," said Cammie softly.

"How you doin' Boss?" This from Roche.

And that was all. Other than a sad and subtle nod from the fair-haired prosecutor, no reply was given or even needed. Cammie stroked Peters' forehead and the two women cried, while Roche—pale and stricken—stood by the window, facing away, crossing his arms, and wiping his eyes from time to time. To Cammie, he looked terrible. Much worse than she was feeling. Yes, Dea Bladet had been like an older sister to her, but only for a couple of weeks, while Roche had lost a very good friend. *No, they'd been closer than that.* "What did the doctors say?" she asked Peters.

"Penetrating knife wound to the spleen." Peters winced as she spoke. "The main complication is internal bleeding."

Roche blew out a breath as if to rid himself of difficult emotions, then unfolded his arms and joined them by the bed.

"Try to get a continuance tomorrow," Peters told them. "I'll do my best from here, but—" Unable to go on, she screwed her eyes shut in a grimace, then lay back and breathed through her pain.

"Okay, that's enough," said the nurse, a large woman who looked like she'd been on her feet for the past twenty years. She leaned over the machines, probably, Cammie thought, to adjust her patient's medication, and then she walked the lawyers out.

In the hallway, Roche asked the nurse about Peters' prognosis.

"We've managed to slow the bleeding, but if we can't stop it, she will need surgery, which means either a partial or total splenectomy. And there's always the risk of infection. So the prognosis is guarded. In other words, it's too early to make any kind of prediction."

"Thank you, ma'am," said Roche.

"We know she's in good hands," said Cammie.

The harried woman smiled thinly, nodded, and then bustled off.

"So what do you want to do?" Roche asked.

Cammie checked her phone. It was two in the morning and her stabbing headache threatened major consequences if she didn't lie down, but the hearing would start at nine. "I need to get ready for tomorrow," she said.

"*We* need to get ready for tomorrow."

"Okay. Can we go up to the neuroICU before we go?"

"Of course."

Roche stood outside Taylor's room with the detectives as Cammie entered alone. She sat with him, holding his hand, talking as though he could hear her. She said how sorry she was that he'd been hurt, that she'd be thinking of him all the time, and that she'd come back to see him as soon as she could. But he just lay there with a breathing tube down his throat, dead if not for the beeping electronics beside him.

Cammie put her face in her hands and wept, sobbing uncontrollably as she asked herself how it all made sense. It didn't. Not to her. But what could she do?

After that Cammie felt nothing but a furious determination to see justice served. So as she and Roche marched out of the hospital, her eyes still burned with tears, but that didn't slow her down a bit on the way to the Hall of Justice, where they worked until the sun came over the hills.

13

A DECEIVING APPEARANCE

Cammie and Roche worked most of the night at the Hall of Justice, then headed home for a shower—separately—before returning to the HOJ and meeting in the lobby.

"How's your head?" he asked, handing her a cup of coffee.

"Thanks," she said as she received it. "It still hurts."

He'd come in a tan wool-silk suit, close in color to that of his sandy locks; she'd opted for a black stretch skirt suit that hugged her hips. With a simple black blouse under her jacket, Cammie's outfit matched her hair as well.

They took the elevator up to the fourth floor, where they accessed the skybridge connecting the HOJ and the Central Courthouse. As they strolled over West C Street, a BearCat came grumbling up to the curb fifty feet below. Out piled Lieutenant Ron Ragasa and his team, who would be stationed in the courtroom at all times as a precaution against the violence surrounding the Southern Trust affair. This was reassuring to Cammie, who felt exceedingly anxious about her first appearance as lead counsel in a murder trial. And it didn't help that Vincent Tyson had been practicing law for twice as many years as she and Roche combined.

"You'll be okay," Roche assured her. "It's just an arraignment. Plus, the facts are on our side."

***

Just before Roche spoke these words, he looked down at the armored police vehicle and was instantly transported back to when he'd sat in its rear compartment with Dea Bladet, and this memory triggered a wave of sorrow that swelled in his chest and flooded his eyes with sharp stinging tears. He drew a calming breath, then turned to Cammie and said she'd be okay, and he meant it. *She will be*, he knew. Cammie was younger than Dea, but just as fierce, and she was off-the-charts intelligent. The night before, when they'd gone over Dea's notes, the charges against Dr. Haukea, and all the applicable legal provisions, Cammie's quick associations, sharp recall, and her capacity for complex analysis had reminded him of Sean Choi. Still, Bladet had been a seasoned veteran, so Roche was hoping the judge would grant them a continuance today, as that would give them time to find stronger witnesses, better evidence, conduct more research, and possibly allow Lynn Peters to get well enough to take Cammie's place.

Having already cleared security on arrival to the Hall of Justice, they came out of the skybridge and directly into the courthouse. There they rode another elevator down to the designated courtroom, outside which they stopped at a second security station. Cammie's bag was inspected, a wand waved over her body, and her dignity diminished as a policewoman patted her down; even so, she felt fine about it, since this procedure would apply to all civilians for the duration of the trial, keeping everyone safe.

Cammie and Roche walked past the spectator seating, or gallery, and into the well, which is the part of the courtroom that is off-limits to the general public. They took their places at the People's table on the right side of the well beside the jury box, and nodded to Tyson and Associates, who glanced up from a hushed conversation at the defendant's table, on the left side.

Also present was Ragasa's team, each man standing six feet apart with their backs to the left- and right-side walls, and a bailiff stationed at the back wall next to the judge's entrance, in addition to the court clerk at a table between the prosecution and the judge's bench, and the court reporter to the left of the judge's bench in an enclosure similar to the empty witness stand on the right side of the bench. Remarkably, there was not a single woman among them.

In the gallery behind Cammie and Roche sat journalists, photographers, several colleagues who'd come to watch, and a group of spectators from the public, which was surprising for a simple arraignment hearing.

Millie Haukea was brought in and seated at the defense table. She wore an orange prison jumpsuit, handcuffs, and her brown hair back in a loose ponytail. Her regal features bore no makeup, and she glared at Cammie and Roche with disdain.

"Pretty smug considering what we've got against her," Roche noted.

"She's got a good lawyer," countered Cammie.

"That depends on how you define 'good.'"

"So Choi sent me a picture of the accident victim," Cammie said, taking the materials she needed from her bag and arranging them on the table. "You won't believe who it was."

"Who?"

"The same Asian woman who attacked me and Lynn."

"That's poetic justice. She got bus-ted," said Roche.

Cammie gave him a tiny smile as the bailiff stepped forward.

"All rise," he intoned. "The Honorable Andrew Toles presiding."

Judge Toles entered the courtroom through the door behind the bench and stepped up to his place on high. He was a tall, broad-shouldered, and big-bellied African American man in his early sixties with short and very curly hair showing patches of gray. Peering down over his glasses, he adjusted his microphone and said in a grave baritone, "Please be seated. This is the matter of the People of the State of California versus Camilla Haukea. The defendant is charged with multiple offenses including two counts of murder in the first degree as well as burglary, data theft, and two counts of attempted murder. Counsel, please state your appearances for the record."

"Good morning, Your Honor," said Cammie, rising to her feet. "Camilla O'Mara appearing for the People. I'm stepping in for Dea Bladet, who was killed last night, as you may know."

"Good morning Ms. O'Mara. Yes, I am aware of that tragic incident, and I'd like to express my deepest condolences to you and everyone else affected."

"Thank you, Your Honor," said Cammie, resuming her seat.

"Good Morning Your Honor, Jonathan Roche, co-counsel for the People."

"Vincent Tyson, Your Honor, appearing for the defendant. We object to the substitution of counsel."

Here we go, thought Cammie.

"On what grounds?" Judge Toles asked.

"Your Honor, Ms. O'Mara lacks the necessary familiarity with this case, which could prejudice the defendant's right to a fair trial. Furthermore, Mr. Roche's involvement as lead counsel in a related matter compromises his impartiality."

Cammie stood to reply, but His Honor stopped her with a massive hand. "Overruled," he said. "As you know, Mr. Tyson, the two cases are distinct as to their legal and factual bases. That you were the defense attorney in the Southern Trust matter does not establish bias on the part of the prosecution—nor on yours, I might add—and there is no evidence that Mr. Roche has acted improperly. As for Ms. O'Mara, I find that she is fully capable of serving as lead counsel here. This trial has only just begun, which means she's as well prepared as Ms. Bladet would have been." The judge shifted his gaze to the defendant. "Doctor Haukea."

Thus dismissed, Tyson sat down as Millie Haukea rose, modestly and with a professional bearing, even in her orange jumpsuit.

"These charges carry heavy penalties," His Honor boomed, "including life in prison without parole. Have you received a copy of the complaint against you?"

"Yes, Your Honor," Tyson answered for her, standing once again. "We acknowledge receipt of the complaint and wish to waive a formal reading of the charges."

"How does the defendant plead?"

"Not guilty," said Tyson and Haukea in unison.

"A plea of not guilty is entered into the record. Moving on to bail. Ms. O'Mara."

Cammie sprang to her feet. "Your Honor, the People request that the defendant be held without bail due to the severity of the charges, the strength of the evidence, the danger she poses to the community, and the significant risk of flight."

"Mr. Tyson?"

"Your Honor, the People cannot possibly have any evidence, strong or otherwise, because Doctor Haukea is demonstrably innocent. She is an upstanding member of the community, and we have many credible witnesses who will testify to that effect."

"Thank you," said Judge Toles. "Were it only for the severity of the charges against the defendant, Mr. Tyson, the court might well hold her without bail, but the violence surrounding this case is even more reason to side with the prosecution. So Doctor Haukea will not be released on bond. Now, the preliminary hearing is scheduled for the Tuesday after next, also at nine. Counsel, make sure all discovery materials are exchanged in a timely manner. Is there anything further from the People?"

"Yes, Your Honor," said Cammie, standing. "We move for a continuance. Mr. Roche and I were only notified this morning that we'd be handling this case. Lynn Peters, our chief deputy, and I were attacked last night, and she remains in critical condition, so our unit is significantly understaffed at the moment."

His Honor nodded. "Yes, I *was* aware, Ms. O'Mara, and I was glad to learn that your injuries weren't more serious. Under the circumstances, I'm inclined to grant your request. How much time do you need?"

"Four weeks, Your Honor."

"Any objection from the defense?" asked Judge Toles.

Tyson stood slowly, almost apologetically. "I'm afraid so, Your Honor," he began. "We are, of course, sympathetic to the People's situation, but a continuance would infringe upon my client's right to a speedy trial. You said it yourself—Ms. O'Mara is just as prepared as Ms. Bladet would have been."

The Honorable Andrew Toles fell silent, seeming to deliberate upon the matter with the greatest concern. Dropping his gaze, he scrunched up his mouth and rested his chin on his fist. Finally he refocused on the opposing counsel and reluctantly delivered his ruling. "You make a good point, Mr. Tyson. In the interest of fairness, this trial will proceed as scheduled, but if any further complications should arise, Ms. O'Mara, you can be sure that the court will respond accordingly. If there's nothing else."

"No, Your Honor."

"No, Your Honor."

"Then we are adjourned."

As Cammie packed up her bag, she glanced over at Millie Haukea, who caught and held her gaze. Haukea's expression was softer this time, and Cammie gave her a nod. It had come as a surprise to her that they shared a first name, and since they were around the same age, it felt like a two-sides-of-the-same-coin kind of thing, a there-but-for-the-grace-of-God-go-I type of situation.

Could the defendant be a good person deep down, or had she passed the point of no return? Was she mentally ill? A wounded soul infected by evil? Born evil? Another possibility, though unlikely, was that she was innocent of the charges brought against her.

Cammie broke eye contact, slung her bag over her shoulder, and nodded to Roche. As they filed out of the courtroom, she wanted to believe that there was hope for everyone, just as all people are capable of malice under a certain set of conditions. Cammie sighed. Johnny held the door for her. His face was calm, those green eyes reassuring. *It's a long road ahead*, she knew as they made their way across the skybridge. *And I've got plenty to worry about besides the twisted mind of an alleged killer.*

***

Later that day in Roche's office, they were discussing next steps over a salad for Cammie and a sandwich for him. "Check this out," he said, chewing turkey and bread, holding his phone up for her to see. A bold headline from the online edition of the Union-Tribune read: **"JUDICIAL OVERREACH? LOCAL PHARMACIST DENIED BAIL IN CONTROVERSIAL RULING."**

Roche read aloud:

> In a shocking display of judicial overreach, Judge Andrew Toles denied bail to beloved local pharmacist Millie Haukea, despite her spotless reputation and the glaring lack of evidence against her.

"I see," said Cammie. "Tyson must be friends with the owner."

"Friends?" scoffed Roche. "I doubt he even knows the word. Listen to this."

The message from this courtroom spectacle is clear: justice is no longer about guilt or innocence—it's about optics, political ambition, and unchecked power. While prosecutors O'Mara and Roche bask in their success, a respected member of the community sits behind bars, being denied her fundamental right to due process.

"So what do you think?" Cammie asked.

Roche wiped his hands with a thick paper napkin. "Seems like Tyson's gonna use every dirty trick in the book, but as long as the judge is solid, we should be okay."

"I agree. Toles was firm but fair. I liked him."

"So did I."

Suddenly the article disappeared and the internet page produced an error.

Cammie peered over Roche's shoulder as he tried in vain to bring it back. "That's weird," she said.

"Maybe the piece was too biased," he suggested. "I'm gonna take it as a good sign."

"Me too," said Cammie with a hopeful smile.

14

DISCOVERY

Vincent Tyson had been pleased by Judge Toles' performance, so much so that he'd wired the man a generous gratuity to his offshore account. He'd *had* him wired a gratuity, to be more precise, for Tyson would never have involved himself in anything that might put him at risk. Not if he could help it. This was why he was still in the game at sixty years of age, when so many of his competitors had been knocked off the chessboard.

At the moment, Tyson was sitting on his oceanfront terrace, his thinking spot, which also served as the place where all of his team meetings were held, his team now comprising only Asher and Dane. For added strength, however, he'd offered Igmar a place at the table. This was a promotion, which meant in theory that every man would now have to fetch his own refreshment, but since Asher was still being punished for killing Kang, the digital mercenary was currently serving as the butler.

In fact, Asher had just been sent to the kitchen for another round since the discussion had been put on pause; Tyson had taken a call from the owner of the largest newspaper in town. The criminal defender remained in his seat as Asher sullenly collected everyone's glasses and trudged inside to refill them. Igmar watched Asher do this with obvious delight while Dane gazed out at the ocean.

"What were you thinking?" the crooked attorney snapped, holding his cell phone to his ear.

"Give me a break! I was in Jamaica," whined a man through the tiny speaker.

Tyson snorted. "That's no excuse. We'd already agreed on the restriction. You're lucky my hacker found the article right away. Get your head out of your ass!"

"Sorry, Vince. Can I make it up to you? What if we ran a series on you and your firm, building you up. Something like, 'Famous Firm Unstoppable' or 'The Real L.A. Law.'"

"I don't need to be built up, Monahan. I need to keep a low profile, which is why I ordered the blackout in the first place. Just stick to the agreement."

Clicking off, Tyson shut his eyes against the pain of disappointment. He shook his head in disgust, taking note of a fresh salty breeze blowing on his face, but it failed to quell his rage. Tyson persisted, drawing it in through his nose. Slowly. Deeply. Letting it fall out naturally as the cawing of the gulls and the sea's soothing rhythm carried him away. Every few seconds a wave crashed softly, but this force was also unyielding, and when the surf was raging it could only be described as hard. *Ah, the ancient duality of nature*, Tyson reflected. Then his eyes snapped open.

Asher was back in his place. "It's gonna be a tough night for Taylor," he said in jest to Dane, the muscular specialist in accidents and suicides, who also held a pilot's license.

"Nah," said Dane. "He won't feel a thing."

They both looked ready. *They'd better be,* Tyson grumbled to himself. Their mission was critical because Dom Taylor could have seen that email before Asher had deleted it, the email sent by Major Wyans of the Honolulu Police about Millie's sealed records and the crimes she'd committed there—allegedly. So if Taylor *had* seen the email and were to regain consciousness, it was a given that he'd speak to the prosecution team about it. Worse yet, he'd most likely mention Millie to his friends, Detectives Park and Walker, whose testimony could conceivably destroy Tyson's case, even with a friendly judge.

"What should we do about Park and Walker?" Igmar asked.

Tyson nodded his approval. "Good question. Let's start with Taylor. The blackout should give us time to wrap up the trial, assuming these two are successful tonight."

By 'blackout,' Tyson had meant all the strings he'd pulled at every major and minor media outlet covering the trial. Through bribery, blackmail, cyber tactics, legal threats, and subtle behind-the-scenes maneuvering, he'd practically ensured that no news of Haukea v. The People would be made public, his main concern being that Park and Walker might learn of it.

"So we'll steer clear of those two for now," Tyson went on. "Because if we go after them and fail, things could quickly spiral out of control. They're MARTAC operators, members of the Harbor Police's SWAT team. What if they got hold of whoever we send after them?"

"What do you mean *whoever we send*?" Asher protested. "It would be me and Dane, obviously."

"Why don't you go get us some chips?" Igmar said with a straight face. Then, at Asher's clear indignation, the giant Swede broke into a grin and burst into a roaring belly laugh.

Tyson smiled, said nothing, while Dane was looking thoughtful. "Or we could just take Millie out and be done with it," the muscular pilot suggested.

"I know," said Tyson. "And that's a very tempting option."

***

"Are you and Taylor close?" asked Johnny Roche. This time they were in Cammie's office, a windowless room in the Hall of Justice, and they'd been busy for hours at a worktable in the corner.

Cammie smiled appreciatively, since Roche had politely said *are* in place of the much darker *were*. "Close *friends*, yes," she replied. "But we've only had a handful of dates. And I don't think it's going anywhere."

"No?"

"He wants someone to stay home and take care of him. You know, fold his clothes, cook his food—"

"And you're a busy professional."

"Exactly."

"And that's what laundromats and take-out are for."

"Right again," she said.

"Is there any news about his chances of recovery?"

"No, but the doctor said they might be flying him to New York for testing."

"What about Lynn?"

"Nothing good there, either," Cammie told him with a sigh. "They couldn't stop the bleeding, so she's having surgery tomorrow. A total splenectomy, which means two months before she can come back to work, and a week before we can even meet with her."

This last comment led to silence and a shared expression of discouragement.

The trial wasn't going well; she and Roche had faithfully delivered to Tyson all the required discovery materials including witness statements, surveillance footage, forensic reports, expert findings, physical evidence, and police reports, while the crooked defender had been filing motion after motion—to exclude, to delay, to withhold certain materials, and to protect supposedly sensitive information. This was to be expected from any opposing counsel, up to a point, but making things much worse was that at every hearing held to argue these motions, Judge Toles had listened carefully, expressed agreement with both sides, then invariably proceeded to rule in Tyson's favor. On anything important, that is. Sometimes he'd throw the People a dry and dirty bone.

So Cammie and Roche knew little about Tyson's strategy, while Tyson would just breeze into the courtroom when the trial started, ready to rebut each and every one of their arguments. Cammie was concerned that His Honor might not be nearly as honorable as he had seemed initially.

They were exhausted after working a string of eighteen-hour days, writing motion responses, preparing and protecting witnesses, meeting with experts, researching the members of the jury pool and drafting the jury's instructions, writing and rehearsing the opening statement, preparing for cross-examination, and the list went on. *And* this wasn't their only case; both had other work to do.

"Do you want to go up to the roof?" asked Roche.

"Yeah," said Cammie, setting down her pen immediately.

They climbed two flights of stairs and emerged from the access door on a perfect sunny day. Nothing but clear sky and they could see for miles. Neither spoke as they took it all in: the deep blue bay scattered with sparkling diamonds, the Coronado Bridge winding its way to the island, a cruise ship docked at the terminal next to the sturdy Navy vessels, and the hills of Tijuana in the distance to their left. At that height, the wind was gusty, blowing their hair in every direction, but the cool air served to clear Cammie's head. It helped her sort something out that had been nibbling at the edges of her mind.

"Okay," she said, turning to Roche. "Let's start from the beginning. We've got a poisoner on our hands, and she's no amateur. Haukea's a doctor of pharmacy."

"Right," said Roche slowly, unsure of where she was headed.

"And her accomplice is an ex-military master of disguise and impersonation. Or maybe she's *his* accomplice."

Understanding dawned in Roche's eyes. He nodded. "Or maybe they were teammates, killing people to force a mistrial."

"Exactly," said Cammie. "Then there's the programmer known as Asher, also an expert in his field, who attempted to kill Choi and Taylor when they got involved—"

"And the martial artist who tried to take you and Peters out. That's four." Roche was keeping count on his fingers.

"There's five, at least. Remember the footage from the courthouse? Someone fired a shot at Morrison Grant, coincidently missed, and too coincidentally missed again, setting him free and enabling him to escape."

"Sounds like a loyal teammate to me."

"I agree. So who's the team leader?" Cammie asked like a teacher, waiting for Roche to draw his own conclusion.

Roche shook his head. No idea. But then his eyes came alive. "Tyson," he said with conviction.

"Why?"

"For his clients. First it was Southern Trust, and now it's Millie Haukea. Take out the opposing witnesses, investigators, and attorneys and the case gets dismissed. So Tyson's who we really want."

"Right. Which means..."

"Which means we need to strike a plea agreement with Millie Haukea."

"But there's a problem," said Cammie. "It's unethical and illegal for us to contact her without going through Tyson, and I can't think of any way to do it."

"Oh, that's easy."

"How?"

"You don't want to know."

"Is it legal?"

"More or less."

"Is it ethical?"

"Ethical?" Roche parroted incredulously. "Cammie. We are up against a gang of remorseless murderers. Dea is dead, and we don't know about Dom. It was by blind luck that they didn't get me, and things could *easily* have gone the other way for you and Lynn as well. Now, I can get Haukea to come in, and I know for a fact that it won't blow up in our face. But it's your call."

Their eyes met. The wind ruffled his thick head of sandy blond hair. Finally, she smiled and said, "You'd make a good lawyer."

He nodded grimly and together they turned to take one last look at the California coastline, as if to show respect or say goodbye. Then they hustled downstairs and set the plan into motion.

***

Millie Haukea lay on her bunk in jail, staring up at the bed above her with her hands behind her head. *He's sorry*, she thought. *I could see it in his eyes.*

"I'll make it up to you," Morgan had promised her in the interview room.

But how was he planning make it up to me? He didn't know Voss was going to set him free. Maybe he'd been planning to escape all along. In any case, he's sorry, which means he might be sober again. And if that's true, then he could be anywhere, impersonating anyone, male or female. He could have even been in the courtroom, watching me in disguise.

Millie knew in her heart that she shouldn't pin her hopes on Morgan to break her out of jail or influence the trial in her favor. But that knowledge was deeply buried. Closer to the surface, her more impulsive self pictured him marching into the courtroom as a juror and shooting her a wink.

It was too easy to dream of freedom, to cling to her fantasy of returning to Hawaii, where she'd been born. Of running away and living there with him—not on Oahu, where she might be recognized, but on one of the smaller islands. Kauai or Molokai perhaps, in a tiny town where people kept to themselves.

I could be a mother!

No. You need to focus on the trial, on working with Vincent. He's been good to you.

But has he really?

Her cell smelled like the inside of a portable toilet, one of those temporary installations found at stadium events or construction sites, and the guards were just as nasty as the inmates. But when Millie was let out for recreation or meals, people tended to leave her alone. Not that they knew she'd been a serial killer, of course, for if that came to light she'd be convicted immediately. Still, she carried herself with a physical confidence that few of the others would be bold enough to test.

So my slip-up on Oahu wasn't all bad. I'm respected here. Why? Because the ability to kill is an adaptive trait. It's in our DNA. Yes, I took it too far, but I can scale it back. Live a normal life.

Can you really?

Later that day, when Millie's group was let out for rec time, she trudged over to a picnic table and took a seat. With her back against the edge of the tabletop, she was watching the various group activities going on when a fellow inmate named Sara ambled over to sit opposite her.

"Hey," said the black-haired tattooed woman, with whom Millie wasn't close—nor did she ever want to be. But sometimes they would eat together and "talk story," as they say in Hawaii.

Millie turned to face her and nodded a lukewarm welcome.

"I've been thinking about your case," Sara said.

"Is that right."

"Yeah, and I had an idea. Did you know I'm a CI?"

Millie shook her head, but had, in fact, heard that Sara was a confidential informant.

"I was looking at thirty years without parole, but I've been working with a DA and now I'm getting out in five. You should do the same. There's this cop named Ragasa at SDPD. Call him. He's easy to find."

"I'll think about it," Millie muttered.

Sara stood and started off, but a few seconds later Millie called out after her. "Hey!"

The other turned her head.

"Don't shut your eyes tonight."

Sara cocked her head, looking thoughtful. Then nodded gravely and turned to go.

Millie gazed down absently at the worn wooden table, brooding over the fact that Sara was to be shanked in her sleep. On the one hand, she felt, that's what anyone who squealed on her fellow cons deserved; on the other, betrayal and broken promises were standard practice in their world, and Sara seemed like a decent person.

At least now she'll have a fighting chance.

15

THE DEVIL YOU KNOW

Two female correctional officers guided Millie Haukea through the drab light-brown corridors of the women's facility, stopping at several security stations along the way. The guards watched her with heightened suspicion and paid more attention than usual to the integrity of her restraints on account of a recent fatal incident: Somehow, three inmates had escaped from their cells the night before, found Sara's door unlocked by coincidence, and quietly filed in to stab her with their shanks. But Sara, who'd been alerted and was lying awake, sprang up to surprise them by attacking first. Using a jail-made stabbing weapon of her own, she'd killed all three inmates before succumbing to her wounds.

'Somehow,' scoffed Millie to herself, eyeing all the guards surrounding her. *'By coincidence.' It might have been one of these bitches who let it happen.* At any rate, Millie wished she could see the video, if only for the entertainment value.

"Good morning, Doctor Haukea," said Lieutenant Ragasa as she shuffled into the interview room, limited in mobility by her shackles. The stocky Filipino nodded to the guards, who left them alone while Millie eased herself into a chair.

"I'm guessing you remember me," said Ragasa, who was seated on the other side of a table. Behind him, in the upper left corner of the room, a camera was aimed directly at her.

Millie frowned and rolled her eyes. *Of course I remember you.*

"I appreciate you reaching out to me," Ragasa went on.

She allowed him a single nod.

"Before we talk, I need to inform you of your right to have an attorney present. We spoke about this on the phone, but for the record, please look up at the camera and confirm that you are voluntarily waiving that right. Voluntarily means no one is forcing you. Okay?"

She looked up at the camera and scowled at it. "Yes. I understand and I agree."

"Thank you, Doctor Haukea. Remember, everything about this conversation is voluntary. Under the fifth and sixth amendments, you don't have to answer any of my questions, or you can answer some of them and not others, and you can change your mind about your lawyer being here at any time. Do you understand?"

"Yes." *He's cute, in a grumpy-older-guy kind of way, with that trim little mustache. And he's in pretty good shape for fifty. Maybe forty-five.*

"One last thing. I also have to inform you that Jonathan Roche and Cammie O'Mara, the prosecutors in your case, are watching us live. They aren't allowed to come in here, or to influence our conversation in any way, but they *are* here at the jail and I'll be speaking to them when we're done. Are we okay so far?"

Millie was sick of all the explanations and niceties. Especially the niceties. She looked away in frustration and blew out a long, impatient breath, but again she gave him a nod.

"I need you to say yes or no."

"Yes."

"Thank you. So why did you want to talk to me today?"

"I'm not sure."

"Is it because your attorney hired you and Morrison Grant to kill Ronald Green and Michael Schmidt?"

"Who?"

"The Southern Trust executives who were murdered two months ago."

Nice try, she thought.

Ragasa was undeterred. "Are you paying for Mr. Tyson's legal services or is he doing it for free?"

Again she saw no reason to reply. *I like your brown skin, Ragasa. It reminds me of mine.*

"You *do* know Tyson's not really defending you. He's defending himself. Using you as a shield."

He was right, of course. But Tyson had been like a father to Millie, the closest thing she'd ever had, anyway. Saved her from life in prison on Oahu, put her through school, and always kept her flush with money. It was a complicated situation. So again she gave no reply. Just stared at the policeman. His eyes were dark and Asian, a little like hers.

Ragasa stayed calm despite her unwillingness to speak. "You stated before that Vincent Tyson is a family friend, but I can assure you that whatever he's done for you, he didn't do for *you*."

Millie let her mind wander as Ragasa went on to explain that the case against her was solid, and that she'd go to prison for life, while her attorney would walk away scot-free and filthy rich.

She knew all that, and it was mostly true, except for the going-to-prison part; Morgan might still help her escape or somehow influence the jury's verdict, and it was also possible that Tyson, who really *was* an intelligent, experienced, and well-connected litigator—and a dirty fighter besides—could convince the jury to acquit her, despite the overwhelming evidence.

But none of that's for sure, she knew. *Maybe I should make a deal and rely only on myself for a change.*

Frustrated, uncertain, stripped of her freedom and therefore furious, she took comfort in an old fantasy, imagining Ragasa on his back and herself straddling him, wrapping her hands around his neck, and watching him die. The thought of it was arousing, and the act itself would deliver a climax of epic proportions.

"Your cooperation could result in a relatively light sentence," he was saying. "You might do as little as fifteen years, maybe ten with good behavior."

Millie watched his lips but tuned out the words, focusing instead on another familiar feeling: anger. She wanted to hit and hurt. Why? It was her heartless father, who'd left her and her mother, never to be seen again. Then Millie's mom had checked out, too, overdosing on hard drugs. Her grandfather, the first man to ever show her love, had taken charge of her then, but he'd had his own demons. And when he'd died and gone to hell, Millie'd been left to the horrors of the foster care system. It was enough to make her want to leap up onto the table, rip that camera from its mountings, and smash it against the floor!

"That's an interesting tattoo you've got there," Ragasa noted, nodding toward her upper chest.

"I don't want to talk about it," Millie said, buttoning her orange jumpsuit all the way up.

"I wasn't looking at you improperly, if that's what you're thinking," he said. "It's just that I saw this TV show once where the bad guy had a Nazi swastika covered up by making it into a divided square just like yours."

"I said I didn't want to talk about it!" Millie shouted, bolting out of her chair, but her restraints wouldn't allow her to fully explode. So she let out a long, piercing scream.

At that moment she made up her mind. It was an impulsive decision and probably the wrong one, but Millie didn't care. Couldn't care. Didn't *love herself* enough to care. Despite Morgan's unreliability and Tyson's selfishness, those two men were familiar figures, unlike the cop she was currently with and the sharks on the other end of the camera. She couldn't trust those three pigs even if she'd wanted to. *Better the devil you know*, she told herself as the guards dragged her back to her cell.

***

The next morning, the same two female correctional officers led Millie to a room similar to the one she and Ragasa had used, but this one was not supplied with a camera nor with any other kind of recording equipment, just a large window through which the prison staff could watch—but not listen to—her attorney-client consultation.

"You'd better behave this time," said one of the guards with a malevolent grin, "or it's the *shoe* for *you*." This was in reference to the SHU, the special housing unit a.k.a. solitary confinement.

Facing forward as she trudged along, Millie didn't acknowledge the woman's remark, which had come across as tough, but in jail the guards held all the cards. She wondered what kind of voice the woman might use if someday they saw each other on the outside.

Tyson was already seated when Millie entered the room. In shackles again, she could only shuffle to the one other chair. Then she lowered herself into it, facing him. After they'd been left alone, Tyson didn't speak; he just kept staring. Savagely, as though he might fly out of his seat and strike her with an open-handed slap.

Millie held his gaze unflinchingly.

"So you met with the prosecution without me," he finally said. With each word, his heavy lips mashed together and parted, and his black eyes seemed to burn the life right out of her.

Even as her heart pounded in her chest, Millie was able to keep her face impassive. "You think I told them something?"

"No," said Tyson, relaxing a little. "No, I don't. Not intentionally."

"Not at *all*," she hissed. Now *she* was the angry one.

"How'd they set it up?"

"One of my fellow inmates came up to me in the rec yard and happened to mention that she was a CI for a district attorney, but she didn't say who. Then she suggested I make contact with a cop named Ragasa."

"It was either Roche or O'Mara," he said with disgust. "Had to be. I could use it against them in court."

"Let it go."

***

Snotty brat! growled Tyson to himself when she told him to let it go. "Why?" he asked.

"First of all, Sara's dead."

"Who?"

"The inmate who told me to make contact."

"Well, that *does* make a difference. Now she can't testify."

"Of course you know *why* they wanted to make a deal with me."

"Of course. And you're right—we need to play it cool, even under the circumstances," Tyson said, knowing there were certain lines that Judge Toles would never cross. For instance, if the prosecution were to produce evidence of Tyson's having hired Millie to kill the Southern Trust executives, they could move to have him removed from the case, citing a conflict of interest, and Toles would be forced to grant that request. *Which wouldn't be so bad*, Tyson thought, *but then they'd charge <u>me</u> for solicitation of murder and I'd lose my human shield.*

"Vince, can I ask you a question?" said his human shield.

Bloody hell, here we go. "Yes, you may."

"How do I know you won't have me killed like the others?"

"Because I gave you my word that I would defend you."

"What about the money?"

Too many questions. Tyson plastered on a tender look, leaned forward, and set his hand on her knee like someone capable of love might do. "Don't worry, honey," he said. "I've always looked out for you, haven't I?"

She pursed her lips and studied her jail shoes. Tyson figured she was debating whether or not she could trust him. As she did this, Tyson's tender look slipped, revealing his hateful impatience for a beat, but before she glanced up he forced the lie back onto his face.

In her amber eyes he saw love and trust, and it made him sick. *She's a pervert! It would be so easy to have her shanked, just like Sara. Then I'd fly to a non-extradition country, alter my appearance, and live in luxury for the rest of my life. I could be in Brazil in a week.*

He gave her knee a loving squeeze. "Don't worry about the money," he said. "Since half the team's either missing or gone, your payday's gonna reach into the afterlife."

That earned him a grin. Millie settled into her chair and heaved a great sigh.

So did Tyson, since he'd just made up his mind to have her executed. His relief was absolute, and he let it show. Naturally, she assumed he was feeling better because *she* was feeling better, which Tyson thought was perfect. "The next phase of the trial is voir dire," he told her, "which means jury selection, and you have a right to attend. In fact, I want you to—"

BOOM BOOM BOOM!

Tyson and Millie turned to face the door.

"Come in," Tyson barked, at which point a large female guard who bore no similarity to anyone he had ever known entered with authority and said, in a natural-sounding woman's voice, "Message from the warden, Mr. Tyson."

Tyson looked up at the officer, who caught his eye as she handed over an envelope. He nodded and she departed. Then he drew from the envelope a folded sheet of paper, which he opened and read, and his eyes grew wide as the implications hit him like a baseball bat.

> I'M KEEPING A CLOSE EYE ON YOU AND THE TRIAL. IF ANYTHING HAPPENS TO MILLIE, YOU'RE NEXT.

"What does it say?" Millie asked.

Two abilities that all good trial lawyers possess are acting and thinking on their feet, and Tyson was one of the best. He shook his head dismissively, rose with an air of indifference, and said, "Oh, it's just bad news about a different inmate. I need to go see about it." Then he leaned over to kiss her forehead as a father might do—or as a young woman who never had a father might need him to do—and told her not worry, that everything would turn out fine.

Then he flew out of the building in a murderous rage.

16

NOCTURNAL VISITORS

It was after sunset when Dane and Asher rolled up to the hospital on their rented bikes, parking in a white zone near an emergency exit. Both were dressed in the same blue scrubs that the doctors wore, bought from the same company that supplied the medical center. They dismounted, shrugged on long white lab coats with real ID badges, hid their features with surgical caps and masks, covered their prints with blue rubber gloves, and set off for the sliding doors at the entrance.

Thus disguised, they met with no trouble in the lobby, and none when they came to the staff elevator, since they had come prepared; on their previous visit, Asher had "accidentally" bumped into a physician and used a custom RFID skimmer to clone her keycard while offering his most profuse apologies.

Alone in the lift, they exchanged a glance. Dane looked far too serious. Mean, even. Asher clapped him on the back to help him loosen up, and then he went inward, taking deep breaths to stave off his fear. The doors slid open on the tenth floor. Fifty yards down the hallway, the same pair of plainclothes policemen sat on either side of Dom Taylor's door. Asher and Dane marched forward as if they belonged there, and stopped in front of the lawmen, who stood with expectant looks.

"We're here to perform a neuro exam," said Asher. "The attending physician ordered an immediate assessment based on new EEG readings."

Dane showed them a clipboard holding a real consultation request with Taylor's name and patient number and a note that corroborated Asher's explanation, all in the attending physician's meticulously forged handwriting and with his signature on the dotted line.

While the officers scrutinized the paperwork, Asher's thumping, pounding heartbeat and recurring thoughts of death threatened to take control of his legs and carry him back to the elevator, but this sense of terror was nothing new to him. Plus, he'd never do that to Dane, who'd then be arrested or killed. And Asher would have to suffer Tyson's wrath, missing out on the life-changing payday he'd been promised. *Or worse*, he reckoned as the cops opened the door and nodded them inside.

With the lights off, the curtains drawn open, and the sky growing dim outside, the room was fairly dark, but they could see Taylor easily; in the center of that space he lay on a bed with wires taped to his chest and his head and everything hooked up to machines.

Dane took his place by the door, reaching under his scrub top for a silenced pistol, the same one he'd used to kill Bladet, while Asher prepared an injection. He drew a syringe from his coat, held it up to eye level, and pushed the plunger up to expel the last of the bubbles and a dribble of the mortal solution. Then, as he leaned over the district attorney investigator to administer the shot, he felt stupid, as tiny air bubbles would be the least of Taylor's concerns. As he brought the syringe closer and closer to Taylor's shoulder, the patient suddenly sat bolt upright!

The man posing as Taylor drew back a heavy fist and slammed Asher in the mouth, then reached under the bedsheets for a hidden pistol while fighting for the syringe with his other hand. "Hey!" he shouted.

Then came the muffled *thwack* of Dane's gun, and the undercover cop instantly lost his strength.

The syringe clattered to the floor.

Asher took the pistol from the dying man, who fell back onto his pillow with a badly bleeding chest wound.

"SDPD!" screamed one of the men at the door, throwing it open but not charging in. "Drop your weapons!"

"Cooper!" yelled the other, also staying out of sight. "What's your status?"

The only reply from the undercover officer was a wet gurgle and a final shuddering sigh.

Dane swiveled his gunsights from the bed to the open doorway, dropped into a crouch, and backed into one of the corners farthest from the threat.

Asher had two guns now. Two pistols and a plan. He took cover behind the bed and held up the guns for Dane to see.

Nodding in understanding, Dane bellowed, "Okay, we're coming out! We give up."

"Slide us your pistols!" demanded one of the officers, still hidden from sight.

So that's what Asher did. He pushed both guns out into the hallway, strode to the middle of the room, and put his hands in the air. Meanwhile, Dane took Asher's place behind the bed and concealed his pistol under the sheets. He, too, held up his arms, but kept one hand lower than the other, close to his hidden weapon.

The muzzle of a pistol appeared in the open doorway, turning the corner. It was followed by one of the plainclothes policemen, who held the weapon straight out in a classic two-handed firing position, rotating into the room by degrees until he had a clear view and an easy shot at Asher.

Then his partner stormed in, training his sights on Dane. "Step away from the bed!" roared this second man, giving Dane no alternative but to comply.

"Easy now," the first one said, stepping slowly toward Asher with a pair of flex cuffs in one hand and his leveled gun in the other. "Put your hands behind your back and turn around."

Asher put his hands behind his back, but he didn't turn around. Instead, he flew past the policeman's outstretched shooting arm while whipping out the syringe from his back pocket, and plunged it into the policeman's neck.

The second cop targeted Asher immediately, but the first was in the way. No shots were fired, at least not until Dane exploded forward to wrest the gun from the second cop's hands. BLAM went the pistol and *thud* went the second cop's body as it hit the floor like a fallen tree.

Asher slipped instantly out of his bloody lab coat and hustled out the door with Dane right behind him. In the hallway, they slowed to a walking pace and fell into easy conversation as staff and security rushed past in the opposite direction.

The elevator doors slid closed. They felt a jolt as the compartment started down. "Well done," said Dane to Asher, whose heart was slamming against the inside of his chest with so much force that he heard the pulsing in his ears all the way down. It seemed to take forever. But soon they were back on their bikes, zooming through the downtown streets, not talking in their helmet comms, just glad to be alive.

***

Crime really pays, thought Asher, who was just as amazed by the nocturnal view from his penthouse suite as he'd been when he'd first acquired it. His building stood in downtown San Diego, with its sprawling expanse of high-rise structures glowing with warm white lights, neon greens, blood reds, and cool electric blues. These colors could be seen in reflection on the rippling black waters of the bay. Rising from downtown's western edge, the Coronado Bridge curved high over the harbor, lit on both sides by lampposts marking its sinuous path to the island. And Coronado itself—one of the costliest tracts of real estate in the county—shone with equal brilliance. Its crown jewel, the famous hotel, was so ornately decorated with vintage-style lights that at night it looked like Disneyland.

Frozen in place in the middle of his sitting room, Asher marveled at this multicolored spectacle. Truly, it was a million-dollar view. "More like four million," he muttered out loud.

"What?" Puzzled, Dane shut the front door behind them and joined Asher where he stood.

"Nothing. Drink?"

"Pleeease," said Dane, feigning desperation as he plopped himself down on a black leather sofa.

"Help yourself. The bar hasn't moved," Asher said. "I'll be back in ten."

Dane groaned and got back up while Asher started down the hallway, at the end of which lay his data center, a secure climate-controlled room that housed the most advanced private computer system in the city. Thirty minutes later, he ambled back into the sitting room to see Dane on the couch with a drink halfway to his mouth.

"So?" Dane prompted.

"Nada," said Asher, stepping behind the bar to pour himself a club soda on ice.

"You mean he's gone? Disappeared without a trace? Never to be found by the greatest brain of all time?"

Asher took a seat on another leather sofa and shot his comrade a frown. "There's no record of Taylor being moved. In fact, his entire medical file has been erased."

"Irretrievably?"

"Yes. I think Choi's been helping the hospital with their IT system." Asher fished around in his blood-spattered scrub pants for a secure cell phone, then drew it out and put it to use.

"Good news or bad?" grumbled a deep voice on the other end of the connection.

"Medium," Asher retorted, setting the device on the table between him and Dane. "You're on speaker."

"Go on."

Asher launched into a retelling of their adventure, and when he came to the part at which the undercover officer sat up in bed—

"I get it," boomed Tyson. "You failed. That's *bad* news, not medium."

"It could have been worse," countered Dane. He took a sip of his drink and set it aside. "It was a well-planned ambush, and we survived."

Tyson harrumphed. "How hard do you think it'll be to find him?"

Asher leaned closer to the phone. "I searched the hospital records, both local and national, as well as the surveillance camera feeds—which I edited—plus ambulance logs and insurance claims, and there's not a single record of Taylor's hospital stay. It's as if he were never there. Do you recall me telling you about Sean Choi, the programmer who works at the DA's office?"

"Yes."

"I think Choi's digitally hiding Dom Taylor and Lynn Peters. And their police protection will be twice as heavy now."

"Okay," said Tyson. "That's second priority for now; there's something that's even more important. I need you to locate Morgan and bring him to me."

"Why?" asked Dane.

"Disguised as a guard, he found me at the jail, handed me a note, and left before I could read it. It said if anything happened to Millie that I'd be next."

Asher frowned. "*Will* anything happen to Millie?"

"Of course not."

"So he *could* be in the courtroom," Dane concluded. "Posing as the bailiff, or maybe the court reporter. Even a cop. Do y'all think he could pull off Judge Toles?"

"Assuming he's sober now, and I think he is, Morgan can pose as anyone," came Tyson's voice. "He could be a different person every day. That's what makes him dangerous."

"Why do you want him so bad, anyway?" asked Asher. "Why not just let him watch the trial and keep us on Taylor? And what about Park and Walker? We could hit them tomorrow."

"Just do as I say. Are you ready for voir dire?"

"I will be," Asher promised.

"So will I. See you tomorrow," Tyson said, clicking off.

A few minutes later, Asher and Dane were out on the balcony leaning on the stainless-steel drink rail topping the barrier, which wrapped around two full sides of the residential tower. This afforded them an even better view than that of the sitting room.

"Where do you look for a master of disguise?" Dane wondered aloud. "I *know* we won't find him at his apartment."

"No," said Asher glumly, stepping away for a second to turn on the jacuzzi. "He won't be at Millie's house, either. And he'll have switched cars, so the tracker's no good."

Dane's face brightened. "I just thought of something," he said. "Even if Morgan's clean now, his old connections should be able to tell us *something*."

"Uh-huh." Asher knew what was coming.

"That means peyote, mushrooms, datura," Dane went on. "You know, the vision seekers, shaman circles. We can hit *them* up later."

Asher finished Dane's sentence, dryly. "But since Morgan was also a cokehead, why not canvass the high-end party clubs?"

"Exactly!" Dane was grinning from ear to ear. "Can I use your phone?"

"Of course," said Asher. Gazing down at the island bridge, Asher finished his cold club soda; it tickled his throat and cooled his body, which was still running hot after the failed operation. *The medium operation.* Chuckling to himself, he next put his mind to work on how to locate his former comrade, and it occurred to him that he could probably hack in to the servers at Fort Irwin. If there was any organization that kept sensitive information on Morrison Grant, it would be the U.S. Army.

The sound of the sliding glass door brought him back to the here and now. Dane was back. "I called a couple girls and told 'em to meet me here. Hope that's okay."

"That's fine. High-class hookers to assist you in your investigation?"

"Yep. It'll make it much easier for me at the clubs."

"I agree," said Asher, leaning on the rail, staring out at the water.

"Hang on," Dane suddenly said, as if he'd just discovered a glitch in his plan, but of course he hadn't.

Asher turned to face him slowly, with half-lidded eyes and a skeptical frown.

Dane plowed ahead as though he were oblivious to Asher's expression. "It's too early to go out, so can we use your hot tub? You'd be welcome to join us."

"No thanks. I've got work to do. And yes you can, but on three conditions."

"Done."

"No smoking or coming, and you have to leave by eleven. I'll be having a visitor of my own and it needs to be clean out here."

"But we can skinny-dip?"

"Sure."

After a third round of drinks in the open air, just as Asher was rattling ice cubes in his empty glass, the hookers rang the bell. He said hello and then disappeared, tidying up the kitchen while Dane poured drinks and played the charming host. Before long, the muscular hitman and his investigative assistants were out on the balcony peeling off each other's clothes. Asher paid little attention to the playful young women, not batting an eye at their jiggling breasts, nor pausing to ogle their clean-shaven lower bodies.

Asher killed the kitchen lights and strode down the hall. *Work before play*, he reminded himself. It was a motto that had always served him well.

17

GOODBYE—FOR NOW

Sean Choi gripped the steering wheel with two tight hands, intensely focused on the cars ahead, which fell behind quickly as he bobbed and weaved between them. *Dammit!* He smacked his hand on the center pad and held it there, doing nothing to relieve his frustration, nor apparently alerting the preceding driver as to the urgency of his mission by the sound of his blaring horn. The clock on the dash read 8:15 a.m. He wouldn't make it on time, but every second mattered.

His morning had begun calmly. Slowly. With a nice cup of coffee and everything neatly laid out for the first of several days in court. He was out the door by 5:45, earlier than usual since he had to be somewhere before going to the courthouse, somewhere fairly distant.

The second reason for his pre-dawn departure was that he'd be executing a surveillance detection run, a technique he'd been taught by his pals in law enforcement. In this case that meant (after scanning the car in the garage for bombs and tracking devices) performing a series of subtle maneuvers on the road such as changing routes, driving in circles, varying his speed, and making sudden stops or turns, all intended to shake off or identify a tail.

So by the time he pulled up at the secret medical facility where Lynn Peters and Dom Taylor were being treated, he'd been sitting in the driver's seat for almost an hour. In his personal vehicle, not the Police Interceptor.

It was at this secret facility that the first disaster of the day took place. It wasn't related to Peters, the chief prosecutor, whose postsurgical progress had been better than expected. No, the terrible news had to do with Taylor.

"It's been two and a half weeks," the neurologist said to Choi as they stood over Taylor's bed. Dr. Slater was a kindly man, older, with a cherubic face, a neatly trimmed beard showing gray, a generous midsection, and dark, incisive eyes. Beside the bed, stacks of machines clicked and beeped, keeping the DA investigator alive. "And there's still no sign of cognitive improvement."

Choi knew what that meant. From his own secure data center at his house—though it wasn't the most advanced system in town and it wasn't a penthouse suite—he had studied everything the doctors had told him, along with other data to which he hadn't been officially privy, learning as much as possible about Taylor's condition and prognosis. Thus, Choi readily understood the significance of the neurologist's words. "A week and a half to go," he said.

"That's right," Dr. Slater replied, nodding appreciatively. "The chances of meaningful recovery drop off at four weeks. But that's based on statistics, and every patient's different. I recommend we wait three months."

"Before what?"

The neurologist met Choi's gaze and held it. Then he looked away. And that heavy silence continued as Choi fought for control of his emotions.

"Can I get you a cup of coffee or something?" asked Dr. Slater after a while.

They sat at a table in a break room and went over the technical details of Taylor's situation. Choi urged Dr. Slater to assign percentages to each possible outcome, which the doctor was reluctant to do, but he did offer recommendations based on his own experience.

Then Choi glanced at his phone to check the time and bolted to his feet. With a final handshake he hustled down to Taylor's room to say goodbye to his closest friend—for now.

Running late and only halfway back to San Diego, Choi was not only in a frantic rush; he was also terribly emotional. He feared he'd never work with Taylor again, or if Taylor did come out of the coma, that the investigator would be so impaired as to have no possibility of a meaningful life. Choi slammed his hand on the horn again, and this time the driver ahead was considerate, veering to the right to let him pass. Luckily, the traffic wasn't heavy, and this gave Choi a chance to consider his role in the case against Millie Haukea. Voir dire would be starting in just a few minutes, which was why he was in such a rush.

A week before, he had overheard Tyson telling Asher that Asher's services would be needed during the trial, particularly for jury selection, so Choi had set his mind to work on what that meant. He'd thought maybe Tyson wanted the hacker to research the prospective jurors, but any prosecutor worth his or her salt could do that. Or simply hire an investigator. *So why would Tyson need such a high-priced technical specialist?* Choi had wondered. *For something criminal.* That meant accessing protected data, but there had to be more. Choi then put himself in Asher's shoes. *What would I do if I had no scruples? I would analyze the prospective jurors not only by what I could learn about them beforehand, but also by how they reacted during jury selection.* By means of this highly illegal technique, Choi knew, Tyson would be better able to decide who he did and did not want on the jury.

So how would Tyson and Asher accomplish that? Choi had thought, reasoning that Tyson would need a miniature microphone and speaker, hidden perhaps in a pair of eyeglasses or in a hearing aid. That would be easy. He and Asher would also use a camera, which was even easier. They could stick it on his briefcase, on a tie pin, or on the same glasses as for the communications equipment. They could stick it anywhere, really.

This explained why Choi was driving so recklessly; still upset after the doctor's news, he needed to be physically present in court to catch the defense red-handed, by scanning the room for signals and blocking them if needed. As he roared along, now only twenty minutes from downtown, his thoughts revolved around the software he was working on. If successful, it would prove that Millie Haukea had been the server at the Convention Center and one of the three intruders at the Hall of Justice, even though the photographs and camera feeds suggested otherwise. The district attorney's office might be able to convict her with that alone.

Choi wondered if Cammie would call him to the stand to testify about this new untested method. *No*, he concluded. *I'll have to work with a recognized expert witness.*

He smelled smoke. Holding the wheel with both hands, Choi eased off the gas and veered into the slow lane, then inhaled through his nose to track the origin of the scent; maybe, he hoped, it was coming from outside the car. But all hope was lost when tendrils of gray smoke came curling up from the floorboards, filling the car's interior and stinging his eyes. Then an explosion from under the car rocked the moving vehicle and sent it careening off the road. The smoke in the air was thick and caustic, and sparks were flying out of the dashboard. As Choi rolled through a field, bouncing over rocks and clunking into ruts, orange and yellow flames leapt up from under the hood. He stomped on the brakes to no effect, so there was only thing left to do: throw open his door and dive out while protecting his tablet. *Good thing I've had some recent practice.*

The car exploded while he was in mid-air, and the fiery blast launched him even farther, scorching his face and singeing his hair.

Choi lay sprawled out in the dirt, face down. His ears were ringing and his mouth was hanging open. A blazing fire was spreading through the trees and grass, rushing toward him, but he couldn't move and couldn't think.

Finally, the imminent danger jolted Choi back to his senses. He clambered to his feet and staggered off in a safe direction to dial 911, then placed a second call to Cammie O'Mara.

"I might not make it in to court today," he said, "but I'm fine." He explained what had happened, told her to keep an eye out for Tyson's jury-rigging tactics, and to expect an email containing new information on Millie Haukea that he'd found the night before.

"Okay, Sean. Thank you, I mean it. But mostly I'm just glad you're okay."

There was a silent pause. Then he said, "Hey, Cammie?"

"Yeah?"

"Knock 'em dead today."

"Funny you should put it like that," she replied.

No one spoke as Choi remembered Dea Bladet, and he figured Cammie was doing the same. Then it occurred to him to break the bad news about Taylor, but he decided against it. *That's a sitting-down-face-to-face kind of topic*, he thought.

"Johnny's here," she said. "Want to talk to him?"

"No, you guys are busy. See you tomorrow or later today."

After they'd ended the call, Choi found a boulder to lean against, turned on his tablet, and let his fingers fly.

18

BOUGHT AND PAID FOR

At precisely 8:00 a.m. Vincent Tyson bounded up the courthouse steps with his three associates, who looked more like an executive protection detail than the legal team they really were. He'd chosen a simple black suit and left his Rolex at home, but his dyed black hair was parted just so and gelled in place. When he reached the screening station in the lobby, none of the deputy sheriffs inquired about the hearing aid in his ear, and the device didn't set off the metal detector. Next came the x-ray machine, a source of great anxiety, but when his briefcase emerged on the other side needing no inspection, Tyson gave the police an affable smile, picked it up, and continued on his way.

Asher's worth every penny I pay him, Tyson reckoned while marching through the halls with his legal team, winding their way to a second screening station at the courtroom doors.

The digital mercenary had built the custom case a few years back. Containing tiny electronics made with a negligible amount of metal and a pinhole camera disguised as a rivet, the leather-bound carryall had made the difference between a fair, impartial jury and a sympathetic one many times, earning Tyson much more in legal fees than Asher had charged him for the work.

Having had no problems at the second security stop, Tyson strode into the courtroom, past the empty spectators' pews, set his briefcase on the defense table, took out what he needed, and placed it on the floor so as to provide Asher with the best possible view of the jury box.

"Looks pretty good," said Asher in his ear. "A little to the left."

Tyson ducked under the table to adjust the angle and muttered a few words to check the audio transmission.

"Perfect. And I can hear you fine."

Ready now for their dirty fight, Tyson and Associates went through their notes, which were extensive after spending the past forty-eight hours researching the prospective jurors, all one hundred and fifty of them.

Cammie O'Mara and John Roche soon took their places at the People's table to Tyson's right, and the SDPD officers spread out along the walls, the clerks sat down at their stations, the bailiff reported to his post at the back wall by the judge's door, and a few members of the press and other interested parties filled the left side of the spectators' pews, or gallery, leaving the right side totally vacant.

Having heard a ringtone, Tyson looked up from his legal pad to see Cammie O'Mara taking a call. She met his gaze, and although he felt like grinning in triumph since Sean Choi's absence at this late hour meant he'd either died or been injured in the explosion, Tyson gave her a nod of apparent respect.

"All rise," the bailiff called out at 8:30 sharp, whereupon the Honorable Andrew Toles lumbered in with his usual limp. Dressed in a flowing black robe, the massive African American man assumed his high place and instructed the bailiff to bring in the first part of the jury pool.

Shortly thereafter, fifty residents of San Diego County took a seat, the first sixteen in the jury box to the right of the People's table and the remaining thirty-four on the right side of the spectators' pews.

Cammie rose to address the judge.

"Good morning, Your Honor," she called out. "May I approach?"

Judge Toles peered down at her over his glasses and waved her forward; Tyson strode up to the bench as well.

"Yes, Ms. O'Mara?" Toles rumbled quietly with the microphone off.

"Your Honor, just a few minutes ago my jury consultant was involved in an extremely suspicious automobile accident. I'm requesting a continuance based on your statement that if there were any further extenuating circumstances—"

"Yes, Ms. O'Mara, I do remember saying that I'd respond accordingly, but the fact is, your jury consultant is not a member of your legal team, and the prospective jurors are already in place. The best I can do is postpone your opening statements until Monday, but we will proceed with jury selection for now. Any objection, Mr. Tyson?"

"No, Your Honor," said Tyson gravely, showing no trace of emotion, but in his heart he was delighted. The trial was off to an excellent start.

***

Cammie shook her head in disgust as she resumed her seat at the People's table with Roche to her right. At that point, Millie Haukea was brought in, clad in an off-white skirt suit and no restraints, her brown hair slightly curled, and a modest amount of makeup. Just enough to give a professional impression.

Cammie had argued against Tyson's motion to allow her to dress in civilian clothes, and even more vehemently when Tyson had asked that his client not be forced to appear in handcuffs, but Toles had ruled in favor of the criminal defender.

Seemingly frightened by her perilous situation, Millie Haukea was the picture of wide-eyed innocence. To amplify this image, Tyson turned to her with a theatrically reassuring pat on the shoulders as she eased herself primly down beside him.

Judge Toles swept his gaze across the sea of prospective jurors, peering down at those in the jury box to his left—Cammie's right—and then at the larger group behind her. "Good morning ladies and gentlemen," he boomed. "Today we will attempt to select from among you a jury of twelve in addition to four alternates. This is a criminal case, styled The People of the State of California versus Camilla Haukea. Will the defendant please stand to face the jurors."

Dr. Haukea did as instructed and took her seat again, at which point Judge Toles read a summary of the charges filed against her in a low, rich, and resonant voice. Then, addressing all the prospective jurors, he said, "Do any of you have a special circumstance or hardship that might prevent you from being able to serve?"

Half of them raised their hands. One by one they cited medical, financial, and age-related hardships, caregiving responsibilities, language barriers, and the like, which didn't surprise Cammie in the least. But she did grow indignant when His Dishonor—as she'd begun to refer to him in her private thoughts—dismissed more women than men, which was significant because male jurors would find it easier to be merciful to this young and attractive defendant, while female jurors would tend to weigh the evidence with greater deliberation. Judge Toles didn't do it blatantly, Cammie observed, not so much as to leave himself open to a claim on appeal, but her suspicion that he was colluding with the defense was now set in stone.

During this long and infuriating process, her phone notified her that an email from Sean Choi had been delivered, which read as follows:

Hey Cammie. This is what I found on Millie Haukea. It looks like her tattoo is, in fact, a covered-up swastika. Her grandfather, who raised her for several years after her mom died of a drug overdose, had been a prisoner of war on Sand Island just off Honolulu. A Nazi soldier. And Haukea must have taken on some of that identity because in high school she joined a group of students with neo-Nazi leanings. An interesting choice for a brown-skinned half-Hawaiian, wouldn't you agree? The whole gang was about to be expelled for hate speech, violence, bullying, and symbolic graffiti when one night at a party, a few of her comrades got drunk and raped her, so the school merely suspended Haukea on the condition that she cover up her tattoo. Hey, I have to go, the police and the paramedics just got here. Good luck!! Full report attached.

As Judge Toles continued to question the prospective jurors, inquiring about any biases, preconceived notions, or conflicts of interest that might prevent them from being impartial, Roche leaned toward Cammie and whispered, "Why didn't you accuse Tyson of jury tampering at the sidebar? I know you saw his hearing aid."

"If he *is* cheating," she whispered back, "then he's definitely got a backup plan, maybe a clean one to hand over in case we object."

"Well, what about a camera? We could have the bailiff search him and all his things."

She shook her head. "By now he could have put a camera anywhere in the room. Plus, Toles is bought and paid for. He'd rule against us."

Roche nodded and sat straight up, returning his attention to the judge, whose commanding baritone would have carried to every corner of the room even without the microphone.

"Do any of you personally know the victims or the defendant?" Toles was saying. "No? What about the attorneys? Has anyone ever been involved in a case with one of them?"

Juror number five raised her hand. Cammie and Roche knew this middle-aged woman to be Betty Stoner, an elementary school teacher. Married with three children. Choir director at a Presbyterian church. Likely to be a strong moral leader and a good candidate for jury foreperson. They wanted her in the jury box. Fortunately, Mrs. Stoner was sitting in the fifth position, meaning she was already there, and there she'd stay unless Toles or Tyson excused her.

"Yes, ma'am," said Judge Toles.

"I get my prescriptions filled at Grimes Pharmacy," Mrs. Stoner explained. "That's where the defendant works."

Worked, thought Cammie.

His Honor nodded. "Do you know her well?"

"No sir," said Mrs. Stoner, "but I did know Connie Riker, another pharmacist who used to work there, but she died."

"Do you think you could make a fair and unbiased decision based on the evidence in this case?"

"I believe so."

"You do have *some* familiarity with Doctor Haukea, do you not?"

"Yes, Your Honor. We've spoken a few times. In a how-are-you-today, fine-and-how-are-the-kids kind of way, with people in line behind me."

"But you *did* know the late Ms. Riker, whose unfortunate death is related to this case. Juror number five, you are dismissed. Thank you."

So Mrs. Stoner rose and walked out of the room with her head held high. The three jurors at the end of her row shifted over to fill her seat, and another one from the first pew strode up to the box to make sixteen. If by that process the pews later became underpopulated, they would be repopulated by the next-numbered jurors waiting down the hall.

By the time the prosecution began its examination, the herd had been carefully thinned in favor of the defense, and Tyson was looking as self-satisfied as if he'd already won the case—and done so on his own.

But it hasn't even started, Cammie reassured herself as she scanned her notes, matching the jurors' names with their faces and thinking ahead.

Roche stepped into the space between the counsel tables and the clerks, ignoring the podium that separated the prosecution and the defense. He positioned himself so as not to show his back to the judge, while also facing the folks in the jury box to his immediate left and those in the pews farther back. "Good morning, ladies and gentlemen. My name is Jonathan Roche, co-counsel for the People," he said, gesturing toward the prosecution table. "And this is Cammie O'Mara, our lead counsel. Both of us are deputy district attorneys for San Diego County."

Cammie had insisted that Roche handle this part of the proceedings so that she could watch the jurors, noting when and why they perked up or nodded in agreement, and looking to see who might be a leader and who a follower when it came time for them to deliberate. In a later phase of jury selection, she and Roche would be allowed to excuse twenty of them without giving a reason, so now, while Roche asked his questions, Cammie was taking notes, adding to the extensive information that they had compiled over the preceding weeks.

"Have any of you ever served on a jury before?" Roche asked.

Some raised their hands, so he followed up with them, inquiring as to whether the trials had been civil or criminal and how they'd voted, paying particular attention to those who were already in the jury box and in the first couple of pews. Then, as Cammie continued to scribble furiously, he asked if anyone had ever been a victim of violent crime. Several indicated that they had.

"Okay, keep your hands up for a second, if you would," said Roche. "I'm about to ask a personal question that might make some of you uncomfortable. But this entire *trial* is personal, and important, so I have to ask."

Cammie watched the jurors. Both men and women were nodding along with Roche. They liked him.

"Have any of you suffered a sexual assault? If not, please put your hands down." Two women kept their hands up, the closest of whom was number twenty-five and seated in the first pew, while the other, number seventy-one, was farther back, so Roche directed his next question to juror number twenty-five. "Ma'am," he said, knowing her name was Marcia Delaney, an itinerant farmhand and an avid gardener whose best friend was a border collie. Roche and Cammie hadn't uncovered Ms. Delaney's lamentable experience, so they'd wanted her in the jury box at first, but not anymore. "It will come out in this trial," he went on, "that several years ago the same type of crime was committed against the defendant. Do you think you could set that fact aside and judge her guilt or innocence based *only* on the facts of this case, without being influenced by any sympathy you might have for her as a result?"

"I'm not sure," said Ms. Delaney, whose blond hair was pulled back in a ponytail. "It was a such a horrible experience."

Roche nodded with respect. "I know and I'm sorry," he said. "But if you were on an airplane and someone asked the pilot if he or she felt able to fly the plane, and he or she replied, 'I'm not sure,' would you be satisfied with that answer? That's how serious this trial is. The court needs a yes or a no."

He's good, thought Cammie. *Strong but sensitive. Smart but down to earth. Handsome but not pretty.*

"Well," said Ms. Delaney, "I really can't be sure until the trial is under way. I'd certainly try to be fair, but I do have many friends who are survivors. Since I have to choose, my answer is yes."

Cammie caught Roche's eye and shook her head.

Roche turned to the judge. "Your Honor, the People move to excuse juror number twenty-five for cause."

"Mr. Tyson?" Toles intoned.

Tyson stood. In a plain black suit, with no fancy watch, and a pleasant expression instead of his customary scowl, the criminal defender looked humble, noble even, and the jury seemed to like him, too. "Your Honor, I must disagree," he said. "Mr. Roche has impressed upon juror number twenty-five the seriousness of the matter, and she has indicated that she is able to remain impartial. So there's no statutory basis for her removal."

"The court shares your view, Mr. Tyson. Juror number twenty-five, you will remain in your seat."

Roche turned to Cammie angrily, but she shook her head with a smile. *Good*, she thought. *More fuel for the fire. Pile it on, Tyson.*

19

OLD TRICKS AND OLD TIMES

"Doing well so far," came Asher's voice in Tyson's ear. "Your next topic is drugs and foster care."

Now twenty minutes into his examination of the jury panel, Tyson hadn't needed to hear he was doing well; his forty years of courtroom experience told him so. Nor had he forgotten the next line of questioning. But it *was* helpful to know that, according to Asher's software, five of the sixteen individuals in the jury box were men with dominant personalities who showed sympathy for Millie Haukea—making them good candidates for the role of foreman—and eight out of sixteen favored Tyson over Roche.

"One of the facts that you will learn about my client," Tyson proceeded to tell the jury pool, first meeting the eyes of those in the box, then walking toward the jurors in the pews, "is that her childhood was less than ideal. When Doctor Haukea was just a girl, her mother died of a drug overdose, and she later spent time in the foster care system, which can be a difficult place to be, as you may know. Ladies and gentlemen, do you believe that a person with a troubled past is innocent until proven guilty? Please raise your hand if you feel that my client would be more likely to have committed a crime based on her background."

No one did.

"Juror number seven's postural and biometric analyses show aggression," said Asher from his data center at home.

Tyson knew the woman's name was Cristina Muñoz and that she was twenty-eight years old, single, and a buyer for a supermarket, but he hadn't uncovered anything else. "Juror number seven," he said to the woman. "Do you have any experience in the foster care system?"

"Yes, I do," Ms. Muñoz replied.

Through a series of patient questions tactfully put, Tyson managed to coax Ms. Muñoz into admitting that she, too, had had a difficult upbringing, but that *she* had never been accused of a crime, unlike the defendant. "People with a troubled past need to be extra careful about what they do," Ms. Muñoz said to Tyson. "If the defendant is here in court, then, yes, she probably fell back into old patterns and did something wrong."

"Move to strike for cause," said Tyson immediately. Then he questioned and moved to dismiss two more jurors who, according to Asher's real-time analysis of linguistic data, would also have been unlikely to sympathize with Dr. Haukea. Naturally, Judge Toles granted all of these motions.

"Okay, we're good," said Asher in Tyson's ear. "By the way, the data shows a ninety-nine-point-nine percent probability that Morgan is not sitting in the jury box in disguise."

***

"Do you think Morrison Grant could be on the jury?" Roche asked Cammie as they resumed their seats at the People's table after lunch.

"No," said Cammie. "He wouldn't want to commit to the same identity for so long. He'd be a sitting duck. It'd be much smarter to pose as a journalist or some random spectator."

"That way he could just disappear," said Roche, nodding.

"All rise!"

The afternoon session was faster and more exciting than the proceedings held earlier. By this time, both sides had gathered information about the remaining jurors' willingness to send someone to prison for life, about their opinions of someone like Millie Haukea, and with regard to the scientific evidence they'd later be shown, whether such evidence was likely to be fact, fiction, or somewhere in between.

Starting with the People, opposing counsel took turns exercising their peremptory challenges, striking jurors without having to give a reason. Both the prosecution and the defense suffered heavy losses, though the prosecution's were more critical. Tyson seemed to know exactly which jurors Cammie and Roche had most wanted to remain in the box, and he excused them all. Then, when it came time for Cammie and Roche to dismiss jurors who they believed might show undue favor to the defense, Tyson would object under a Batson challenge and His Dishonor would invariably sustain those objections.

By four in the afternoon a supposedly fair and impartial jury had been sworn in, given instructions, and dismissed until the following Monday. With a smack of his gavel, Judge Toles boomed, "We stand adjourned," then disappeared through the door to his chambers.

"Fair and impartial," scoffed Cammie as she marched up the aisle to leave.

Roche said nothing as he held the door for her. He looked too angry to speak.

Back at the defense table, Tyson and Associates were still packing up, and doing so with an air of great celebration. Their triumphant laughter followed Cammie and Roche to the front entrance, pursued them in the streets, and taunted them all the way back to the Hall of Justice.

***

"Get your ass up, Haukea! Your lawyer's here to see you," a sturdy correctional officer barked a few days later.

Millie rose from her bunk, turned to face the wall, allowed the woman to restrain her, and shuffled off to the attorney-client meeting rooms. Once seated and left alone, she wondered what Tyson had come to say or talk about; in her mind, everything had been settled the day before.

The moment he stepped through the door, a rush of euphoria lifted her into the heavens. Morgan had gotten everything right. The ten-thousand-dollar tailored suit, the Rolex watch, and the perpetual scowl. The upright posture and a practiced swagger. A specially padded undersuit plus masterfully applied stage and prosthetic makeup. Only she could have known this wasn't Vincent Tyson, Attorney-at-Law.

"I told you I'd get you out of here," he began, in a voice matching that of the criminal defender.

"Are you sure no one's listening?" she asked, tucking her brown bangs behind her ears.

"Yes, I'm sure. These are privileged conversations," Morgan said, nodding toward the window where an officer stood watching. "The only thing he can do is read our lips, which I doubt he's capable of, but let's turn away just to be safe."

As they did, she asked, "How are you?" making an effort to keep the *are you still using* out of her voice, but that's what she wanted to know, so he heard it loud and clear.

"Never better," he said seriously, with a convincing amount of eye contact. Still, the question hung in the air.

"I've been thinking," he said, breaking the silence.

Millie leaned closer, drawn to the confidence in his eyes. It seemed they might be running away together after all. As he spoke of his plans to get her out, she imagined sitting on the porch of a beachfront cottage with a baby on her knee, and him in the water fishing. With a throw net, the Hawaiian way.

"I'm gonna need some time," he was saying. "And remember, don't tell Tyson anything. The only reason he hasn't tried to kill you is that he knows I'm keeping an eye on him. Speaking of which, you might see me in court as a spectator. If you do, don't smile, wink, or show any other sign that you know it's me."

"I wouldn't do that," she assured him.

He stood to hand her a business card with Tyson's name but a different number on it. "I'd better go. Let me know when your attorney-client conferences are so I don't show up here at the wrong time."

"Okay," she said, rising to offer him a handshake. As she did, she blurted out, "I love you."

"I love you too, babe," he told her with a grin, a genuine expression that looked out of place on Tyson's features. "We'll be together before you know it. It'll be just like the old days."

***

"Hey man!" came Jeff Walker's exuberant voice in Sean Choi's now-aching ear. "Thanks for the call."

"Don't thank me yet, brother," said Choi into his smartphone. "How was your guys' assignment?"

"It was good. Missed home, though. What's goin' on?"

"Taylor's in a coma. He was in a so-called 'accident' related to a murder trial we're working on. Well, that *I'm* working on."

"Can I see him?"

"No," said Choi dejectedly. "No one can. He's being treated at a secret location. Lynn's there, too, but she's okay. Just got out of surgery."

Choi went on to provide some of the details surrounding the case, but he didn't think to mention Millie's name, as he wasn't aware that Walker had had any past dealings with the defendant.

"What do you need?" Walker asked with evident concern. "Detectives? A tac team?"

"SDPD's on it for now, but I'll keep you in the loop."

"Thanks, bro."

"Would you tell Park for me?"

"Will do. Hey, why don't you and Dulce come over for dinner this weekend? Maybe we can get Maggie and Crawford over here, too."

"I'd love to," said Choi. "You know I would. But things are too crazy right now. I'll see you soon for sure."

"Okay. Good luck, brother."

The call left Choi even more discouraged than before. Besides being on his way to sit in silence with his closest friend while the four-week cut-off date loomed closer and closer, now he felt a sharp pang of nostalgia, a longing for the times when they'd all get together in someone's back yard—"all" meaning Walker, Tina (Walker's wife, Choi's wife's sister), Dulce (Choi's wife), Park and Carla, Dom Taylor, Lynn Peters, and everyone's kids. With each passing day, Choi was growing increasingly scared that Taylor would never make it to another one of those get-togethers.

"Who was that?" asked Dulce, wheeling herself up as he prepared to leave.

"Walker," answered Choi. "I gotta go, honey." He felt his throat seize up and his eyes cloud over with stinging emotions, but fought against them long enough to kiss his gorgeous wife goodbye, head out the front door, and climb into the new and improved Police Interceptor. Fleet management had issued him the SUV for continuous use, partly for the protection it offered against further threats, and also out of necessity, as his old car was literally toast.

It wasn't until Choi had completed a surveillance detection run and come to the long stretch of road leading to the medical facility that he realized why he was so upset. It was the cost of fighting for justice. The high price of going up against remorseless crooks whose only boundaries were the lines established by the law. *These thieves don't care who they hurt*, Choi knew from experience. Angry tears poured down his cheeks as he roared east, thinking of Dulce, his reason for living and the sweetest person he knew. Six years earlier, she'd been paralyzed from the waist down in a motorcycle crash orchestrated by a gang of smugglers. Then came David Goode, who'd been gunned down on that same case. More recently, John Seley, Ayla Sami, and Ali Hassan had made the ultimate sacrifice while fighting crime. Mayor Pat O'Connell, too. And now Dea Bladet. Choi nearly lost control of the Interceptor as he brooded over Dom Taylor's chances of following them all to the grave.

But Choi did not lose control, nor would he ever stop fighting for justice. That's what made those backyard barbecues so much fun. Breaking bread with heroes, with clean-hearted people who knew how to laugh for real, despite and also because of the casualties of war.

Which is not to say, Choi further reflected as he trudged into Taylor's room and prepared for two days of work at a desk provided by the neurologist, that he didn't sometimes dream of an easier life. Or wish that it would all just come to an end. At the moment, for instance, he was hurting so badly that he tried and failed several times to send an ordinary email. In the end, he just folded up his laptop and hung his head.

20

SUITING UP

"Good morning," said Roche. "Can I help you with that?"

"Thanks," Cammie replied over the top of a box, which he took from her hands, then closed the door with his hip.

As it was a Saturday, she'd come casually dressed, sporting light blue jeans—which fit her nicely—a blouse in royal blue, and simple black flats on sockless feet. She'd pulled her black hair into a ponytail that swished back and forth as she ventured inside.

"I thought we could work in here," he said, nodding toward the living room, where there was brown leather seating and thick white carpet from wall to wall. He set the box on a central coffee table. "Have you eaten breakfast?"

Her delicate features lit up. "Yes, thank you."

"Coffee? Tea?"

"Coffee. Please," she said, placing her bag on the couch.

By the time Roche came back with two steaming mugs, she had unpacked her box and arranged its contents on the coffee table: one thick file for each of the charges against Millie Haukea. With a clipboard in one hand and a pen in the other, she sat upright on the edge of the couch, watching him. Eager to begin.

He settled into a recliner, and over first sips they spoke of the explosion that had destroyed Choi's car. "Here's the forensic report," Cammie said, handing it across the coffee table.

The first page of the document noted that if there had been an incendiary device in the vehicle, the only place it could have been hidden was deep in the exhaust system, because Choi had already scanned the engine compartment, the car's interior, and the underside for bombs. On the second page, the report concluded that any such sabotage would have employed a timer set for a certain hour, and that the incendiary device would have been custom-engineered to burn itself up completely, since no foreign material had been found in the exhaust system.

Frowning, Roche handed it back. "Expert saboteurs, engineers, martial artists, snipers, et cetera." He shook his head. "It's Tyson."

"I agree," she said. "But unless someone's willing to testify against him, we've got to go with what we have." She returned the forensic report to its folder and picked up a different file. "So let's start with the charges. Murder in the first degree, count one of two. What can you tell me?"

"Okay," said Roche, leaning back into his soft recliner, where he always sat in that room. "The victim was Ronald Green, the private equity director for Southern Trust's San Diego branch. While attending a dinner at the Convention Center, Green died of a severe allergic reaction to tropomyosin, a protein that had been mixed into his steak tartare, along with ricin, which made everyone at the table sick in order to cover up the crime. Initially, the evidence was weak, just five photographs of a suspected server known as Clarissa, who appeared to be overweight, with long blond hair and a fair complexion. But further information subsequently came to light."

"The evidence was weak?" scoffed Cammie, playing devil's advocate. "The pictures look nothing like Doctor Haukea."

"Not to the human eye, no. But it's the same person, and the evidence to that effect is one of the twin pillars of our case."

"Good. Hey, Johnny, can you do something for me? When I was watching you in voir dire, the jurors seemed to like you, so maybe *you* should give the opening statement. Just for fun, would you pretend you're talking to the jury?"

"For the record, I disagree," he said. "You should give it." But then he stood, took a few steps back, and faced her from a distance as if she were sixteen people wondering whether or not to believe him. "As I was saying," he continued in a deeper voice, projecting it farther than necessary for that little room, "to the human eye, those five photos do not match the defendant's current or natural appearance. But the evidence will not only show that Doctor Haukea is closely associated with a master of disguise trained by the U.S. Army, but also that the photos conclusively match other images of her—one of which is a video recording in which she commits some of the other crimes she's being charged with today. These matches are based on an assessment of multiple characteristics such as facial expression, ear shape, body proportion ratios, and other technical features that will be thoroughly explained to you in due course." Roche retook his seat across from Cammie, who was staring at him with an open mouth and admiration in her dark, perky eyes. Then she clapped and favored him with a heart-stopping smile. But Roche pushed his excitement down to where it belonged, managing to keep it off his face.

"We're gonna have to do a lot better than that," he reminded her. "The trial starts in two days. Speaking of which, you're lead counsel. You have to give the opening statement, and don't tell me you're not good at it."

She nodded reluctantly. "You're right. But you speak well. I liked your big voice, and that was quick thinking on your feet."

"I try to avoid using the podium," he explained. "It gives me more freedom to connect with the jurors, but without a mic we really have to project. Okay," he said sharply. "Your turn. Second count of murder one."

So they traded places, he taking hers on the couch while she circled the coffee table to stand facing him.

"Ladies and gentlemen," she intoned, in a comical imitation of Roche's deep stage voice, scoring a laugh. But then she grew serious. "Before we move on to the second victim—another Southern Trust executive, the late Michael Schmidt, I want to make it clear that the defendant is a doctor of pharmacy, an expert in the effects of drugs and other biologically active chemicals on the human body, and that includes poisons. Now, you will hear expert testimony that Mr. Schmidt died of acute nicotine poisoning and that chemical analysis of his cigarettes showed a six-hundred-fold increase in nicotine concentration compared to the normal amount. You'll see video footage of a man in disguise switching these doctored cigarettes for Mr. Schmidt's regular pack, and plenty of evidence that this same man is a close associate of Doctor Haukea's. Finally, we intend to call two more experts to the stand—one who will declare that the chemical profile of the soil in the defendant's garden contained nicotine alkaloids and other compounds related to the rest of the charges, which I'll address in a moment. The other expert will discuss the discovery of the lab equipment and plant material that had been missing from the defendant's house when it was searched. He will testify that this material not only matches the toxins used in the murders but also the soil in the defendant's garden. Keep these facts in mind as we move forward—because the pattern doesn't end here. Thank you."

Roche held his applause, as it wasn't time to celebrate; he and Cammie needed to show up to court with this kind of "A" game every day if they were going to have even the slightest chance of winning the verdict. But he was stunned. Cammie was going to kill it. And the evidence against Haukea was strong.

They switched places again, Roche going back to his usual spot and Cammie to the couch. A long conversation ensued, about the witnesses they'd call to the stand, the questions they'd ask, Tyson's likely objections to those questions, Tyson's cross-examination of the said witnesses, and the possibility of Roche and Cammie conducting re-direct examination to refute certain points that Tyson might try to make. After they'd plowed through all of that, it was time for lunch.

***

Cammie rested her arms on Roche's balcony, blew out a breath, and swept her gaze along the most extensive concrete pier on the West Coast of the United States. Stretching nearly two thousand feet into the sea, the Ocean Beach Pier was completely deserted, currently closed due to damage caused by storms. Sadly, the damage was permanent, as the iconic landmark was beyond repair. Cammie then looked straight ahead at the soft, sandy beach, following it to the left for a mile. She saw groups of surfers with boards tucked under their arms, talking animatedly, children playing with innocent abandon, and couples holding hands as they plodded along. This brought to mind her brief romance with Dom Taylor, which had ended before it really began. She sighed. It hurt. It physically hurt her to think that the doctor was talking about letting him go.

At that exact moment, a breeze picked up and brushed across her face. The fresh, salty smell was heavenly. That and the waves, rolling toward her, curling, crumbling, pushing up the beach and falling back down, time and time again, much like her own breathing, brought her back to center and restored her sense of peace. That's when Roche called out from the kitchen, "Food's ready!"

She turned to pull open the sliding glass door, just past which, she saw, he'd set a table for the two of them.

"Please," he said, gesturing for her to sit. Smiling genuinely. He had great hair.

"So they can't fix the pier?" she asked once they'd both settled down to eat.

"Nope," he replied. "I'm on a committee that's working with the authorities to replace it."

The food was delicious: thick spaghetti noodles fried in fresh garlic and olive oil, with hunks of chicken, two different cheeses, and a big salad in the center of the table.

"What a great place to live," she remarked between bites.

"It's not as flashy as the beaches up north."

"But a lot less crowded, right? And more locals than tourists?"

"Yeah. What about you? Where do *you* live?"

"North Clairemont," she said. "It's nice. Kinda like OB—built a while ago and not much renovation since. So it's relatively affordable."

"*Relatively* being the operative word."

They ate in a companionable silence for three crashing waves, and then Roche asked, "So where'd you go to law school?"

"Here. At USD," she said, setting down her water. "That's how I met Lynn Peters. She was on the scholarship committee. You?"

"Berkeley Law."

"I notice you didn't say Boalt Hall."

"No racism allowed in *this* house," he declared. "I like to think of myself as an ally."

"Me too. Speaking of which," she said, dabbing at her mouth with a white cloth napkin, "how far should we go with the Nazi club? Should we fly one of them over from Hawaii? We'd have to set that up right now. And what about Haukea's tattoo?"

"No. It's not worth the trouble. As for the tattoo, I'd love for the jury to see it, but I'm sure Tyson won't put her on the stand."

"No. And you can't see it on the mugshots, either. You're right. Her background's interesting, and probably relevant, but the probative value's just not there. Mind if I have some more salad?"

"Mind if I serve you?" Roche returned, piling it on as she held the plate. "It makes me wonder how I would've turned out if I'd gone though what Haukea did."

"Thanks," said Cammie. "That's plenty. You're not feeling *sorry* for her, are you?"

"It doesn't matter whether I do or not. I believe in consequences for actions."

She nodded in agreement. "What kind of situation did you grow up in? Seems like you turned out okay."

"It wasn't easy. My mom drowned in the jacuzzi when I was ten. She was passed out drunk."

"I'm sorry to hear that." A moment elapsed between them, a respectful silence split only by the crying of the gulls outside. Then Cammie offered a private truth of her own. "My mom and dad are divorced. Both are still alive, but sometimes I wish that were only half true, if you know what I mean."

He nodded gravely.

"My dad was a lawyer, but he lost his license to pills and hookers. And *we* lost everything, hence the scholarship."

Their eyes met and held. Cammie could feel his pain as she shared her own. The energy between them drew her in, narrowing her vision until all she could see was him.

But then the moment passed, snapping her back to reality like a book popping shut. They ate a little more, with a drink to wash it down, then rose and made for the living room again. As she took her place on the sofa, Cammie wondered if she'd said too much.

"Okay," said Roche, back in his usual place. "Now for the charges pertaining to the break-in at the Hall of Justice: two counts of attempted murder."

"Right," she said briskly. "Aconitine in the coffee grounds, intended to kill Sean and Dom, and she almost pulled it off."

"Do you want to go through this like we did before? Standing up and I'll be the jury?"

"I'm too full," Cammie said with a smile. "Thank you for lunch, by the way."

"My pleasure," Roche said, glancing up from a forensic analysis.

He meant that, Cammie knew by the honest gleam in his eyes.

Roche looked back down. "The soil composition shows significant traces of aconitine and nicotine. Ricin, too."

"Right. And that's the *second* of our twin pillars." Cammie consulted a different report, the test results from the burned and buried evidence found in East County. "Those same compounds were detected in multiple pieces of laboratory equipment, along with tropomyosin. And there's one more thing. Have a look at page six."

"I know," said Roche with a winning grin. "Matching fingerprints."

He and Taylor could be brothers, Cammie thought. *Dom's darker and taller, but they've both got broad shoulders, the same lantern jaw, and the same determined look in their eyes. Each a warrior and a scholar, but to different extents and in different arenas.* Suddenly she wanted to check on Taylor. "Should we give Choi a call?" she asked.

"Sure," said Roche.

She reached for her phone, pressed a few buttons, and set the device on the coffee table between them.

"He's right here with me," said Choi through the speaker. "But there's still no improvement, unfortunately. Lynn's doing well, though. How are you?"

Cammie looked to Roche, who leaned over the phone. "Pretty good, man. Thank you. Just getting everything ready for Monday. Are we still on schedule with Doctor Brown?"

"Yes. He's flying in tomorrow and I already sent him the outline."

Then they spoke with Choi about his own testimony, which would involve the Hall of Justice, the video footage captured by his backup system in the potted plant, his near-death experience caused by the poisoned coffee, and the theft of data from the computer network.

"When will you be back?" Cammie asked.

"Tomorrow afternoon."

"Okay, let's meet at my place as soon as you can. I'd like to run through your direct and cross. We'll be there all day."

"How does five p.m. sound?"

"Perfect."

By then it was dark, so Roche insisted on walking Cammie to her car. "What time do you want to get started tomorrow?" he asked, setting the box in her trunk.

"Would eight be too early? I'll have the coffee hot. But it's gonna be pizza for lunch, I'm afraid. I'm not much of a cook."

"Sounds good."

The next morning they went right to work on Cammie's opening statement: rehearsing, revising, recording, remarking, and repeating. It took them all day to do it, with a break for pizza, which Roche seemed to thoroughly enjoy. When Choi showed up at five, Cammie ran him through his direct examination, and Roche played Tyson's part, doing his best to poke holes in Choi's testimony, to force him to contradict himself or catch him in an error, but the technical analyst was too smart for that and beyond well prepared.

When there was nothing left to do, Cammie wrapped them both in big hugs and stayed on the porch, waving as they pulled away. She felt incredibly fortunate to be working with such bright and dedicated individuals, both of whom, like her, were proud to be on the right side of the law. At that instant, a surge of emotion took hold of her, coursing through her body and ending in chills.

The next morning, Cammie would be charging into battle, and thanks to her teammates, she was as ready as she could be.

21

FRUIT OF THE POISONOUS TREE

Cammie's heart was pumping, thumping so hard in her chest that she feared she might suffer a medical emergency. She sat up from a restless sleep and turned to the clock. It read four a.m. Soon she'd be standing before the superior court in the most significant appearance of her career thus far. She kicked off her sheets and set her feet on the floor. Headed to the kitchen for a hot cup of coffee. Sat at the table to review her notes and ran through her opening remarks one more time. She nailed it, word for word. After getting ready and stepping into her best skirt suit, Cammie scanned her car with the new detection equipment that Choi had brought over the night before and drove to the HOJ, where she met up with Roche and crossed the skybridge to the Central Courthouse.

"How you feelin'?" asked Roche as he and Cammie reported to their posts at the prosecution table. He'd chosen a black suit with a sleek, modern cut, coincidentally matching her own outfit.

"I'm ready," she said while unpacking her things. "What about you?"

"Me too," he said with a grin, pouring her a glass of water from a pitcher she'd requested be on the table that day. "You're gonna do great."

"All rise," announced the bailiff.

Judge Toles lumbered in, took his place at the bench, and called the court to order.

"Good morning Your Honor," said Tyson, rising to speak before the jury was called in. "The defense moves to suppress the evidence obtained at the Cleveland National Forest site."

Judge Toles peered down from the bench wide-eyed, cocking his head and raising his brows in a show of astonishment. "On what grounds?" he boomed.

"The search was performed in violation of my client's Fourth Amendment rights because the warrant was based solely on an anonymous tip. No geolocation data was used nor any witnesses produced that might have suggested Doctor Haukea's presence at or near the scene. So, at the moment the warrant was signed, there was no observable connection between her and the land in question. For all we know, the prosecution could have planted the evidence and made that anonymous call themselves."

Cammie flew to her feet. "Mr. Tyson," she snapped, "the People find it ironic that you should object to a supposedly baseless search and proceed to make an *actually* baseless claim against us." Then she wheeled on the judge. "Your Honor, the anonymous informant gave the defendant's name, a specific location, and an accurate description of what would be uncovered there. The officers observed the site, which is on public land, meaning no expectation of privacy, and identified a large mound of freshly disturbed earth. Then they followed procedure and secured a warrant. That's not fishing. That's careful investigation under judicial supervision. All done by the book."

Tyson frowned, shook his head, and turned to the judge apologetically, as though he were embarrassed to be wasting His Honor's time and ashamed on the prosecution's behalf. "The affidavit for that warrant simply repeated the tip," he said, "without adding a single independent fact. And SDPD failed to confirm any information before they started digging. They were merely hoping to find something that might match their theory, which under California law is insufficient to establish probable cause."

Now Roche bolted out of his chair. "In this *legal* search," he thundered, "SDPD uncovered materials that had been conspicuously missing from the defendant's home. The laboratory equipment matches the substances used in the murders as well as the chemicals in the defendant's garden soil. They found the plants the defendant tore out of her garden! To suppress this evidence would be judicial error at the very least, and *could* be considered misconduct." Then he leveled his fiery gaze on Tyson. "And the timing of this desperate motion couldn't be more unethical. Above and beyond its total lack of foundation, we should have been notified *weeks* ago."

Judge Toles leaned toward his microphone to reply, but stopped with his mouth half open.

Having silenced the judge with a look, Tyson interjected, "We found the affidavit yesterday, Your Honor. It had been misfiled in the discovery packet. After reviewing it and realizing that it was flawed, we acted as swiftly as we could."

"That's enough," said Judge Toles, raising a meaty palm. "I've read the search warrant, the accompanying affidavit, and all subsequent documentation. On that basis, I find that the affidavit failed to provide an adequate foundation for probable cause, and the law on this issue is clear. The motion to suppress is granted. All evidence retrieved from the Cleveland National Forest site will be excluded from these proceedings."

"You've got to be kidding me!" roared Roche.

Judge Toles turned his gaze on the prosecutor. "You may object for the record, Mr. Roche, but the ruling stands."

"I do so object."

A rumble of voices rippled through the spectators' pews, diminishing only when Toles pounded his gavel.

Roche could not take his eyes off the crooked judge as he lowered himself into his chair, and Cammie also took her seat. After the jurors had filed into the courtroom, she rose again and stood before the jury box. Her heart was racing, even faster than expected, but she felt ready, having practiced her stage voice, while strategically positioning herself closer to, farther from, and facing certain imaginary jurors, just as Roche had shown her.

At a nod from Judge Toles, she launched into a heavily edited version of the remarks she'd spent so much time rehearsing.

"Ladies and gentlemen of the jury," she began, with the confidence of someone thoroughly familiar with the facts of the case, and also with every applicable legal provision and principle. Yet as she paced before the two rows of jurors, their faces grew blurry, and blinking would not bring them back into focus. "Good morning. We are here today to—" was all she managed before a wave of nausea cut her off. The room was spinning. Her mouth was watering uncontrollably. As Cammie fought the urge to vomit, she had to grab the rail to stay on her feet.

"The People request a recess!" Roche called out, springing up to assist her.

"Your Honor, we object to these theatrics!" Tyson exclaimed. "Since the prosecution was prevented from introducing illegal evidence, they must now resort to this thinly veiled stalling tactic."

"The court disagrees, Mr. Tyson," said Judge Toles sharply. "We'll take one hour to make sure Ms. O'Mara receives immediate medical attention. After that, either she or Mr. Roche will present the People's opening statement. In the meantime, everyone please clear the courtroom to make way for the paramedics." He smacked his gavel. "The court will stand in recess."

Roche rushed to Cammie's side as the spectators filed out. The bailiff called 911. Judge Toles retired to his chambers, and in the midst of this commotion the clerk took the pitcher from the People's table and soon returned with a fresh one.

***

"You did well," said Cammie two hours later. She'd been treated for dangerously low blood pressure, then felt well enough to watch as Roche delivered the opening, after which Toles had granted a two-day continuance. It had struck Cammie as odd that Toles had allowed this postponement, since it seemed like a chance for her and Roche to regroup. *It must serve the defense in some way*, she'd figured, but hadn't been able to imagine how. Once His Dishonor had adjourned for the day, Ragasa's team had left their posts along the walls to escort her and Roche back to the Hall of Justice, which is where they now sat, in Cammie's office, both of them in a terrible state of dismay.

"I did not do well," Roche retorted bitterly. "If I had, I would have given the signal and Ragasa's team would have shot Tyson, Toles, Haukea, and everyone else who's involved in this conspiracy. Like in the old days, when the mob would just string up a thief and hang 'em in broad daylight. *That* was real justice!"

"Except when it wasn't," Cammie said, smiling weakly and opening her eyes halfway. She was at her desk, leaning back in her swivel chair with a wet washcloth resting on her forehead. Roche, who sat opposite her, had dimmed the lights and set a trash can beside her in case she started to feel sick again.

"I know, I know," he grumbled. "Hey, while you were in the bathroom, I got a call from SDPD. They sent the pitcher for testing and have detained the court clerk pending the results."

"Great," she groaned. "So what now?"

"We've still got the garden soil."

"It's not enough."

"No. Without the laboratory equipment there's no tropomyosin and no matching fingerprints." Roche let out a tight, uncomfortable breath and they both fell silent. After a while he said, "Let me call Lynn. Should I put her on speaker?"

"Yeah, but don't tell her I'm listening."

"Hey Johnny," came their chief deputy's voice from the phone on the desk. "How did it go today?"

"Horrible," he said, and proceeded to break the news.

"But Cammie's feeling better?" Peters asked.

"Yeah, she looks okay."

"Looks okay? Is she there? Am I on speaker?"

Cammie shot Roche a withering look.

"No, no, no, no," Roche said quickly. "She's down the hall in her office. I just came from there."

"Well, don't give up. That's the important thing. Something's gonna shake loose, I'm sure of it."

Roche and Cammie rolled their eyes at each other. *Easy for her to say.*

Roche went downstairs to fetch Cammie a sports drink, and then they spent several hours reassessing the strength of their case. It wasn't pleasant work. The discussion centered around which witnesses they might still be able to call and who would have to be released. This was depressing enough in itself, but when added to the possibility of dropping charges against Dr. Haukea or cutting her a deal, it was so intolerable that dinner together was a grim and melancholy event. Cammie and Roche barely touched their food, hardly spoke, and their faces told a story of utter defeat.

22

REVIVAL

Roche took care of the check, leaving a tip large enough that it hurt him to do so, but the waitress looked like she could really use it. Once his and Cammie's plates had been cleared away, they nodded to each other and headed out into the night.

They trudged along the sidewalk in silence mostly, with the occasional hollow observation and dispirited nod in reply. But then they heard music. Roche looked up. At the top of some steps just ahead he saw an open door. Light poured out of it, along with a sound so moving that they both came up the stairs as if pulled by some magnetic force.

"Oh my God," murmured Cammie.

'Oh my God' is right, Roche thought as he swept his gaze over a vast assembly of African American worshippers. Everyone was on their feet, swinging their bodies to a loud syncopated rhythm. A poster on the wall informed him that this was day two of a week-long revival featuring guest preachers, choirs, and extended worship led by a different church every night. Today's service was being conducted by a Pastor Williams from Hillside Baptist Church.

An attractive woman sitting nearby noticed their presence and hurried to catch them before they could leave. "Come on in, y'all," she shouted over the music. Her beaming grin was so friendly that Cammie and Roche turned to each other, shrugged, and followed her inside. As the woman strutted up the aisle to the beat, showing them to an open spot, Roche found himself bobbing his head in sync with the driving force of the song in progress. "I'm Lynda Goode," she told them, squeezing their hands in welcome with another warm and lovely grin. Then she skipped back to her post near the door.

Up on the chancel, the organist raised his arm to give a signal, cutting off the band and choir at a climactic point, producing a split second of silence followed by a roaring cacophony of hallelujahs, amens, and thunderous applause. As the commotion died down, he played an exquisite progression of chords with no real pulse, just a slow, shifting series of concordant clusters of notes to soothe the crowd. Some worshippers took a load off, and others stayed standing as the band joined in to mark the beat. Then the choir added their voices—the tenors, the altos, and lastly the sopranos with their bright and plaintive calls. Now with the full strength of the ensemble and the congregation singing along, this vast but simple space resounded with such passionate gratitude that Roche's heart began to swell with something he hadn't felt in a very long time. Maybe never before. As he looked around at all these humble folks, clad without exception in what he knew were the finest clothes in their closets, who had all come together on a Monday night—meaning after many hours of tedious, low-wage work—and whose smiles assured him that the color of his skin was not a problem, Roche's despair over the case against Haukea began to melt away. These people had *real* problems, and yet, despite being trapped at the bottom of a deep hole that they'd been forced into, they'd come with their heads held high and ready to count their blessings.

As the tune built in intensity, more and more worshippers took to their feet; many began to dance at their places or in the aisles. The drummer drove a faster tempo and the bassist smacked his strings in accord. Before long, the entire group of gathered souls was stepping from side to side, clapping as one, rejoicing together. And this set the stage for the pastor to step in front of the choir. The charismatic leader lifted the mic to his lips and launched into a daring solo. A thousand arms waved in the air as his great voice soared over those of the choir. "Let's take it up!" he bellowed halfway through, cuing the band to shift the melody a whole note higher. The effect was like that of shifting from fourth to fifth in a Formula One racer—finally coaxed into exploding, the house erupted in a frenzy of pent-up emotion.

When the hymn was finished, the congregation was slow to wind down. For at least five minutes, as the organist played calming chords, scattered cries still rang out from among them and one man charged down the aisle shouting in such a strong release of feelings that no man in his right mind dared to stand in his way, including and especially not Roche.

Finally, wiping his brow with a linen cloth, Pastor Williams instructed everyone to take their seats. His sermon started softly. He went slow. Took his time. Early in this performance, he offered a reading from the Bible interspersed with observations pertaining to the message and supported by examples from his own life—from theirs as well, for this was a massive family with shared traditions and common understandings despite its being composed of several different groups. He'd ask for amens and encourage those assembled to participate by saying he wished he could get a little help or that someone out there was hearing him. A few times he told everyone to turn to their neighbor and repeat something he'd said, some short but significant point or a meaningful phrase.

In this way the message built—in community, constructed by call and response. At certain admonishments there'd come a smattering of applause; at stronger points that landed like punches there'd be a full ovation or the deacons might stand in agreement. All the brothers and sisters were free to urge the pastor along with loud exclamations such as "Say it!" or the more provocative "Well?"

As this built into a crescendo, tears poured down Pastor Williams' face, and he made no effort to wipe them away. He exhorted his people to stay on the path. To wait just a little while longer. To hang on no matter how hard things got. And they responded. One by one, in a growing chorus of amens, hallelujahs, and thank-you-Jesuses, they rose to their feet again, no longer weary, filled with pride, power, and love.

"What was your favorite part?" Roche asked Cammie on the walk back to the Hall of Justice. The cool air felt heavenly.

"Fellowship time," she replied with a dazzling smile, her first of the day.

Roche had been amazed at how long fellowship time had lasted. When he was young, his mother had taken him to several different churches, and one thing they all had in common was the passing of the peace or greeting time. But it had been nothing like what he and Cammie had just experienced. For fifteen minutes, the band had rocked on while every brother and sister in the house intermingled, and the children were free to fool about. The idea was to reach everyone you could in that time, especially folks you didn't know, and this resulted in Cammie and Roche being wrapped up in big women's arms and rocked against their massive bosoms. Which, given their current emotional state, had been more than a welcome occurrence.

"What about you?" Cammie asked.

"I can't decide between the music and the sermon."

"A-men," she said. And that's when her cell phone rang.

***

Sean Choi had been present in the courtroom when Judge Toles had ordered the exclusion of the evidence found in East County. Then, when Cammie had turned pale at the beginning of her opening statement, he'd rushed to her aid along with Roche and Ragasa. He'd also stayed to watch Roche give the opening instead, but after Judge Toles had unexpectedly granted a long continuance and smacked his gavel to adjourn, Choi had hurried outside to make a call.

"Sorry I couldn't pick up, Doctor Slater," he said when the neurologist answered. "It's been a crazy morning."

"No problem, Mr. Choi. I was calling to give you a little bit of good news."

Choi's heart leapt. "That's great!" he exclaimed. "Did Taylor move a finger or something?"

"No."

"Um, did his brain waves show increased activity?"

"Nooo," the specialist replied, stretching out the word in a leading sort of way, as though he might have been smiling when he said it.

Choi was scared to take a third guess. He didn't want to get his hopes up, but by the sound of the doctor's voice, it seemed he hadn't really been calling to share a little bit of good news. It was great news.

"Taylor woke up," said Choi, with a slowly spreading grin that lit up his face.

"Yes, he did, and he's been asking for you."

"I'm on my way."

Not long after that, Choi and the bearded, big-bellied neurologist were striding toward Taylor's room along with Lynn Peters, who was clad in sweats, slippers, and a blue hospital gown.

"He started showing signs of improvement yesterday," Dr. Slater told them. "But I didn't want to let you know until I was sure about his progress, which has been nothing short of incredible."

"Hey buddy!" said Taylor, sitting up in bed.

"Not so fast," said the neurologist. But that didn't stop Choi from throwing his arms around his hero. Nor Taylor from doing the same to his.

Meanwhile, the doctor spoke with Lynn Peters. "I found him sitting up this morning, insisting he was fine."

"Sounds like Dom," the blond-haired chief prosecutor replied. "But he's not *really* fine, or is he?"

"No. Of course not. But he *is* exceptionally strong. Most people don't even speak this early, let alone pull off their monitoring equipment and attempt to visit their fellow patients."

"I made it halfway there," said Taylor, grinning with pride. "But then I fell."

Peters smiled, too. She seemed pleased that Taylor had thought of her so soon, and only slightly angry that he'd done something so reckless.

"Your dizziness will subside quickly," Dr. Slater told his patient, "but you'll be weak for quite a while."

"How long is 'quite a while'?" Taylor asked.

"For most people it's a month or more. I'll give you folks some time alone."

After Dr. Slater had left, Peters and Choi tried to fuss over their friend, and they brought up simple topics such as the "winter" weather and some local news, but Taylor wasn't having any of it.

"Listen," he insisted in a hoarse and raspy voice. "One of the last things I remember is getting an email from a Major Wyans in Hawaii, on Oahu. He'd seen a BOLO notice for any suspects matching the characteristics that SDPD had indicated at the time—a female poisoner in her twenties or thirties. All his message said was that he'd been involved in a case ten years ago related to poison and murder. I'm gonna call him right now."

"Take it easy, big guy," said Choi. "You can hardly talk."

"It's from the breathing tube," Taylor croaked, shutting his eyes against some kind of sudden pain. Choi figured it was a headache.

Peters laid a hand on Taylor's shoulder. "Let us bring you up to speed on things. If you're feeling okay after that, then we'll call Wyans."

So Taylor rested his head on a pillow as they told him about the explosion at the condo in Mission Bay, the one that had put him in a coma. He had no memory of it. Then they broke the news of Dea's murder, the attack on Peters and Cammie, and the intrusion at the Hall of Justice.

"*That's* why I couldn't find Wyans' email anymore," Taylor said with new understanding. "When I first got it, there was a file attached, but I couldn't open it on my phone."

"And that file's the reason why the crooks deleted the email and tried to kill you. Tried to kill us both, actually," Choi explained. "I called to see how it was going at the condo, but you weren't picking up. So I pounded a cup of coffee and headed over there, but the coffee had been poisoned during the break-in. I got violently sick on the way there, and when I arrived, you were across the street being treated by the paramedics. That's when I collapsed."

"I appreciate you coming after me," Taylor said with a meaningful nod.

Choi frowned and shook his head. "I should have gone with you."

Soon Taylor had been brought up to date on everything else—namely, that Tyson was probably running a team of hired killers and that Judge Toles was almost certainly in Tyson's pocket. "Let's call Wyans," Taylor said. "I'm feeling okay."

So Choi looked up the number for the Wahiawa Police Station, dialed it, and handed him the phone, but the officer who answered was sorry to report that Wyans had died in a freak accident just a few weeks earlier.

"Riiight," said Peters after they'd ended the call. "Just like all seven of the Southern Trust victims."

"I need to fly to Hawaii," Taylor said.

Peters pressed her lips tightly together.

"And somebody needs to be there to watch his back," Choi added helpfully, smiling.

"Fine," Peters said, shaking her head theatrically as if she feared she were making a serious mistake but going through with it anyway. "I can set that up. But not until the doctor gives the all clear."

"The all clear for what?" asked Dr. Slater on his way back in, but he didn't receive an answer. "Mr. Taylor needs to rest," he told them, "but you're welcome to use the break room."

While heading down the hall to that location, Choi turned to Peters. "We have to move you and Dom to a different facility."

"I'll be discharged in a week," she protested.

"Dom will be too, but it doesn't matter. Assuming Asher knows about the bomb that caused my car accident, then he also knows where the accident occurred. So it won't be long before he tracks you down."

"Okay. I'll take care of it. You've got enough on your plate," said Peters on the way into the break room. They had just settled into facing chairs when Peters' cell phone rang and she picked it up. "Hey Johnny," she said. "How did it go today?"

Choi suddenly realized that he'd been so excited about Dom's recovery that he hadn't told her about the excluded evidence and Cammie's medical emergency in the courtroom.

"Well, don't give up," Peters said into her phone. "That's the important thing. Something's gonna shake loose, I'm sure of it."

"Why didn't you tell him about Dom?" Choi asked after she'd clicked off.

"I thought Cammie might like to hear it from him." Peters eased herself to her feet. "You know what? I better head back to my room, take it easy for a while. You'll wait here, I guess?"

"Yes ma'am." Choi rose to see her out, then resumed his seat and took out his laptop. Later, he and Peters headed back down the hall to visit Taylor again, who seemed to be feeling even better than before. Early in the conversation, Peters brought up a crucial point. "We have to keep everything confidential, Dom, especially your recovery, because we can't risk alerting Tyson or putting anyone else in danger."

"Will do," he said. "What about Cammie and Roche? Can we tell *them*?"

"Yes, but that's as far as it can go. Make sure they understand that."

Taylor nodded and reached for his phone, catching Cammie just as she and Roche were leaving the revival.

***

Finally, thought Kang as she completed her stretching routine with no pain at all for the first time since the bus crash. Having had three weeks to devise a detailed and wonderfully exciting plan, she paused to fill her lungs and calm her mind so as not to rush into action.

The sun was just peeking over the eastern mountains as she prepared a cup of tea in the kitchen, flashing back to the resistance training she'd undergone for two decades, starting when she was only a child. Her teachers had rolled bamboo over her bones to break them slightly, conditioning her shins and forearms against major fractures. They'd done the same to her torso, using sandbags and stones, and she herself had hardened her hands by punching thick wooden boards and concrete slabs for years.

Kang's masters had also taught her to fall correctly, by tucking her chin, dispersing energy, and relaxing the body on impact, and they'd made her practice it—*through my tears,* she recalled, stepping out onto the balcony to take her first hot sip—until she'd done it properly every time. As she'd risen in rank, the budding martial arts master had practiced muscular engagement, building up core and tendon strength, and all of these hard-won qualities had helped her to avoid skeletal, spinal, and internal injury when the bus had slammed into her car.

Kang further recalled the "exercises" that had developed her mental toughness and resistance to pain; in her mind's eye she watched her six-year-old self being deprived of sleep, forced to sit in icy water, and made to hold the horse stance for half a day. These early memories were so unpleasant that as the sun lifted clear of the hills, a lonely tear traced its way down her cheek and fell into the canyon below.

Still, Kang knew, the important thing was that she had survived the ordeal, and without major trauma. As she'd lain there bleeding in the twisted wreckage of her brown sedan and Asher had come running up in the guise of a concerned citizen, she hadn't passed out from the pain or overreacted. She'd feigned unconsciousness. And when Asher had glanced around nervously to make sure he wasn't seen, then wrapped his weak little typist's hands around her throat, she had held her breath and slowed her pulse such that he would think she was dead.

As one of the only people in the world who knew the location of Asher's downtown penthouse suite, Kang had something truly special in mind for the weaselly programmer. But first, she'd empty Tyson's safe.

23

A CHANGE OF PLANS

Vincent Tyson clasped his hands behind his back and cast his gaze out over the ocean. He stood at his third-floor picture window, watching as a big burnt-orange sun inched ever closer to the end of the Earth. He drew a great breath, but it wasn't sufficient; still he was desperate for air. And the coastal view upset him, since he'd soon have to leave it behind. He wondered how long it would take for him to forget this sprawling expanse of blue liquid beauty after he'd left San Diego. Agents interested in buying the property were already circling like sharks, just like his opposing attorneys, just like SDPD, and, if he wasn't careful, Tyson knew, just like the feds would soon be doing. This brought Millie Haukea to mind, the only person with whom Tyson had any semblance of a good relationship; that, too, was doomed, as was his glorious career in Southern California and the very existence of his aging body.

It was a Friday, the end of an exhausting week in court. Millie's trial had recommenced the previous Monday after a generous continuance, about which Tyson made a mental note to ask Judge Toles. The prosecution had already called the majority of its witnesses, having painted a fairly clear picture of Millie's guilt for the jury, but on cross-examination the criminal defender had cast a cloud of doubt over that testimony and even scored a few points of his own.

"Doctor Hawley," Tyson had said to the forensic analyst employed by SDPD to assess the chemical composition of Millie's garden soil. "Isn't it a fact that the genus *Aconitum* is used for medicinal purposes?"

"Yes," the expert replied. "But only in tiny, controlled doses. Aconitine is better known for its toxicity. As a poi—"

"Thank you." Tyson had then proceeded to question the scientist about castor beans and tobacco, obliging the man to acknowledge that ricin and nicotine, these plants' chemical constituents, were also traditionally used in herbal medicine. "So Doctor Hawley, wouldn't you agree that an herbalist such as Doctor Haukea could have been growing these plants without any malicious intent at all?"

"Objection, Your Honor," said Roche from the People's table. "Calls for speculation."

"It's his field of expertise. I'll allow it," His Honor ruled, looking displeased, as though he'd wanted to side with the prosecution but his strict code of ethics prevented him from doing so.

"It's possible," Dr. Hawley conceded. "But—"

"No further questions."

And so it had gone. Cammie O'Mara then called Lieutenant Ragasa to the stand, who declared that he'd found Millie Haukea and Morrison Grant together when he and the SWAT team had executed the search warrant at her house, thus establishing a connection between the defendant and a suspect wanted for the same criminal offenses.

Then Tyson rose to conduct the cross-examination. "Did it appear to you, Lieutenant, that Mr. Grant was living at my client's house?"

"No."

"Did you witness any physical contact between them?"

"No."

"Any verbal communication hinting at something more than a casual acquaintance?"

"No, but that doesn't mean—"

"Could it be, sir, that my client merely allowed Mr. Grant onto her property for a short visit, and only grudgingly, as she indicated in her statement?"

"Your Honor," Cammie O'Mara had protested, "once again Mr. Tyson is asking a witness to agree with an interpretation of the defendant's intent or state of mind. There's no way for him to know. We object."

"And you are overruled," Judge Toles boomed, peering down at the feisty attorney. "Mr. Tyson is simply asking the witness whether it is *possible*, based on his professional observations, that Doctor Haukea told the truth. Answer the question, please, Lieutenant."

This gave Ragasa no choice but to recognize the unknown status of Millie's relationship with Morrison Grant, the expert in impersonation and disguise.

Then Cammie O'Mara had called Sean Choi to the stand, who spoke about the break-in at the Hall of Justice. She started and stopped the video footage of that incident while he provided a detailed narration. Tyson had to admit that Choi and O'Mara had been very well prepared; even so, the images of Millie weren't clear, since they'd been taken from an unfavorable angle and at a distance, and her hair had been tucked under a cap.

On cross, Tyson had only a few questions for Choi, who admitted that the hacker known as "Asher" had yet to be identified or located, and since Tyson had already weakened the connection between Millie and Morgan, the fact that Asher and Morgan should appear in a video with an unidentified female seemed relatively inconsequential.

The following Monday, the prosecution would be calling its final witness: a second expert who had the potential to seriously damage Tyson's case, but the criminal defender didn't foresee any major problems, what with the excluded evidence and Judge Toles' continuing support.

A curious circumstance jolted Tyson out of his recollections—the window he was peering through had been left unlocked. Considering the long odds of an intruder being able to slip past the guard house, then scale the flat rear façade of his home while bypassing his home security system, Tyson concluded that either he or Igmar had forgotten to secure the window. Absently, he re-engaged the lock while still studying the ripples that stretched out into infinity before him. The sun had fallen halfway below the horizon line, but its top half still painted the waves in a sparkling golden swath that ran right toward him.

The doorbell rang, and so with a final glance at the dying day, Tyson drew the curtains and clomped downstairs to the first of his two evening appointments. Shortly thereafter, he was seated at the table on his backyard terrace facing Dane, Asher, and Igmar with the ocean spread out before them.

"I don't think we're going to find him," said Asher. "I've looked everywhere. The surface web, the deep web, the dark web, even classified networks. The U.S. Army has no clue as to Morgan's current location."

"You taught him too well," said Dane, who then turned to Tyson. "And I've checked all his known associates and hangouts. Not a trace."

"Wonderful," said Tyson. "But how did you rack up a twenty-five-thousand-dollar tab in seven days?"

"I had to hire a team." Dane shot Asher a grin, which the latter mirrored conspiratorially.

Tyson scowled at them both. "Is there any good news at all?"

"Yes," said Asher. "I found the facility where Taylor and Peters were being treated."

"How?" asked Dane.

'How' doesn't matter, Tyson thought, feeling his anger rise.

"Well," said Asher, apparently quite satisfied with himself, "I traced all deliveries of medical supplies to any location within a fifteen-mile radius of the accident—nice job on that incendiary device, by the way."

"Thank you," returned Dane, whose bloated pride in his bomb, which had failed to achieve its objective, was enough to make Tyson want to flip the table over, drinks and all.

"What do you mean *were* being treated?" Tyson snapped. "Taylor and Peters were gone?"

Dane's smile fell off his face. "We were too late. By the time we got there, the facility was already abandoned. We did catch a nurse as she was leaving, who told us under duress that Taylor and Peters had been moved, but she didn't know where to."

"She also said that Taylor came out of his coma," Asher added, cringing in anticipation of his boss's reaction.

"That's *not* good news!" Tyson screamed, red in the face by that time.

"No," Asher admitted, "but at least we know where he is—Oahu. A script I'd written weeks ago alerted me to a non-commercial flight with no listed passengers, which departed earlier today from San Diego to Honolulu. It's a small jet leased to a shell company with buried connections to the U.S. Attorney's Office. That's the agency leading the Southern Trust investigation."

"I'm aware," said Tyson dryly.

"So I popped the security system at Honolulu International Airport and found Taylor and Choi in today's camera feeds. From there it wasn't hard to—"

"That's enough," said Tyson. "Igmar, you and Asher are going on vacation."

"It'll be a *permanent* vacation for Taylor and Choi," the giant blond knew.

"Yes. And Dane, now I *do* need you to remove Detectives Park and Walker, because if Taylor or Choi manage to learn anything in Hawaii, that's who they'll contact."

"Park and Walker are SWAT team operators," Dane said. "I'll need to hire a team to assist me."

"Fine," Tyson grumbled. "As long as they're not from Carnal Bliss Incorporated."

After everyone had left, Tyson fixed himself a second drink and sipped it until the appointed time, at which point he made his way down to the sand and headed north, strolling casually along the moonlit beach as if he'd only gone out for some air. Soon he caught the fragrant scent of pipe tobacco and spotted a bulky silhouette in the distance, looming ever larger as His Honor limped forward and Tyson strode toward him.

"I didn't think you'd make it all this way," Tyson jeered, stopping a few feet short.

"Yet here I am," came the judge's deep and resonant reply.

"Do I need to worry about you?"

Judge Toles puffed away for a moment, looking thoughtful. Then he said, "No. But I *am* concerned about the risk."

"Which explains why you've been finding for the prosecution."

"Yes. But that's just for the sake of appearances. And there's something else."

"Oh?"

"My clerk received an anonymous letter threatening his wife if he didn't bring to court an unopened bottle of Visine manufactured before two thousand ten and squirt a third of it into the People's pitcher of water."

"I don't know anything about that."

"Of course you don't."

"Sounds like something a pharmacist might dream up. I'll speak to my client."

"See that you do. Any more stunts like that and we're done. I don't care about the money anymore."

"There's more at stake than just your compensation," Tyson retorted ominously. "Much more. Enjoy your weekend."

Tyson spun on his heel and cursed Toles all the way back to his house. Suspecting that the weak-minded judge might declare the buried evidence admissible despite having been instructed to the contrary, Tyson had asked Millie how the prosecutors could be made sick just before their opening statement. Fortunately for everyone—except the People of the State of California—Toles had found for the defense on the matter of the buried evidence.

Maybe I should take his family before he really starts causing trouble, Tyson mused while crossing his open-air terrace and storming inside. Once up in his room, he glanced at his wrist and was instantly comforted by the sight of his Rolex. He thought about putting it in the wall safe, but gave in to exhaustion, leaving it where it was as he flopped onto the bed. Soon he was fast asleep.

It wouldn't have mattered either way. Determined to strip him of that watch and the contents of the safe, Kang slipped quietly out from behind the curtains and set to work.

***

Judge Toles also fumed as he headed for his own coastal residence, but it was a righteous anger that drove him there, the fury of a man no longer able to cower before his own greed, nor before the wrath of the man with whom he'd just met. Charging forward as he'd done in the old days, forgetting about his knee, he thought back to the proud young man he'd been at one time. So sure of himself on and off the football field. Ready for anything.

It would be a hard and dangerous road, Toles knew. Yet as he stopped to rest his gaze on the pale yellow moon and its mirror image below, a light wind swept over him, an ancient whisper telling him he wouldn't be doing it alone. This assurance surged though his body, crackling with electricity, giving him goosebumps all over his skin. Then, with new pride and purpose, Judge Toles drew back his pipe and hurled it out to sea like a quarterback aiming for the endzone.

24

THE WATCH AND THE WINDOW

"You okay?" Choi asked while traveling five hundred miles per hour at an altitude of forty thousand feet.

"You know I don't like flying," replied District Attorney Investigator Dom Taylor, who sat across from him at a dark and glossy table.

"You *do* look a little green. But we can talk, right?"

"Sure."

"So I spoke with the new head of the Wahiawa Police Station, a Major Nakamura. She's expecting us."

"A woman in charge," said Taylor. "That's refreshing. What do we know about her?"

"Former Navy pilot. After that, she worked patrol and then as a detective on the south side of Oahu. That's where most of the crime occurs on the island. When Major Wyans had his so-called 'accident,' she was promoted and sent up to Wahiawa."

"How far is Wahiawa from the North Shore?"

Choi looked puzzled. "About ten miles. Why?"

"Walker's always talking about surfing Pipeline. I'd like to see it if we can."

"There'll be killer waves this time of year."

At the airport they found a blue Honda SUV waiting for them in the parking lot with a set of keys under the mat that not only started the car but also let them in to a little house in Wahiawa, where they'd be spending the weekend. An hour later they were pulling up to the police station.

"Howzit," said Major Nakamura, who stood to greet them in her office. The head of district two was trim, strong, and confident. Apparently of Polynesian and Asian descent and somewhere in her thirties, she studied their credentials before offering them a pleasant smile, a firm handshake, and a couple of chairs at her desk. "What can I do for you gentlemen?"

"Thank you, ma'am," said Choi as he and Taylor sat down. "As you may recall from our phone conversation, Taylor here received an email from Major Wyans before Wyans passed away."

Taylor nodded. "We believe his death was not an accident. In response to our BOLO notice for any female poisoner in her twenties or thirties, he made reference to a ten-year-old case matching that profile, and that's what we're here to talk to you about."

Major Nakamura gave no reply.

"Does the name Millie or Camilla Haukea mean anything to you?" Taylor pressed.

"I *am* familiar with the case in question," she finally answered. "But that's all I can say at this time. Is there a number where I can reach you?"

"No," said Choi. "We're off the grid at the moment."

She nodded. "Call me Monday afternoon." Then she handed over her card and stood, signaling the conclusion of the meeting.

Taylor and Choi thanked her, shook hands again, and headed back to the Honda.

"That sounded promising," said Taylor as he started the engine. "But now we've got two days to kill. Does Haukea have any family on the island?"

"Nope," said Choi, looking down at his tablet and scrolling through data.

"What about her employment history?"

"She doesn't have one."

"Education, then."

"That's where this gets interesting," said Choi. "The University of Hawaii has no record of her attendance, even though she's stated she earned her undergraduate degree there. Same thing with her early schooling. And I only know where she went to high school because I found a buried newspaper article on the rape."

"What rape?"

Choi realized he'd forgotten to loop Taylor in on Millie Haukea's history in Hawaii, so he took a moment to do so, detailing her mother's drug overdose, her racist grandfather, and the neo-Nazi student group that was expelled for what they did to her. "All of it was extremely hard to find," Choi said. "Invisible to the general public, and beyond the usual reach of law enforcement."

"So her history was erased by a professional. Maybe by Asher," Taylor suggested.

"Definitely by Asher."

"So now what?"

"The only lead I could find was a couple of those students who got expelled. They're still here, living up on the North Shore."

"Let's get to it," Taylor said as he slammed the car in gear.

***

Kang stole out of the shadows and crept up to a snoring Vincent Tyson. *Ugh*, she thought while slamming a syringe into his thigh and pushing in the plunger with her thumb.

"Hey!" he shouted immediately, and his arms shot out to grab her, but she took a step back and watched as the sedative took effect. Two minutes later, he was still face up on the bed but unconscious by then, bound by zip ties at the wrists and ankles and no longer wearing his Rolex.

Kang did not consider herself a skilled safecracker, but she did know how to extract information from unwilling subjects, so she simply waited, settling into a seated meditation pose and breathing deeply, clearing her mind until Tyson began to stir. At that moment she opened her eyes, leapt to her feet, switched on the lights, and asked, "What's the combination to your safe?"

"Help!" Tyson screamed. "Somebody hel—" but she silenced him with a rock-hard fist to the nose that produced a crunch and a steady flow of blood.

"Make any more noise and you'll regret it, Vincent," she said. "If you won't tell me, I'll start by breaking your fingers, and it will only get worse after that."

"It's my birthday."

She gave him a puzzled look. "Happy birthday, but I am still going to torture you."

"No, the code is my birthday."

Kang strode directly to the large framed painting of a courtroom scene and took it off the wall to expose the safe. Then she entered the code, swung open the door, and stared open-mouthed at many stacks of bundled bills, gold bars, rare coins, and a box of gems she'd heard about but never seen. Hurriedly, she filled her bag, and was halfway out the window when she turned to say, "You're a handsome man, but your actions make you ugly. I never respected you."

And then she was gone.

***

As Taylor nosed the blue Honda SUV out of the Wahiawa Police Station's parking lot, Choi gave him directions to Kamehameha Highway. They headed north, driving through pineapple fields on the way to Haleiwa (pronounced hah-leh-EE-vah), the largest town on the North Shore with five thousand inhabitants. They rolled past surf shops, a grocery store, boutique shopping opportunities, and a little marina to the left. As the road widened into a highway again, they crossed a short white bridge over a river that flowed into the ocean. They passed Waimea Bay and Sunset Beach, and also left behind the Banzai Pipeline, the famous reef break Jeff Walker had spoken so highly of, but Taylor didn't notice. He was paying attention to Choi's report on their next destination.

"Velzyland Beach," the technology analyst said while consulting his tablet. "Another popular surf spot but with a bad reputation for drugs and crime. Home to a few old apartment complexes, which are some of the last buildings in the area that haven't been torn down to make room for the ultra-rich. Take the next left. We're headed for one of those apartment buildings. Incidentally, Velzyland is where Millie Haukea's mother was found dead."

Focused on the road ahead, Taylor acknowledged receipt of this information with a curt nod. "I need to know who we'll be dealing with when we get there."

Choi glanced down at the pistol on his partner's hip and hoped that it wouldn't need to come out of its holster. "Right," he said, swiping and tapping on the screen until he found what he was searching for. "Jonathan Mathers and Jodi Hernon. Caucasian, both twenty-eight years old with prior arrests, his for aggravated assault and hers for possession of a controlled substance with intent to distribute. They live in Apartment 3B, on the third floor.

Adjacent units 3A and 3C are occupied by individuals showing similar criminal records."

"There's a tactical knife in the glove box. Put it in your pocket," said Taylor, braking to a stop near a long three-story building with peeling gray paint. "And stay behind me at all times."

***

Kang had known she couldn't just run down the stairs and out the front door, since it would trigger a silent alarm that would double-lock that door and immediately deploy a team of armed guards to her location. So the exit point had to be the same one she'd used to enter, but now she'd be leaving with a heavy bag slung over her back. She shot a final glance at Tyson, who still lay on the bed with a bloody nose, writhing with fury but restrained, so unable to sit up or use his limbs in any way. She delivered her parting words, then swung her other leg out the window to assume a sitting position, facing outward. Just then, Tyson rolled off the bed and crashed heavily to the floor.

Stifling a laugh, she placed both gloved hands on the windowsill and dropped into a hanging position while rotating to face the house. The descent would be easier than the upward climb, she knew, but also more dangerous. She glanced down at the second-floor balcony and let go of the windowsill, landing on the railing below and balancing there. The weight of the bag nearly tipped her over backwards, but she leaned forward just in time. Then she hopped forward and down from the railing to the balcony floor and turned yet again to peer down at the night-lit grounds, verifying that her route of escape was clear. Seeing nothing amiss, she shrugged off the bag, dropped it to the ground below, climbed over the railing, hung down from the balcony as before, and let go with her hands, rotating one hundred and eighty degrees in mid-air such that she was facing away from the house as she fell into a forward somersault.

"Freeze!" screamed a man in the dark from behind her. "Turn around slowly with your hands up!" Kang did as she'd been ordered, laying her eyes on three security guards, two with pistols trained on her and the third with her bag in one hand and a flashlight in the other.

Half blinded, she couldn't figure out why—

"Wondering why you didn't see them from up there?" gloated Vincent Tyson he came strutting out the front door, followed by a fourth member of the security team. "I told 'em to hide under the balconies and take you by surprise. Figured you'd drop the bag so you could roll."

Tyson was armed. With dried blood running from nose to chin and violence gleaming in his eyes, he looked ready to whip up his assault rifle and dump an entire magazine into her body. Yes, it had been a tactical error to drop the bag, but only a minor one. Regardless of whether or not it was on Kang's back, she wouldn't have been able to escape. And the distance from the second floor to where she now stood was twenty feet, a fall that had needed to be broken one way or another. But how—

"How did they get here so fast?" Tyson asked, irritating her even more. He had always been able to read her mind. "I never showed you where the panic button was, did I? When I first saw the window you'd stupidly left unlocked, I called the security company and told them to be ready, just in case, so they dispatched more guards and stationed them close by. Then, when I rolled onto the floor and hit the button, they came running up in seconds and acted according to my earlier instructions. What else was an intruder gonna do but empty the safe? So I knew where they should wait. Hook her up," he told the guards.

"I'll come back to work for you," she offered, slowly positioning herself so as to deal with the approaching pair of men, the closest one first.

"It's too late for that," Tyson spat out, lifting his rifle to his shoulder and taking aim. "You're going to prison."

The two guards were almost within striking distance. They'd holstered their weapons, but one of the other guards was targeting her, just like Tyson. "Down on the ground," the closest one said.

Kang ignored the order and watched their hands. The closest one was holding out a pair of flex cuffs while the other one had his arms up in a fighting position, ready in case she offered resistance. They stopped just out of reach.

"Turn around," the first guard said.

"Restrain her!" shouted Tyson.

At once Kang flew forward, shooting out a flat hand to chop at the first man's throat, crushing his larynx. While he staggered back and dropped to his knees, she darted behind the other man, twisted his arm behind his back to force compliance and drew his pistol from his holster with her other hand. She held the gun's muzzle to his temple. "If I am going to prison then so are you, Vincent. I'll tell the police about your arrangement with Judge Toles, about the kill team, Southern Trust, everything."

At that, the two remaining guards lowered their pistols an inch and glanced at each other with uncertain expressions.

"I wish you hadn't said that," Tyson growled, taking aim at those unsure guards and shooting them dead. He also put a bullet into the man choking on the ground before swiveling quickly back to Kang and her human shield.

She fired first, missing Tyson but completing the distraction by shoving the last guard forward in Tyson's direction. In a flash she sprinted past the right rear corner of the house and didn't stop running until she'd vaulted the wall surrounding the gated community and had made it to her car.

While speeding home, Kang could not stop thinking about the bag she'd left behind. *It was the life-changing payday that Tyson still owes me, plus interest.* She brooded over this for some time before deciding that ultimately it made no difference. *Easy come, easy go. At least I'm alive.* Relaxing her grip on the wheel, she drove in relative peace for miles, but then the word "stupid" echoed in her mind, gnawing at her until she grew furious once again. *Why does it bother me so much that Tyson said I was stupid to leave the window unlocked? It is such a minor point. But an important one! Nothing I do is without good reason.*

When she'd first broken in, he hadn't been home, but suddenly he'd pulled up in the driveway, so she'd scrambled to hide as he'd clomped up the stairs. She simply hadn't had time to lock it again.

Speaking of time, she joked to herself, holding up her arm to admire the golden watch hanging loosely from her wrist. *I'll get ten thousand for this, at least. Who's stupid now?*

25

A HELL OF A WEEKEND
PART ONE

"There's a tactical knife in the glove box. Put it in your pocket," Taylor had said, braking to a stop near a long three-story building with peeling gray paint. "And stay behind me at all times."

So Choi popped open the glove box to see a large folding knife with a black handle. He took it out and used the thumb stud to engage it, which was easy because of the spring assist. The thick long blade glinted in the sunlight. He touched the edge with his thumb; it was razor sharp.

"Ready?" Taylor growled from the driver's seat.

Choi nodded. He'd never killed anyone before, not directly, but he knew from experience that in his line of work one must always be prepared for sudden violence. So he slipped the folded blade into his pocket and followed Taylor up two flights of stairs, keeping his hands in his pockets, the knife in his hand, and his thumb on the thumb stud.

"Don't worry," said Taylor. "We're just here to talk."

To Nazis, thought Choi, whose pulse was fast, his dread cold and intense. As they approached the door, the muffled sound of death metal music grew increasingly loud.

Taylor knocked hard. "San Diego District Attorney's Office," he bellowed.

The door came halfway open, letting out the blasting noise, and a scraggly face appeared. It belonged to a white guy with long, stringy sun-bleached hair.

"Jonathan Mathers?" Taylor asked.

"And you are?"

"District Attorney Investigator Dominick Taylor. You're not in trouble."

The guy flitted his gaze over to Choi.

"And I'm Sean Choi, investigative analyst for the San Diego DA's Office. We just want to ask you a few questions."

"Yeah, I'm John Mathers." He almost had to shout it over the raucous noise, but then he nodded to someone inside, the volume came down, and he invited them inside.

The three of them spoke while standing in a grimy living room until Mathers asked them to have a seat. He introduced Jodi Hernon, who offered them beer, which, she said, was all they had to drink. That and tap water.

Choi and Taylor politely declined.

All in all, it was a pleasant meeting. Despite their crude tattoos and a clear history of questionable decisions, Mathers and Hernon seemed honest and kind. When asked, Mr. Mathers indicated that yes, he and Ms. Hernon had been among those expelled from Waialua High and yes, they'd been present at the time of Millie Haukea's sexual assault.

"But it didn't happen like she said it did," Ms. Hernon explained.

"It was a big drunken mess," Mathers said. "But she was in there willingly. 'Least it seemed like that to me. I left the room before everything went to hell."

"She was in there *more* than willingly," Hernon volunteered.

Choi nodded. "We're having trouble finding information about Haukea's time here on the island. Do y'all know what she did after high school?"

"She got clean," said Ms. Hernon, who was so thin and pale that it pained Choi to look at her. "Went to college down in Manoa. Engineering, I think."

"She was a great swimmer," Mathers added. "I know she got a job as a beach lifeguard. I used to see her down at Sunset and Pipe."

***

"I got a message from Cammie," Choi called out the next day, to Taylor, who was busy doing pushups in the living room while Choi was in the garage kneeling beside a couple of motorcycles he'd discovered there. "Are you well enough to be working out?"

"What'd she say?" Taylor asked, appearing in the open doorway. He wiped his sweaty face with a towel.

Choi stood up. "She and Roche are getting ready for Doctor Brown's testimony on Monday, working all weekend. She asked about you."

Taylor shrugged, frowning slightly as if he didn't care. "She was just being nice. You were using a secure connection, right?"

"Absolutely. On both ends." Choi hesitated for a moment, then asked, "Did you two get a chance to talk?"

"Yeah." Taylor stepped into the garage to have a look at the bikes. "I called her just as she was leaving some church service. And she came to visit me before I left."

"Is it over?"

Taylor nodded while inspecting one of the two black 650cc sport bikes. He pressed hard on the seat and handlebars to bounce its suspension.

"They're ready to go," Choi told him. "One year old, low miles, fresh oil. I checked the brakes, batteries, throttle, clutch, idle, everything. Do you want to take them up to Haleiwa Joe's tonight?"

Taylor's grin was a definite "yes."

After their visit to Velzyland, they had driven back down the road to Sunset Beach, parked there in a tiny lot, and been astounded by the size of the winter waves. As they got out, an onrushing liquid mountain began to crumble, then crashed on the shore with such great force that the ground trembled under their feet.

With this forceful noise recurring on their right, they'd headed down the beach, holding their shoes in their hands, and found themselves in the midst of a sizeable gathering—of photographers, surfing fans, wet surfers resting, dry surfers stretching, bikini-clad girlfriends, children playing, and vendors hawking their wares.

"Walker can handle waves like *these*?" Taylor asked as they plodded onward.

"He's better than most of these guys," Choi answered.

They recognized the Banzai Pipeline not by any signs or directions given by locals, but by logical deduction; fifty yards ahead, a massive commotion was under way, dwarfing the one they'd just left behind. An announcer using a PA system was calling out surfers' names, scores, heat times, and other pertinent information while a cheering crowd filled the beach and adjacent areas.

Choi had to hand it to the guys and gals out in the water. The freefalls they were taking before the bottom turn were two stories high, and the water under them only four feet deep, with razor-sharp coral on the ocean floor just waiting to tear them apart.

"Looks like a lifeguard station up ahead," Taylor noted. They'd passed a couple of towers along the way, but this was a regular first-aid installation, a large tent-like shelter staffed with professional rescuers watching the event through binoculars. So they trudged closer, diagonally up the beach face toward the tent.

"Captain Kate Harris," said the woman in charge, sticking out a strong and friendly hand. Neither she nor Taylor said a word after that, still shaking hands while looking into each other's eyes. Hers were hazel and they sparkled with enthusiasm.

After producing his credentials, Taylor said, "We'd like to talk to you about a former lifeguard named Millie Haukea. Do you know her?"

Harris froze.

"Earlier today we met with a Major Nakamura of the Honolulu Police," Choi said. "But she needs to check with her superiors before she can talk to us. We're supposed to call her on Monday."

Captain Harris recovered from her shock. "Oh, Rose? She's a friend of mine."

"Speaking of friends," Choi went on, "Our buddies Tony Park and Jeff Walker worked this beach as lifeguards, but only for a week and it was a long time ago. You don't happen to remember them, do you?"

"Tony Park," Harris mused cryptically. "That *was* a long time ago." Then she was back to business. "Yeah, I think we'd better talk, but first I need to speak with Major Nakamura. Plus, we're really busy here, as you can see. So let me call her and I'll get back to you later today or tomorrow."

"We're flying under the radar," said Taylor. "But we can call *you*." So she jotted down her number and gave it to him.

"Mahalo," he said in Hawaiian, meaning *thank you.*

She flashed the brawny investigator a delighted smile, which resulted in another awkward moment—for Choi—with Taylor and Harris grinning, standing close, and speaking with only their eyes. Then she nodded once and went back to work.

The next morning, Taylor gave Harris a call. She asked whether eight p.m. was a good time to meet her and Major Nakamura at a restaurant called Haleiwa Joe's, and that's where Choi and Taylor were taking the bikes.

***

Before Kang broke in to Tyson's house and barely escaped with the Rolex, there'd been a meeting down on the terrace, in which Asher had told Tyson about the suspicious flight he'd detected, and Tyson had immediately sent him and Igmar after Taylor and Choi.

So Asher and Igmar had also boarded a private jet leased by a shell company with no passenger manifest, but unlike Taylor and Choi, they landed at a private airstrip on Oahu. This occurred just before sunrise on Saturday morning. Asher and Igmar found a cargo van waiting for them, checked in to a hotel using fake IDs, and Igmar hit the gym while Asher hacked in to the Wahiawa Police Station's security system.

The pale-faced programmer called up the camera feed and watched on his laptop with interest as Taylor and Choi met with an Asian or Polynesian policewoman. Then he went straight to work, learning Major Nakamura's name and her home address. Later that day, he and Igmar followed her to a restaurant called Haleiwa Joe's, and that's where they were currently sitting, in the parking lot, waiting for a call in the cargo van before heading inside to see who the major was meeting with.

Asher's phone rang. "It's Tyson," he said before picking up.

"Put him on speaker," said the giant blond.

"Hi guys," came a deep but very nasal voice. It was as if Tyson were pinching his nostrils shut. "There's been a change of plans. I haven't heard from Dane, which makes me think Park and Walker might have gotten to him first, so I need you to take Taylor and Choi alive."

"How will we fly them home?" Igmar asked.

"Drugged. We'll say they're sick."

"Understood. What about Major Nakamura?"

"Send her on a permanent vacation."

Igmar smiled.

***

Through her rear-view mirror Major Nakamura saw the cargo van pull into the parking lot right behind her, but she wasn't aware that it had followed her all the way there. And the sky was dark by then, so as she strode into the restaurant, she didn't spot the two goons watching her from the van's front seats.

"You look nice," said Captain Kate Harris, rising to greet her in the reception area.

"You look nicer," Nakamura replied, and it was true. The major had just come from her house after fixing dinner for her family, while the senior North Shore lifeguard had chosen a colorful blouse and tight light-blue jeans. With her auburn hair down and an artful touch of cosmetics, Captain Harris looked better than any other woman in the busy establishment.

They were shown to a table for four in the middle of a rowdy crowd. To Nakamura it looked like an even split between locals and tourists. They chatted awhile, waiting for their drinks, and after a toast and two first sips, she asked, "So did you sign a nondisclosure agreement?"

"Yes," said the lifeguard. "You?"

"Yeah, me too."

"Do you want to go first?"

"Okay," said Nakamura. "Obviously this is off the record."

"Same goes for me."

"Agreed. It was two thousand thirteen. I was a rookie cop. My FTO, Sergeant Jake Bonamassa, was investigating a series of murders at UH Manoa. All the victims were male, all drugged with flunitrazepam, the date rape drug—except one who got some old formulation of Visine—and all of them had been led to a secluded location and manually strangled."

Captain Harris drank from her pink frozen daiquiri, set it down, and replied, "I met Bonamassa years later when he was running your department."

"Back when Wyans was his sergeant."

"Yeah. Big Hawaiian guy?"

Major Nakamura nodded sadly. "Your turn."

"Okay. You probably know most of it, so the short version is, I took a job as an ocean safety officer—that's where I met Millie—and she got caught 'working,' you might say, with the North Shore Thrill Killer, who turned out to be our boss."

"Working *under* him, I'd say," Nakamura quipped, and they both burst into a laugh. "I know what happened next. Hoping for a lighter sentence, she confessed to everything. Her part in those crimes and the frat party murders, which she'd perpetrated by herself."

"Then came the cover-up," said Captain Harris.

"We had her," Nakamura went on, scowling. "The confession, the DNA evidence, witnesses, but some fancy lawyer came in and got her off, sealed the case records, forced a media blackout—"

"And silenced the witnesses through nondisclosure agreements," Harris finished for her.

"*And* made some of the witnesses disappear," added Nakamura. "Including Bonamassa and Wyans."

A silent moment ensued as the implications of that statement hung in the air.

"So where does Taylor come in?" Nakamura wanted to know. "By the way, we can't tell him anything. Not officially."

"I know," said Captain Harris. "We could be sued."

"Or worse."

Harris nodded. "Turns out he's a good friend of a couple guys who were working with us as lifeguards when everything went down with my boss."

"The North Shore Thrill Killer."

"Correct. She actually tried to kill one of those guys, but I don't think Taylor knows that. And *they* don't know Taylor's investigating Millie now for different crimes. We could tell him that."

"We *should* tell him that."

Harris's phone lit up and rattled on the table. She picked it up. "Hello?"

"Captain Harris, this is Dom Taylor. We're on our way, but you and Major Nakamura need to get out of there immediately."

"What? How did you know we got here early?"

"As we speak I'm looking at the camera feed from the parking lot outside and there are two men headed your way. One's a big blond guy and the other's wearing a black baseball cap. Both are armed and dangerous and they're coming for *you*. We'll go straight to Haleiwa Joe's, but if you can get away, go to the beach where we met yesterday. We're five minutes out. Run!"

26

A HELL OF A WEEKEND
PART TWO

Major Rose Nakamura leapt up from the table and yelled, "Honolulu Police! This is an emergency!" She pointed to the exit farthest from the restaurant's front doors. "Everyone out, right now!"

Chairs scraped against the floor and people started moving, but not nearly fast enough, so Nakamura drew her Glock 19 and aimed the pistol at the ceiling as if she might fire it, screaming, "Go, go, go!" then "You, too!" at the waiters and the kitchen staff staring at her from behind the counter.

The noise of the crowd was chaotic as the patrons stampeded out to a grassy space by the marina. Meanwhile, two other things occurred: The front door crashed open to admit an enormous blond man carrying a shotgun, and Nakamura reached for Captain Harris's wrist and yanked her down behind their table, the only cover available. "We're going, too," the policewoman told her friend, flicking her chin toward the same exit used by everyone else.

Harris nodded quickly. She looked frightened but capable.

Nakamura peeked over the table. The giant was coming closer. As he moved from the reception area into the main dining room, he passed a large fish tank to his right, her left. "Police!" she shouted. "Drop your weapon!" Hoping to cause him to slip or stumble, she took two-handed aim from a kneeling position and fired at the aquarium, which shattered and burst, drenching the man, but he didn't fall. And now he was right on top of her.

It's over, she thought.

But the huge man just stood there, wide eyed, with his weapon pointed at the floor. All he needed to do was raise it and fire.

"Come on!" said Captain Harris, darting toward the side exit.

Nakamura walked backward, following Harris while training her sights on the sopping-wet attacker. He appeared to be in shock for some odd reason, so she didn't pull the trigger. As she came out onto the patio, still targeting the wet man, she heard Harris say, "Rose?"

Then a male voice. "Drop the gun."

An icy bolt of fear took hold of the major, paralyzing her for a moment. Then she slowly pointed her weapon to the sky and turned around. A second man wearing a black baseball cap stood behind Harris with a pistol to her head.

Now it was over.

***

Taylor stuffed a prepaid phone into his pocket and hustled out the front door. Down on the street sat Choi on one black bike, with another beside him and the engines running. Taylor popped on a helmet as he strode toward the waiting motorcycle, swung a leg over it, flipped up the kickstand, and gave the throttle a twist. The bike leapt forward and whisked him away.

As he raced along the highway, pineapple fields whipped past on both sides and Choi was right behind him. Taylor felt lucky to be working with such a brilliant wingman. It had been Choi who'd detected the suspicious non-commercial flight and tracked

Tyson's men to a hotel, then remotely accessed the camera system at the restaurant and seen the cargo van pulling into the parking lot.

Having made the ten miles in under five minutes, Taylor and Choi roared into Haleiwa, bounced up into the parking lot, braked to a hard stop, and found the restaurant bustling with post-crisis activity.

A quick sweep told them everything they needed to know; the dining room was deserted except for a woman scooping up fish on the floor and dropping the frightened souls into buckets full of water; Nakamura and Harris were not among the shell-shocked patrons milling about, but their cars were still on the property and the cargo van was gone. Just to be sure, Taylor and Choi jumped back on the bikes and raced up to Banzai Beach, which they found deserted, so then it was on to the crooks' hotel.

***

Captain Kate Harris had never been more frightened in her life, and that meant quite a lot. Usually on the life-saving side of the terror equation, she was accustomed to killer waves, major injuries, and even dead bodies, but now she found herself in a situation where life-*taking* appeared to be the dominant factor.

She and Major Nakamura were sitting side by side against a wall in a hotel room with their wrists bound behind them by silver duct tape. Their mouths had been taped shut as well. Straight ahead, the smaller of their two captors sat watching them from a chair with a pistol in one hand. His face was thin and deathly pale, his head covered by a black baseball cap, and the man's massive partner stood next to a table at the window, peering out through a tiny space between the curtains. He was also armed, with the same black shotgun he'd brought into the restaurant, and a row of grenades lay on the table beside him.

"We should switch rooms in case Choi finds our registration," the smaller one said.

"Good idea," the blond one agreed. So he left in a hurry and pounded on the door to the adjacent room. Seconds later Harris heard a burst of shouting that ended abruptly, followed by two thuds and a telling silence.

"Okay, let's go," said the smaller one, helping them roughly to their feet. First Nakamura, who palmed one of the grenades on the table and stuffed it into the back of her jeans when the crook turned back for Harris.

A few minutes later, everyone and everything was in the same configuration as before: the hostages sitting against the wall, the minder in the chair, and the giant man peeping out from between the curtains, but the number on the door was different by one, so was the number of grenades on the table, and, presumably, there were two dead bodies in the bathroom.

***

Sean Choi gunned his black bike's engine, taking the lead as they sped into Wahiawa since he was the one who'd studied the map. As agreed, he stopped two blocks away from the target hotel, and from that vantage point he and Taylor could see the cargo van under the lights of the parking lot.

Based on that evidence, Taylor dug out his burner phone to call the police. Then he pocketed the device and said, "You brought your knife, right?"

"Yes," said Choi.

"I'd give you a gun..." said Taylor, patting his holstered pistol.

"But it would be a felony for me to carry it. I know."

With a single nod, they took off running in separate directions. Choi's job was to circle around the back and look into the target room through the bathroom window, while Taylor would sneak past the pool area and do the same from the front side. Their objective was to ascertain whether Nakamura and Harris were there, and if so, whether the women were in imminent danger. If they weren't, then Taylor and Choi would meet in the parking lot and wait for the police.

As Choi drew closer, he dropped into a walking crouch. Partially concealed by the long grass surrounding him, he pulled out his knife and flipped it open, but when he came to what he thought was the target window, the room appeared to be completely vacant. *Why?* he asked himself. *Because they moved!*

Choi wished he'd thought to grab their comms, but they'd left the house in too much of a hurry. Now there was no way to let Taylor know he was walking straight into a trap.

***

Captain Harris was still sitting against the wall in the new room, with Nakamura next to her, the pale-faced crook straight ahead, and the giant one peering through the curtains next to a table full of grenades—minus one.

"Taylor's out there," the blond giant said while reaching for his shotgun. With the weapon in his hands, he put his back to the door, drew a deep breath, and blew it out as he charged into battle. Gunfire kicked off immediately.

At that instant Major Nakamura caught Harris's eye and shot her a pointed look, a wordless expression as both of their mouths were still taped shut.

Harris glanced down at Nakamura's hands. Behind her back, the major held the grenade she'd taken from the other room. Clearly, the plan was to attack the smaller crook, who by then was looking out the front window. Harris couldn't imagine how Nakamura intended to execute that plan without injuring herself, but she did trust her more experienced friend. Maybe the grenade was non-lethal.

Nakamura swiveled around on her rear end, facing away from the distracted crook. She leaned forward and down in a protective position and shot Harris another insistent look, so Harris quickly did likewise. At that point the major pulled the pin and flipped the device toward their captor and both women screwed their eyes tightly shut.

The blast felt to Harris like a thousand needles piercing her ears at once, leaving her dizzy and disoriented; a sharp ringing drowned out all other sounds. And a brilliant flash like that of lightning also filled the room for an instant, disrupting her vision despite the precautions taken. But she could still see, more or less. So as she swiveled back around, she saw that the smaller crook's situation was far worse than hers. He staggered forward, blinked with unseeing eyes, and dropped to a knee, struggling to recover from the blast.

Someone was shaking Harris's shoulder. Startled, she whipped her head around to see Sean Choi. He was shouting something but she couldn't hear what it was.

Choi frowned at her uncomprehending expression while using a knife to free her wrists. Hurriedly, he did the same for Nakamura, then led them into the bathroom, where they had to step over two bloody bodies to escape through the broken window.

***

"Get to the front parking lot! The police are on their way!" Choi screamed at Major Nakamura and Captain Harris, but they didn't seem to understand. So he pointed insistently in that direction until they did as he'd instructed. Then he hustled back into the hotel room to prevent Asher from joining the fight by the pool, which he knew was in progress because he'd seen Igmar step out into battle and heard the ensuing gunfire. Taylor would have his hands full as it was, without the arrival of a second shooter.

As he came out of the bathroom and into the bedroom, Choi forgot to peek around the corner, so he charged straight into a gunshot. CRACK! Despite the ballistic vest he wore, the impact felt like he'd been hit with a giant sledgehammer. Instantly Asher rushed forward, attempting to clobber him on the head with a pistol.

Big mistake, thought Choi, who stepped neatly aside as his rival ran past, shoving him straight into the wall. Then he wrenched the pistol out of the man's hand and slammed it into the back of his head.

When Asher dropped to the floor, it was as if a magician had vanished the bones from his legs, so Choi felt safe leaving him there as he raced to the front door, pushed it open—carefully this time—and was horrified by what he saw. Next to the night-lit pool lay Taylor on his back with the giant Scandinavian in a mounted position, strangling the life out of Taylor and repeatedly smashing his head into the concrete deck.

Choi wasn't a great shot, so he stepped closer, aiming the gun with both hands and his finger on the trigger, lining up the larger man in his sights. Suddenly he was tackled from behind, thrown forward onto the deck. *It's Asher! He's stronger than I gave him credit for*, Choi thought while scrambling for control of the pistol.

It was two on two, with both pairs of combatants in the same configuration—bad guy on top—except Taylor was no longer resisting, Choi noted to his dismay. But then he remembered something he'd learned about Igmar when he'd first laid eyes on the giant man, weeks earlier while recording a conversation in Tyson's back yard. Choi had later gone home to dig into Igmar's past and discovered that Tyson had adopted him in Sweden following a boating accident in which Igmar's entire family had perished, and Igmar, then four years old, had nearly drowned. That kind of trauma, Choi reasoned, even as he fought with Asher, was likely to have left Igmar with an aversion to water or swimming. *Possibly a pathological aversion.* "Roll him into the pool!" he called out to Taylor.

But this gave Asher the advantage. The hacker clambered into a superior position, drew back his forearm, and smashed it into Choi's face, knocking him out.

***

Minutes earlier, as Choi hustled around the back of the hotel to peer into the target room, Taylor had snuck into the swimming area, where the shimmering turquoise glow of the water brightened the circle of doors surrounding it. Taylor knew Asher's and Igmar's room number, so he executed a stealthy approach. The unit was straight ahead, and the lights were on inside.

His main concern being that Harris and Nakamura might be facing immediate bodily harm, Taylor crept up to the window with his pistol drawn and peeked through a crack in the curtains. There was no one inside.

A door crashed open to his left and a shotgun fired, but Taylor wasn't hit. As he whirled around to see Igmar, a familiar clatter sounded at his feet, followed by a concussive bang and a flash as intense as the light of a welding torch. Temporarily blind and fearing a second blast of buckshot, Taylor could only charge in the direction of the giant man. The two of them collided. He felt his torso being seized by large and muscular hands, and his body lifted into the air with ease. Then he was slammed down on the concrete walkway, landing on his back and head.

They rolled around, punching each other and vying for position in a shifting tangle of arms and legs, edging closer and closer to the pool. When Igmar found himself on top, he immediately clamped his ham-sized hands around Taylor's throat and put all his weight into the choke.

Seconds away from falling unconscious, Taylor caught the gist of Choi's instructions, so he mustered the last of his strength to trap the Swede with his legs and roll into the pool.

***

"I'm sorry about Choi," said Captain Harris softly, standing close to Taylor with one hand on his chest and the other on his arm. "You'll find him."

Taylor could only nod.

"And thank you for saving my life," she went on, gazing up at him with those big hazel eyes. "Stay in touch?"

Full of mixed emotions, all of them bad, Taylor was not fully present in the sweet kiss that followed, but he sure wanted to be. Their connection had been instantaneous, a mutual recognition of something pure, something ancient. Or was it just hormones? In any case, he wrapped the senior lifeguard in a strong embrace and planted another one on her cheek. Then, as he returned to his motorcycle, the smile dropped off his face, and while riding back to the safe house he scowled, brooding over the event that had angered him.

The police had arrived in time to drag a half-drowned Igmar out of the pool and take him into custody, while Taylor had clambered out of the water in search of Choi, but the technical analyst was no longer on the premises. Neither was the cargo van. Dripping wet,

Taylor had sprinted back to his bike, caught up to the van on the freeway, and followed it to a private airfield, but he'd lost his ID in the fight, so the armed idiots at the security gate wouldn't let him pass. They gave him so much trouble at the checkpoint that by the time they finally relented, Taylor could only race up behind Asher's moving plane, get hit by the jet blast, and watch as it lifted off. Screaming curses into the hurricane-force wind, Taylor swore he wouldn't rest until he'd found his best friend and brought him home.

27

CLEAR AND TERRIBLE INTENT

"Good morning, Doctor Brown," said Cammie O'Mara to the man on the witness stand. In his mid-sixties, he looked eminently believable in a shirt, tie, and jacket that were old but carefully preserved.

Roche watched the jury as the research professor laid out his qualifications with just the right mix of good-natured familiarity and distinguished pride in his education and experience. The sixteen San Diegans were listening attentively, and they smiled when the doctor did, which Roche knew was crucial because if Judge Toles were to disallow Walker's and Park's testimony for any reason, then the People's case might have to depend on what Brown was about to state under oath.

"Doctor, could you give us some idea about the kind of research that you do?" asked Cammie, who in a navy-blue skirt suit and matching low heels looked comfortable sharing center stage with her expert witness. Judge Toles presided from on high while the defense team analyzed every word and Millie Haukea sat watching with practiced indifference. Back in the gallery, a hush fell over the spectators, who may have sensed that the defendant's guilt or innocence would largely depend on what Dr. Brown had come to say.

"Of course," he said, with jolly features that now fell serious. Intensely focused. "My specialty is multimodal biometric identification. Think of facial recognition, which uses computer algorithms to recognize or verify a person's identity based on their facial features. For instance, when law enforcement looks for a match between a suspect and a database, or when we unlock our phones by looking into the camera."

"Can you be more specific, Doctor Brown?"

"Certainly. In facial recognition, the computer first identifies key landmarks such as the position of the eyes, nose, and mouth—and converts the whole of the face into a mathematical representation. This usually involves measuring distances and angles between landmarks or applying deep learning models to extract a unique 'faceprint' or vector. The extracted faceprint is then compared to a known database or a second faceprint for identification."

"Thank you, Doctor. That seems clear enough," Cammie said, glancing at the jury. Most of them were nodding in agreement with her. "So what's the difference between that and multimodal biometric identification?"

Roche found himself distracted by his co-counsel's hair. It was short, silky, and midnight black. Stylish but not glamorous. Like Cammie's witness, whom Roche had had the pleasure of getting to know over the weekend, she displayed a rare combination of down-to-earth basic goodness and razor-sharp skills in her chosen field. *Classy but cultured. Powerful and yet precise.*

"Well, Ms. O'Mara, multimodal biometric identification is the next generation of identification technology. It's essentially the same process as what I just described but at a higher and more reliable level. 'Multimodal' means two or more sets of biometric markers, so not just facial features or expressions. We also use other static measurements such as ear-to-shoulder and neck ratios, posture, body shape and proportions, and 3D imaging—in other words, video footage of body motion, lip movements, hand gestures, and other factors, all of which, when represented mathematically, makes the identification process much safer and more accurate."

"Did you and your team use this technology to identify the defendant?"

"Yes we did. By comparing known photographs and video of Doctor Haukea to the images taken at the Convention Center and the security footage from the break-in at the Hall of Justice, we were able to determine that the person shown in all of these media is the same individual, despite the fact that her appearance had been altered."

Vincent Tyson jumped to his feet. "Objection, Your Honor—the doctor's conclusion is based on his own proprietary algorithm, a new combination of techniques that has yet to be peer-reviewed and legally validated. His conclusions are therefore speculative."

Judge Toles peered down at Cammie over his glasses. "Ms. O'Mara?"

"Your Honor, under the Daubert standard, the factors to consider are testability, peer review, error rates, and general acceptance in the relevant scientific community. Each of the biometric methods used by Doctor Brown has individually been the subject of extensive peer-reviewed research, with clearly documented and published error rates, and they are regularly employed in forensic identification by international law enforcement agencies."

"I'll allow it," Judge Toles told Tyson, holding the criminal defender's gaze for a long and very loud moment of silence. Then: "You may proceed, Ms. O'Mara."

"Doctor Brown, when you say that the defendant's appearance was altered, do you mean that she was wearing a disguise?"

"That's exactly right. I believe that she used prosthetic makeup and a body suit at the Hall of Justice and the Convention Center in addition to dying her hair and skin."

"No further questions, Your Honor."

"Mr. Tyson," rumbled the judge into his microphone.

Tyson stepped up to the podium between the two counsel tables. "Doctor Brown," he began, "thank you for being here. I'm sure you can agree that the important thing, the only reason any of us are here today, is to learn the truth."

"Yes."

"With that in mind, how many times would you say you've appeared as an expert witness in a court of law for the express purpose of identifying a defendant?"

Cammie stood at once. "Objection. Relevance."

"Goes to credibility, Your Honor," said Tyson without turning to look at her.

"Overruled," said Judge Toles. "Doctor Brown?"

"I really couldn't say."

"More than ten?" Tyson pressed.

"Yes."

"More than fifty? A hundred times?"

"Approximately fifty times."

"Thank you Doctor. Let's use that number. Of those fifty court appearances in which you were called to identify a witness, how often were you hired by the prosecution as opposed to the defense?"

"Every time."

"Every time?" Tyson echoed, feigning surprise. "Now, on those fifty occasions, did you ever declare that the defendant was *not* the person in the video footage or the photographs entered into evidence?"

"I did not."

"Is it your testimony, then, that you have only ever been employed by the prosecution and that you have never failed to point your finger at the defendant?"

"Your Honor!" Cammie shrieked.

"Withdrawn," said Tyson quickly. "Doctor, now I'd like to discuss the video footage recorded at the Hall of Justice. Does your algorithm use some kind of quality metric to adjust for factors such as poor lighting and blocked features of the subjects?"

"Yes it does."

"How did your program process *this* recording in terms of quality and what was the average score?"

The scientist frowned thoughtfully, pausing for a moment before giving his reply. "The system assigned each frame a quality score from zero to one, and then it gave more weight to better frames in its analysis. That's the beauty of the multimodal approach; we can still make—"

"The average score, Doctor Brown."

"Zero point five five."

"Fifty-five percent? That sounds low."

"Yes, but—"

"What kind of error rates are associated with this new technology of yours?"

"It's not mine and it's not so new," retorted the scientist, who by then was red in the face. "Facial recognition was developed in the 1960s."

"All right," said Tyson evenly. "Let's talk about facial recognition. What kind of accuracy can one expect with facial recognition alone under the conditions present in the Hall of Justice recording?"

"A single modality system can show error rates of ten to thirty percent under challenging conditions, but that's why we combine it with other data. Multimodal systems can reduce those rates to five percent or less. In our case it was five percent."

"So your computer program is ninety-five percent certain that my client is the person in those images."

"Yes, but there are other factors we weren't allowed to consider."

"Thank you, Doctor. No more questions."

"Redirect, Your Honor," said Cammie, taking her place at the podium.

Roche cringed. She was treading on paper-thin ice.

"Doctor Brown," she proceeded, undaunted. "What is the total amount of compensation that the San Diego District Attorney's Office is paying you for your work on this case, including all research and reports?"

"Two thousand dollars plus expenses."

"And how many hours would you say you've spent on this trial so far?"

"Including this trip? Over two hundred."

"That's less than ten dollars an hour. I imagine you make better money at your job as a college professor."

"Not *much* better." That earned him a laugh from the spectators. He smiled. "I'm actually losing money because I can't do any private consulting while I'm here."

"So why did you come, Doctor Brown?"

"In the interest of justice, Ms. O'Mara. To serve my community."

"Thank you. Just one more question. When you and your team conduct these studies for the prosecution, don't you usually make recordings and take photographs of your own to aid in the identification of the subjects?"

"Objection!" Tyson called out from his seat. "She's leading the witness."

"I'll rephrase," Cammie replied, rolling her eyes. "Doctor, would you describe the process that you and your team normally follow when conducting these studies?"

"We are usually permitted to take photographs and video of the defendant."

"Were you allowed to do so in this case?"

"No."

"Why not?"

"Objection, Your Honor! That's irrelevant to these proceedings!" barked Tyson, now on his feet, glaring at the judge with hateful menace.

Toles gazed off in the distance as if weighing his options, then looked down at the podium and raised his brow expectantly.

"This is for the record, Judge," Cammie argued, flashing Toles an equally threatening look, one that warned of a claim of misconduct.

Roche felt sick to his stomach, but Toles surprised him and everyone else by nodding with stern determination and saying, "You may answer the question, Doctor Brown."

"We were not allowed to study the defendant because Judge Toles ruled against it," the witness stated. "He deemed the use of high-intensity cameras and scripted movements excessive."

"Thank you," said Cammie, waiting for a beat as that sunk in. "Now, you stated earlier that the similarity score given by your algorithm was ninety-five percent. In your expert opinion, if you had been able to capture those images as you normally do, what would the score have been?"

"Higher than ninety-nine point nine percent."

"No further questions."

Vincent Tyson rose, slowly this time. "Your Honor, may I have a few questions on re-cross?"

"You may not. The People have raised no new issues."

Tyson's face turned purple and his knuckles went white as he balled up his fists, staring at the Honorable Judge Toles with clear and terrible intent.

***

At the midday recess Cammie and Roche marched down the courthouse steps with their boss beside them; the trio was escorted by Lieutenant Ron Ragasa of SDPD and three members of Ragasa's team, two in front, two behind.

"Let me take y'all to lunch," Lynn Peters said. The wind swept her golden hair sideways, blowing it in tandem with Cammie's black strands like two tall and perfect palm trees. Peters wasn't moving with her usual grace, as she was still recovering from major abdominal surgery, but she did come down the concrete risers with confidence, which in Cammie's opinion had to have been bolstered by the concealed firearm she was carrying under her jacket. Cammie tucked away a mental reminder to find out how she could carry one, too.

In short order, Cammie, Roche, and Peters had settled around a corner table in an uncrowded eatery; Ragasa and his men had taken a position at another one near the glass front doors, through which they watched the entrance on the street. As the waiters brought bread, butter, and water, the attorneys spoke of minor topics, under the unspoken agreement that the most pressing issue should be saved for when another person arrived.

So Peters, who'd been present at Dr. Brown's testimony, caught Roche's eye and said, "You looked like you were about to hurl when Cammie went up for redirect."

"Oh yeah," he replied, barking a laugh. "That was a close call. We figured Tyson would try to paint Doctor Brown as a gun for hire, and that meant we'd have a choice—either fight back or let it go. And you know how Judge Toles had been ruling for the defense, but recently gave us a generous continuance when Cammie got sick in court?"

"Yes," said Peters, nodding now. She understood. "Doctor Brown has a secret."

"His sister was murdered years ago and the killer was never found," Cammie explained. "So the risk—and this is why *both* Johnny and I wanted to hurl—was that after my redirect, if Tyson had been allowed another cross, he would have asked Doctor Brown whether he takes every case he's offered for minimum wage."

"And Brown would have said no," continued Roche, "that he only works on trials involving serious crimes and only when the defendants seem particularly guilty."

Lynn Peters nodded. "At which point Tyson would have moved to strike all of Doctor Brown's testimony and Judge Toles would have been forced to do so."

"Exshactly," said Roche with a playful smile. "But Cammie's smart. Minutes earlier, Judge Toles had overruled Tyson on a crucial objection regarding Brown's proprietary algorithm, which was encouraging, so she took a calculated risk, betting that Tyson either wouldn't know about Brown's past, or that he wouldn't dig into it on re-cross, or that Toles wouldn't allow any re-cross at all."

"And it paid off," said Peters to Cammie. "Then you took an even *bigger* risk by going after Toles, but I know you wanted to account for the five-percent error. I would have done the same thing."

Cammie nodded. "Yeah, that would have been reasonable doubt. But it seemed like Toles was finally coming around, so I went for it."

"Well done," said Peters as she rose from the table. "Hey Dom."

"Hey yourself," said Taylor, who had returned from Oahu two days before and already explained what had happened there.

Cammie and Roche stood as well, not so much to welcome Taylor, but to greet another lawman they'd never met.

"Lieutenant Bill Coffin, Harbor Police," said a tall white-bearded fellow with a military haircut. Coffin extended a strong and friendly hand.

Lieutenant Ragasa was also among the newcomers, having left his three men at the table by the door.

Food was ordered and eaten as this larger group met to coordinate the investigation not only of Sean Choi's disappearance, but also that of Jeff Walker and Tony Park, whose testimony against Millie Haukea would almost certainly lead to her conviction.

Peters had asked Lieutenant Coffin to attend the meeting because he was the commander of MARTAC, the Harbor Police's maritime tactical unit, whose members included Park and Walker.

"We're basically a SWAT team," Coffin explained, "except we do much of our work in the bay." Then he swept a sympathetic gaze around the table. "Chins up, everybody, we'll find 'em. We've got our best people working on it."

"We do, too," said Lieutenant Ragasa. "I've got undercover guys following Tyson and watching his house but there's been no unusual activity so far."

"He's an old dog. Knows every trick in the book," Taylor said glumly. He hadn't even looked at his plate. "*My* best guy's gone, but if I know Sean, he'll be doing everything he can to help us. Park and Walker, too. In the meantime," he asked Cammie, "can't you subpoena Major Nakamura and Captain Harris?"

"You said they didn't want to testify," she said. "In that case, it could take us a month or more to get 'em here."

"They're afraid for their lives."

"Believe me, I understand," Cammie said.

"I'll talk to them."

"Let's just focus on finding our guys," said Lynn Peters. "I know y'all have got your best people on it but I just thought of someone who might be even better."

28

DULCE AND THE FAMOUS DETECTIVES

Lynn Peters rapped her small but solid knuckles on a black wooden door, and lifted her face to the camera monitoring her from above.

A dark-haired woman swung it open. "Hello Lynn," she said with a hollow smile, extending both arms in welcome.

Peters stepped into the offered embrace, then said as she pulled away, "Maggie Garcia, meet Cammie O'Mara and Johnny Roche."

Cammie shook Maggie's hand and looked into her almond-shaped eyes. They were beautiful, as was the rest of her—dark and unflinching, too.

Maggie led them inside along a wood-floored hallway with Peters walking beside her and the attorneys behind.

"How's Dulce doing?" Peters asked.

"She's okay," said Maggie. "Hasn't slept yet, though."

The passageway opened up into a new-smelling living room that was neat and clean but limited in size, just like the house itself. There they met Dulce, Sean Choi's wife. She could have been Maggie's twin, with long, glossy dark hair, smooth cinnamon skin, and a trim and shapely upper body. "Nice to finally put a face with the name," Dulce said, rolling her wheelchair forward to shake Cammie's hand. "Sean's always talking about you."

Then the third sister came out of the kitchen, drying her hands with a towel. She was slightly older—Cammie guessed her age at thirty—and displayed the same family resemblance. "Tina Garcia," she said as Cammie shook her hand.

"Tina's married to Jeff Walker," Lynn Peters explained.

"The famous Walker. I hope we get to meet him soon," Roche said, stepping forward to meet Tina so enthusiastically that Cammie felt a pang of envy.

The mood in the house was flat and somber with two exceptions. Tina had trouble cornering those two rambunctious exceptions, but ultimately managed to scoop up her daughters and then said goodbye.

"I have to go, too," Maggie said. "But I'll be back with dinner."

"Thanks, sis. Please," said Dulce to her guests, "make yourselves at home while I get us something to drink." Then she propelled herself into the kitchen.

"She's a systems analyst like Choi," Peters told Roche and Cammie as they all took a seat in the living room, forming a rough circle on sofas and cushioned chairs. "And she's just as good as he is."

Dulce returned with a selection of cold cans in her lap, one of which she handed to Lynn Peters.

"You look tired," said Peters, thanking Dulce with a nod. *Pop* went her can of sparkling water.

"I've been working non-stop since Sean was kidnapped."

"Have you found anything?"

"No," Dulce replied sadly, wheeling herself into an open spot in the circle after handing out the other two drinks. "I tried the easy things first. Buildings in town connected to Tyson, anything owned by shell corporations or obscure LLCs. *Pero nada.*"

As the woman went on, Cammie found herself mesmerized. She'd always considered herself pretty, and had been told as much her entire life. But the Garcia sisters were next-level attractive, like movie stars, and Dulce most of all.

"… since Asher was the one who took him," Dulce was saying, "I thought he might accidentally give us a clue."

"How?" asked Roche, clearly fascinated.

"Every hacker has a signature style," Dulce told him. "The malware he writes invariably talks to his servers in the same way—in short bursts of traffic, like Morse code. And he tends to use the same kind of backdoor every time. So I built a filter to flag those criteria, but he's really good at covering his tracks."

"What about power consumption?" Peters asked, also with marked interest but for a different reason. "Sean told me y'all have a computer room, a big one. So Asher would, too, right?"

"That's a good idea," Dulce said, "but he can make his usage look normal, even when it isn't. Plus, he could easily fake traffic and power logs."

"Setting a trap for us."

"Yeah. It's a mess. Do you want to see our data center?"

Dulce led them to a study with twin computer stations on the side walls and racks full of equipment between them. She rolled herself to the right and parked at a long varnished shelf that served as a desk, woke the monitors with the mouse, and set her fingers into motion.

As she worked, reminding Cammie very much of her buddy Choi, Dulce provided running commentary: "The only thing I could think of was that Sean might try to leave us a trail. 'Digital breadcrumbs' is how we say it. So besides monitoring network traffic, I've been deploying scripts to scrape all the building management interfaces in the county—lighting, security, fire suppression systems, HVAC, electricity metrics, that kind of thing."

As line after line of unintelligible code scrolled rapidly down the screen, Cammie became ever more disinterested. Her head was so full of trial strategy, witness testimony, technical details, rules of evidence, and legal provisions that she found it difficult to absorb anything more. Yet Roche and Peters seemed enthralled as they leaned over Dulce's shoulder to watch. Especially Roche. Cammie noted with some dismay that her co-counsel was standing close enough to the lovely analyst to be able to smell her hair, and so, as Peters continued to offer ideas and ask good questions, Cammie tapped him on the shoulder. "I need some air," she said. "Do you want to take a walk?"

They said they'd be back and stepped outside, strolling along two parallel rows of small homes with front-yard gardens, not talking much. Before long they came to a grassy park dotted with tall and leafy trees. Two boys were horsing around in a pool, and a woman sitting nearby on a lounge chair looked up from a paperback novel. Cammie nodded to the woman—their mother, she figured—as she and Roche sat in the shade on a black metal bench.

"Tomorrow's a big day," said Roche, alluding to Tyson's opening statement and the start of his witness testimony. "Let's run through his case."

"You read my mind," Cammie replied. "Okay. Some of them will testify as to Haukea's altruistic devotion to the homeless."

"How much do you want to bet Tyson told her to do charity work in case she got in trouble?"

"I wouldn't put it past him. Then he'll call a few supposed friends of hers, who'll swear that she gives them herbs from her garden when they get sick."

"*Supposed* being the operative word," Roche noted. "He's also got experts standing by, ready to declare that multimodal identification is totally unreliable. But you're ready for that."

"Yes I am. Finally, a group of Haukea's former colleagues up in Ventura will march into court one by one to assert that on the night of the break-in at the Hall of Justice, she was at a cocktail party with them and could not possibly have been here in San Diego."

Roche nodded quietly, studying his shoes. Tyson's case was strong. Totally false, but strong nonetheless.

"Johnny, we *have* to find Park and Walker. If we don't, we'll lose the verdict."

Roche frowned. "To hell with the verdict. We have to find Choi. But Park and Walker, too. They're probably all in the same place, don't you think?"

"Yeah, I do." Cammie sighed. They were surrounded by chirping birds, up in the trees, and the cacophonous noise only increased her anxiety. She wished the DA's office would send *her* to Hawaii for the weekend. She imagined herself in the tropics, sprawled out on a lounge chair with warm golden sand beneath her, palm trees blowing in the wind up above, their long fronds softly rustling, and Johnny Roche standing there in swim trunks. His bulging muscles glistening in the sun. He'd hold up a bottle of tanning lotion and ask if she needed some. She'd think about it for a second, then say yes, and he'd rub it all over her body.

It was a ridiculous idea. Besides being just friends, the two of them had too much to prepare for. And unless a miracle occurred, Tyson would be wrapping up his case in a week, likely after planting enough seeds of doubt in the jury's minds that they would have no choice but to set Haukea free. And if that happened, given the murderous looks the defendant had been flashing her throughout the trial, Cammie would never feel safe again!

***

A few days earlier, Sean Choi had been knocked unconscious, then bound and gagged and driven by Asher to a private airport on Oahu. Kept medicated until Dane and his goons had dragged him into Asher's penthouse suite in San Diego, Choi was not fully aware of those events. The first thing he was sure about was being shoved into a very cold room.

"There he is!" exclaimed a hearty voice, a familiar one.

Choi blinked repeatedly until four blurry outlines came into focus. First he saw the man who'd spoken, his old pal Jeff Walker, and then the massive Tony Park. Both came quickly forward to make sure he didn't fall.

The other two people in the room were older, sixty or thereabouts: a worried African American couple who had no idea why they were there. Introducing themselves as Charles and Lenora Whitfield, it wasn't until everyone had settled down on the carpet and Choi had gone through the entire story, meaning Southern Trust, all the parties involved, and the rest of the details concerning Millie Haukea's trial, that the Whitfields realized they'd been kidnapped in order to keep Judge Toles from siding with the prosecution. Toles was their brother-in-law.

"Millie Haukea?" repeated Tony Park, an Asian man in his mid-thirties who was just as large as Igmar but in much better physical condition. His shirt was torn, and his knuckles bruised and bloody. "That's a name I never thought I'd hear again."

"Yeah, I thought the case was closed. She confessed to everything," added Walker. He was almost as muscular as his fellow detective but smaller in stature and with short blond hair. "At least that's what the Honolulu Police told us when we left the North Shore." He turned to Park. "Man, that was a long time ago. Remember you met Carla on the flight home?"

"How could I forget?" Park quipped, making double reference to the importance of his relationship with his wife and also to his photographic memory.

"This was a server room," Choi said, judging by the industrial HVAC vents in the ceiling, the acoustic panels on the walls, several three-phase outlets below that, and fiber-optic jacks where the baseboards should have been. But now the space was just a cold and empty prison cell with no windows, an exceptionally secure single entrance, and cameras watching them around the clock. No one had any equipment or supplies, except for Park's watch.

As Walker told the story of how he and Park had been captured, the Whitfields stood, stepped away, bowed their heads, closed their eyes, and spoke in low, passionate voices.

Choi wasn't religious—nor were Park and Walker—but he knew they were being monitored by desperate crooks with little reason not to kill them all, so praying didn't seem like a bad idea.

***

Just outside the secure entrance to Asher's former data center—or command center, as he sometimes preferred to call it—a hallway led back to the large sitting room with the bar in the corner, the jacuzzi on the balcony, and that stunning view of San Diego Bay and Coronado Island. Gathered there at the moment, seated on the black leather couches and reclining chairs, were Vincent Tyson, Asher, Dane, and Dane's three hired guns. This latter trio looked like they'd been run over by a convoy of armored trucks, and only Dane seemed to be in decent spirits. Tyson was listening with impatience, Dane's men were groaning in agony, and Asher sat indignant at a folding table piled high with electronic modules, screens, and cables everywhere as the muscular accident specialist recounted the events that led to Park's and Walker's abduction.

"So that's why I was incomunicado," Dane was saying to Tyson. "Me and my team staked out Walker's house, waited till it was empty, disabled the security system—"

"With remote assistance," Asher interjected.

"Disabled the security *with remote assistance*, waited for Walker's wife and daughters to come home, and tied them up.

When he came home from work, it was easy to take him, 'cause all we had to do was threaten his family."

"So what went wrong?" Tyson asked, staring pointedly at the three suffering men.

"Tony Park is what went wrong. We had Walker call him, saying he needed help with something in the garage, but we didn't know about Park's fighting skills. Could have used some remote assistance on that one, ol' buddy."

"*You* should have done your homework," Asher fired back.

"Anyway, we finally got him down between the four of us, but these guys took a beating, and I think I broke my hand."

Tyson felt like raising his empty glass to Asher as a signal for the same again, but he knew the kid would be offended. Besides, the digital mercenary had suffered enough already, what with the difficult trip to Hawaii and being told to dismantle his computer room. "So what happened to Toles' family?" Tyson asked. "I told you to bring me his wife and kids."

Dane shrugged. "I think he sent them away. The brother-in-law was the best we could do."

Tyson heaved himself up and trudged over to the corner bar. The drink he started fixing himself was a badly needed one. The trial was still going according to plan—barely, and only because he'd taken these four new prisoners—but now that Captain Harris and Major Nakamura had been told about it, if either one of them should come to California to testify with regard to Millie's earlier crimes, then the scales of justice would tip sharply in the People's favor.

And there was another problem, an even more serious one: Since Igmar had failed to dispose of Taylor and gotten himself arrested, the Honolulu Police either already knew that Igmar was Tyson's adopted son, or they would discover that fact, given enough time. Dreading the risk that these new circumstances posed, Tyson poured a second measure of liquor into his glass, doubling the dose. And this gave him an idea! *Two measures, one glass. Two birds, one stone.* Inspired now, he whipped out his encrypted phone and placed a call to his contact in the organization, who agreed to help Igmar escape. Then he dialed the Honolulu Police, identified himself as Igmar's attorney, and asked to speak with his client. In a short coded exchange, he told Igmar to wait for a clear opportunity to flee from custody, which he said might present itself at any time.

"I'm also gonna need a favor before you come home, but I'll fill you in when the time is right. Okay buddy, we'll see you soon," Tyson said, clicking off.

In order to pull off this new plan of his, Tyson would need to place a third call, but that would happen later, and he'd have to time it exactly right.

29

ONE LAST JOB

Igmar, Tyson's enormous butler, had committed several serious crimes, including the aggravated kidnapping of a police officer—Major Nakamura—and the attempted murder of District Attorney Investigator Taylor, who was also a sworn agent of the law. As a result, Igmar was not treated gently by the Honolulu Police. Dragged roughly out of the pool at the hotel, he was placed under arrest and taken to HPD headquarters, where he was booked and questioned.

"I want my phone call," he repeated many times.

"Absolutely not," he was told just as often.

"But I have the right to an attorney."

"Yes, you do. We'll contact one for you or bring in a public defender, but we're not about to hand you a phone. Once again, what's your real name and who are you working for?"

Igmar knew he was safe at the moment, since his identity had been deliberately obscured. And he was certain Tyson was pulling strings behind the scenes, so he just lowered his big blond head and shook it to indicate refusal.

Fortunately for the police, DAI Taylor had told them everything he knew: that Igmar was the adopted son of Vincent Tyson, who, in turn, was a defense attorney on the mainland and probably a criminal himself. So when Tyson eventually called and demanded to speak with his "client," the police had legal grounds to monitor the conversation, although this proved to be of little value since Igmar and Tyson spoke in code.

Within twenty-four hours of that telephone call, a key member of the Honolulu Police Department had received a convincing sum to help Igmar escape and withhold the news of the breakout for as long as he could. Thus, Igmar was now speeding north, having been furnished with a car, a burner phone, plenty of cash, a shotgun, and a ski mask.

"You made it," said Tyson in Igmar's ear as the giant Scandinavian sped along. "That's great. Harris and Nakamura are at Harris's house right now. I need you to go there, hit them both, then get your ass to the airfield."

"Thanks Da—" Igmar started to say, but Tyson had already ended the call.

***

"Appreciate you coming over," said Kate Harris to Rose Nakamura. "I haven't felt safe since Haleiwa Joe's."

"That's normal," the head of the Wahiawa Police Station told her friend. "But you handled yourself well."

"Thanks," said the senior lifeguard, popping open the fridge. "Drink?"

"I'm on call tonight, so just water please."

They headed upstairs to the second-floor balcony and sat at a table under a soft blanket of clouds, imbued by the sun from behind with warm and gentle colors.

"Dom Taylor called me today," Kate Harris said.

"Oh? How'd *that* go?" replied the other with a mischievous grin.

"It was a real nice talk."

"I'll bet. Was he trying to get us to testify?"

"Not really," said Harris, brushing a stubborn curl of auburn hair away from her face. "Maybe a little. But he understands. Said it's the bloodiest trial he's ever been on. Eight murders and eight failed attempts."

"How long did you talk for?"

Harris gave a secret smile. "Two hours."

"See?" said Nakamura. "Maybe it *is* going somewhere. I liked him."

"Me too," said Harris, sipping her wine while gazing up at the sky. Night would fall within the hour.

Nakamura's phone lit up on the table. The caller ID said 'Unknown.' She picked it up and said, "Nakamura."

"You're about to be attacked," came a deep voice in her ear. It sounded like an older man.

"Who is this? Hello?"

The line went dead. Nakamura bolted up from the table and drew her pistol. "Lock yourself in the bathroom," she said. "Right now. And call 911."

***

Millie Haukea stepped into her cell, flopped down on her bunk, faced the wall, and punched it hard. Her cellmate didn't say anything, knowing better than to bother her. Millie had just returned from seeing Morgan in the attorney-client meeting room. He'd been disguised as Tyson, but not with the same attention to detail as before; his makeup had been slightly off and he'd forgotten to wear the fake Rolex, but it was the eyes that really gave him away. They'd looked tired and unfocused. Shifty. Guilty.

"You're using again," she'd said.

"It was days ago and just a little bit," he admitted, turning away from the observation window in case anyone was trying to read his lips, and she did the same. "But I'm clean, and ready to bust you out of here."

"You don't think I'll be acquitted?"

"Maybe, but even if the jury lets you walk, there's a lot of things that could go wrong before then."

Morgan was right. The DA's office had made a fairly good case against her despite the inadmissibility of the buried evidence. Millie gauged her chances at fifty-fifty currently, but all that was needed for everything to go to hell was for Walker to escape or for Harris and Nakamura to change their minds about testifying. Not to mention the danger posed by Tyson, who, Millie suspected, would give her up or even kill her to save himself. "So what's the plan?" she asked.

"The best time to do it is when you're in the Courthouse Commons Tunnel," he said, alluding to the new underground passageway that connects the jail to the courthouse. "I'll be on the inmate transport team in a sheriff's deputy uniform. I'll take charge of you and slip you a handcuff key, which you'll use to free your wrists as we walk. Midway through the tunnel there's an alcove with a storage room where the cameras can't see us. I'll have civilian clothes and fake badges stashed in there, and we'll exit through a side tunnel used by the maintenance crews."

"Okay," she said slowly, stretching out the word with hesitant approval.

"Check this out," he said, placing his briefcase on his lap. He clicked it open to pull out the construction plans, on which he pointed to all the features he'd just mentioned. "I can handle this," he assured her. "Then we'll run away together, like we've always planned."

Millie leaned forward in her chair to rest her elbows on her knees, hung her head, and gazed down at the industrial carpet. It was thin and brown.

"I *know* I can do it," he said, "but it's your call. If you change your mind, just wear your hair down that day and I won't do anything."

"What day?"

"The day of the closing arguments. Okay?"

She nodded slightly, still looking down. Goodbye was a standing handshake, with hollow confidence on his end and bitter disappointment on hers. Both were too preoccupied with their emotions to realize that Morgan had left his briefcase behind.

Now, back in her cell, let down and inconsolably angry, Millie slammed her fist into the wall once again. She closed her eyes and wished that life were fair. That she were six years old again. Reaching back for one of her earliest memories, she saw palm trees rustling in the humid, fragrant wind of her island home. At the foot of the trees, she was playing in the sand with her mother. The good version of her mother, happy and alert. *That's the tough lesson about drug addicts and abusers, and drugs and abuse, and all the other people and things we know better than to get involved with*, she thought. *They're bad for us. Messed up but not all the time. Even the worst sin or sinner is connected to something pure and good, however ancient, distant, or tenuous those ties may be. That's what makes them dangerous.* On that windy day, Millie recalled, she had looked up at her mother's lovely face, and they'd beamed at each other in mutual, perfect, palpable affection, and Millie had wished more than anything that her mom would stay like that forever. But she hadn't. Two years later she was found face down in the sand with a needle sticking out of her arm.

And here I go again, this time with Morgan. I'm clinging to the memory of his sober self, whom I only ever see on rare occasions, while ignoring the obvious truth. Do I have a soft spot for people doomed to fail? Maybe I'm doomed to fail, too, and maybe that's precisely why.

After graduating from high school, Millie had cleaned up her act and done well in college, but in time her deeply rooted fear and abysmal self-esteem had been triggered by the stress of achieving, so she'd rushed into the promising arms of evil. Then felt betrayed and gotten clean again. Then been tempted and fallen again. Over the years, this cycle had often repeated itself, so she knew all the familiar signs. And she was seeing them now. For the millionth time, Millie realized, she was pinning her hopes on a false promise. Even if Morgan *could* get her out and they made it back to Hawaii, she'd eventually find herself upset, and again she'd take the easy way out. *I always have, and I always will.* Deep down, Millie knew that the best course of action would be to plead guilty and spend the rest of her life in prison.

***

Igmar's heart thundered in his chest as he pulled the car to the curb and sat behind the wheel, sorting out his thoughts. *Don't take too long,* he told himself, *or you'll lose your nerve.*

No one was closer to Vincent Tyson than Igmar, who had known for years that when his adoptive father inevitably fell into the hole he'd been digging for himself, he would desperately clutch at the people around him, dragging them down to share his fate. And now, after eating the man's leftovers for thirty years—both literally and figuratively—Igmar reckoned they were even. He'd already made up his mind to do this one last job as a token of his appreciation, but as he sat there in the car, he determined that once it was done he'd go his own way. With the cash in his pocket and the many skills he'd acquired, he'd be fine. That settled, he pulled down his face mask, grabbed his shotgun, and charged into violence.

***

Kate Harris sat with her back to the bathroom door, dialing 911. It was locked, as was the door to her bedroom, but neither barrier would do much good against a determined intruder, especially if he was anywhere near as large as the man who'd come for them at the restaurant.

Startled by gunfire on the ground floor below her, Harris leapt up, climbed into the bathtub, and lay face down, forgetting that she was still on the line with emergency services. Her breath was coming in short little gasps, and her heart was beating so frantically and with so much force that she thought she might pass out from anxiety.

She heard her friend screaming downstairs, and more cracking shots went off. Then came a second yell, from a man this time, followed by a boom like that of a cannon.

A heavy silence descended on the house, but it was worse than all the noise. *Is Rose dead?* Harris asked herself. *What about the intruder? What's he doing? Maybe climbing the stairs right now, coming for me!*

"Ma'am? Are you all right?" came the dispatcher's voice crackling through the cell phone, which was sitting on the floor, out of her reach.

Then a weak cry drifted up from below. It was Rose! But Harris couldn't move. She closed her eyes, forcing herself to belly breathe as Nakamura called out again: "Kate? He's dead, but I need help."

So Harris flew down the stairs with a racing pulse, and followed her friend's moans to the kitchen. There she found Rose pale white and bleeding to death from a gaping wound on her thigh. Nearby, the same huge man who'd kidnapped them lay face up with a hole in his head and a shotgun on the floor.

"What's your blood type?" said Harris, rushing to a drawer for a wooden spoon and an apron in the cabinet.

"A-positive," Nakamura mumbled as her eyes fluttered closed.

Harris dropped to her knees in a spreading pool of crimson liquid, wrapping the apron strap around her friend's upper thigh. Leaving herself a loop, she slipped in the spoon handle and twisted it tightly. Then she wadded up the rest of the apron and used it to apply pressure to the bleeding wound. "Hang on, Rose," she said.

When the ambulance pulled up outside, Harris called out to the paramedics, guiding them to her location. "Shotgun wound. A-positive," she told the woman in charge as they all hurried in.

"Thanks," said the EMT, replacing Harris's hands with her own to keep the pressure on.

In under a minute they got Nakamura on a stretcher and back on the road. This left Harris with the dead man, waiting for the police. As she sat on the kitchen floor, clenching her fists, she swore she'd travel to California to testify.

30

PAYDAY

Forcing a smile, Judge Toles opened the door to greet Vincent Tyson, Tyson's three associates, Cammie, and Roche, who all marched into his chambers and took a seat on one side of his massive desk. The ornately carved worktable was a monument to the arbiters of justice who had come before him, having stood in two earlier courthouses before they were demolished and the current one built. It was a fitting throne for such a large man, though on that day His Honor's broad shoulders hunched forward and his usually sharp eyes were bloodshot and dull.

As he dropped into his swivel chair, Toles said to Cammie and Roche, "I've read your motion to submit additional evidence." Then to the defense: "As well as *your* brief in opposition." Then to all five, speaking to them in turn: "And now that I am fully informed, I find that reopening the People's case would be unfair, unfounded, and prejudicial. Sufficient basis has not been laid to allow testimony from either Jeff Walker or Kate Harris, and a presentation of the facts surrounding Doctor Haukea's first murder trial—in which she was acquitted—would unduly influence the jury."

At that, Cammie's anger at the judge's obvious misconduct finally bubbled up and over. "I'm filing a motion for recusal!" she snapped.

Instead of returning fire, Judge Toles simply looked at her, let out an anxious breath, slumped back in his chair, and said, "You are certainly entitled to do so."

But Cammie wasn't done. She whirled on Tyson. "You filthy crook!"

The criminal defender didn't even glance in her direction. "Your Honor, please," he said.

Judge Toles gave neither support nor rebuke to either side, so a shouting match ensued, with Roche leaping to his feet and jabbing an accusatory finger in the air toward Tyson, whose three associates responded in kind, and Tyson himself, remaining seated, finally turned to Cammie. He eyed her for a solid five seconds as his lips curled into a mocking grin and the yelling continued around them. Then Tyson stood, offered the judge his hand—which the judge refused—and strode out the door with his associates in tow.

***

Once outside, Tyson stopped and said to his team, "I'll see you tomorrow," though it wasn't true, and so with a triple nod they marched back to their office. Tyson had other pressing matters, none of which were related to the trial but they did require deep and ordered thought, so he strolled off in another direction, circling the block as his mind tackled a lengthy list of things to do.

The in-chambers conference had been a great success, not only because of the judge's favorable ruling, but also because Tyson had reached behind Cammie O'Mara to drop a tracker the size of a vitamin pill into her bag while she'd been staring at him and Roche had been busy in the shouting match. This victory aside, however, the rest of Tyson's carefully laid plans were crumbling beneath his feet.

First there was the fallout from Hawaii. Yes, they did have Choi, but Igmar hadn't managed to capture Taylor, nor to kill Harris and Nakamura. Tyson came to a potted tree at the corner and turned left, wondering what he should have done differently. At least part of his strategy had been successful; Igmar was dead and therefore unable to identify, locate, or testify against him. But Tyson had figured the brute would have no problem taking care of two women before he was killed by law enforcement. *Got that one wrong*, he lamented. So now Captain Harris was on her way to San Diego to declare that Igmar and Asher had kidnapped her, and worse, that Millie was connected to those two men through Tyson, who years earlier had made her sign an NDA regarding Millie's "alleged" crimes on the island.

Fortunately, none of that mattered anymore. Now that Toles had ruled Harris's testimony inadmissible, her pilot might as well turn that plane around and set it back down on the runway. Still, the steps Tyson had taken to cover up Millie's Hawaiian killing spree hadn't been completely on the level and they wouldn't hold up under scrutiny; he'd always known that. And this was just one more reason to make his getaway now, among many others. For instance, Millie could change her mind and tell the police everything. Morgan, too. And all the feds had to do was dig deeper into Southern Trust, and they'd find a trail that would eventually lead to consequences Tyson didn't even want to imagine. So it was time to go. He'd have to call his contact in the organization for one last favor.

Tyson's phone buzzed in his pocket. He took the call.

"Mr. Tyson, this is the San Diego Central Jail. You forgot your briefcase in the attorney-client meeting room."

Tyson was puzzled. He didn't reply right away, but then he understood, and his mouth twisted into a malevolent grin. "Thank you," he said. "I'll be right over."

***

Disguised as Vincent Tyson, Morgan strode out of his attorney-client conference at odds with himself. On the one hand, he felt light, almost giddy, almost high while smiling at the correctional officers who checked him out of the jail. It was a familiar feeling, that old pre-deployment quickening, a sensation he'd long since learned to enjoy. In the Army, the new guys always hated it—just as he had, initially. Many would vomit or lose control of their bowels. But not Morgan. He had never lost control, and he knew he never would. As he stepped into the hazy late-afternoon sunshine, he thought ahead to the next day's operation. There were many moving parts to consider, but he had done his homework and pulled all the right strings. He was sober now, feeling good, and it was all because of Millie. He loved her. He really did.

On the other hand, as he strolled back to his car he felt terrible about the way he and Millie had left things when they'd said goodbye. He with perfect confidence in his plan, but she with a crushing look of disappointment on her face. *Why? Was it the drugs? I'll never touch the stuff again. Or if I do, it'll only be occasional, and just a little pinch. That's the way to do it.*

Then a little voice spoke up, calling out from the farthest corners of his mind. *But you've never been able to leave it at 'just a little pinch,'* it said.

Yes, I have, he insisted. *For a while. And then I screw it up. But now I have a reason not to screw it up. Millie and I are gonna have kids.*

Morgan grinned as he sauntered through the streets, picturing his future children playing in the sand with their mother looking on, while he was knee-deep in the ocean, fishing the Hawaiian way.

The people on the street were smiling at him, and some had even waved, but it was because they'd thought he was Vincent Tyson. In any case, Morgan felt strong again, a master of his craft, looking just like Tyson to the very last detail. *I've even got the same briefcase.*

The sudden knowledge of his mistake hit him like a bus. With a hollow feeling in his gut, Morgan spun on his heel and hustled back to the jail. Thankfully, they had it waiting for him at the attorney check-in window. Flooded with relief, he stepped back out into the sunshine. But ten happy strides later, he heard a deep male voice calling his name.

His real name.

That hollow dread came instantly back, much colder this time. He whirled around to see the real Vincent Tyson parking at the curb, then heading his way on foot. Not in a threatening manner, so Morgan held his ground.

"Didn't you say I'd never find you?" Tyson gloated as he drew closer, wearing the same black suit as Morgan was, and interestingly, he seemed to have forgotten to wear the Rolex, just as Morgan had.

Morgan's heart was thumping harder than it had in many years. Yet he detected no bulge in the other man's jacket, no weapon in his hand, and no other threat in the vicinity. So, he figured, this was a chance encounter, and since he was still in fighting shape while Tyson was long past his prime, he felt safe. If it came down to a fight, he'd be the victor for sure.

"What were you thinking?" Tyson continued. "You were my number-one guy."

"I'm still number one," Morgan sneered, already swinging his briefcase like a giant boxer's uppercut.

Caught under the chin by a tooth-rattling blow, the real Tyson crumpled to the sidewalk, completely unresponsive. Morgan patted him down and came up with a thick black wallet, which he pocketed—for the cash, the credit cards, and the real ID. Then he sprinted off, making sure to remember the briefcase this time.

***

"I'm wearing a black suit," Tyson had said to Dane on the phone, "and I don't know about Morgan. But he'll either attack me or run away as I approach, and I won't do anything. Got it?"

"Got it."

"Good. Now, get set up on the roof of the same building Voss was supposed to hit him from. You remember, the one where you landed the helicopter and picked up Kang that day? But you'll be shooting at the entrance to the jail, not at the courthouse. If he shows, he'll either be coming out or walking in through the front doors. And he might be holding a briefcase. I won't. That's another way to tell us apart. Aim for the upper chest, then get the hell out of there. I'll take care of the corpse."

"Understood, boss. Just one question: How do you know he won't shoot you?"

"It's illegal for an attorney to bring a gun into a jail."

Dane hung up, grabbed a folding sniper rifle, stuffed it into a backpack, hopped on a motorcycle, raced to the indicated location, ran up the filthy staircase, came out onto the rooftop, and dropped into the prone position, all in under ten minutes. It wasn't until he was peering through the rifle scope sighting the jail's front doors that his breathing returned to normal.

He didn't have long to wait. A few minutes later, Dane saw his boss strolling happily into the jail—that carefree attitude being his first clue that it wasn't really Tyson—and coming back out with a briefcase—his second clue. Then Tyson's car pulled up at the curb and the real criminal defender got out.

It was with few reservations that Dane lined up his former comrade's chest in his crosshairs. *We all make choices in life*, he thought. *And Morgan made his.* Then he completed the trigger pull—CRACK—and ten minutes later he was back in Asher's penthouse suite.

***

"How'd it go?" Asher asked from the makeshift data center by the windows in his sitting room.

"Hit him in the heart from three hundred yards," Dane replied as he came in, shrugging off his backpack and dropping onto a sofa, joining his hired men.

Asher raised his eyebrows with newfound respect. *Three hundred yards? That's a good shot.* He had to admit his partner in crime had acquired many useful skills, from staged accidents and suicides to piloting planes and choppers, and now marksmanship, which Asher figured he must have picked up from Voss—*may he never rest in peace.*

Asher turned his attention back to the monitors, which showed his involuntary guests sitting against the wall in his empty data center, and it occurred to him that when this job was over he and Dane might form a more permanent sort of partnership. With the sensitive information he had copied from Dom Taylor's computer at the Hall of Justice, all kinds of lucrative opportunities had opened up—blackmail, political manipulation, framing, feeding information to defense attorneys, monitoring active investigations, or just selling the data were a few of the ideas that came to mind.

Before long, Tyson returned from disposing of Morgan's body, and he, too, took a load off in the main living area. He nodded to Dane and Dane's men, then set Morgan's briefcase on his lap and clicked it open. "That little bitch," Tyson growled while sifting through the papers inside.

"What?" said Asher from across the room.

"Millie and Morgan were planning to escape. I've tried to be patient with her, but that ends now. Can you get a bomb into the courtroom by tomorrow morning?"

"Of course I can." Asher was familiar with that room, so he immediately thought of the air conditioning unit on the wall above the jury box. It wouldn't take longer than five hours to assemble the explosive device, falsify the failure codes and a backdated work order, then report to the courthouse as a repairman. *In a decent disguise this time.*

"Good," said Tyson. "I need a two-minute time delay, a remote control effective at a half a mile, and no possibility of escape or survival."

"No problem. I'll leave the remote control in your office," said Asher, whose agile mind had already processed the given requirements and skipped ahead to an extra detail he'd be adding just to challenge himself. A cruel little trick.

Tyson caught Dane's eye next. "I'm sure we can all agree that things don't always go according to plan, so I need *you* to make sure Ms. O'Mara doesn't make it to court tomorrow. Preferably never again. She's got a tracker in her purse and you can use my phone to find her. Here. Keep it," he said, tossing over the cell. "And I've got good news for you guys—it's payday, but we need to go down to my car. Grab a couple of sturdy bags."

In the kitchen, Asher rolled out the refrigerator to reveal a door, which slid open at the turn of a key. He, Dane, and Tyson stepped into a private elevator that glided straight down to the basement, where Tyson led the way to his black sedan and popped open the trunk. Under the spare tire cover was a locking compartment that swung open to expose a large black duffel bag. Tyson extracted two gold bars, one for each of them. "These are worth over nine hundred grand," he said. "Apiece. Now listen up. I'll be catching a flight tomorrow morning, so I don't know when we'll talk again. Maybe never. Just keep our guests alive until tomorrow, and once the bomb goes off I don't care how you get rid of them. And cover your tracks."

They assured him that they would.

With a single nod, Tyson stepped into the black sedan, shut the door, and squealed out of the underground garage.

Asher turned to Dane. "I'm heading out for a while," he said, "so watch the cameras and make sure your guys are ready for anything. Remember what happened with Tony Park."

"Yeah, but now the prisoners are locked up and their wrists are taped up."

"Just stay alert. And don't leave until I get back. One more day and life'll be a lot better for the both of us."

31

BAD GUYS AND BLACK EYES

Sean Choi's gaze followed a small metal tube that ran from an HVAC duct on the ceiling down to a dull gray service panel on the wall. The service panel wasn't locked. To access the controls inside, all he'd have to do was pull the metal tab and swing the cover open. Which he could easily do, even with his wrists taped together, but the problem was that his captors would see him through the camera feed.

"Earth to Sean," said Tony Park, the massive Asian detective and former Navy SEAL.

"Sean here," said Choi, sitting with his back to the wall like everyone else. He was on the far left, then Park and Walker, and on the right end was Charles Whitfield—Judge Toles' brother-in-law—and Whitfield's wife, Lenora.

"Man, it's crazy watching you think," said Walker, the blond-haired detective. "You really *were* in outer space."

Park leaned toward Choi and spoke in a whisper. "We have to do something or we're dead, and I've got an idea."

Five minutes later, Choi raised his arms, giving the signal that he needed to use the restroom. He kept them up until the door came open, and two guards positioned themselves just inside the door. The lead one nodded to Choi, his signal to stand.

As Choi got to his feet and stepped toward the door, Walker also raised his taped-up wrists, but the guards shook their heads.

"You know the rules," the lead one said.

The odds are two out of three that the guy closest to you will have a broken nose, Tony Park had whispered to Choi before the guards came in. *You should be able to tell by looking, but hit him either way. As hard as you can.*

"You might as well let *me* out, too. It'll save time," said Walker, clambering to his feet with a dumb-looking grin, pretending he had no idea how serious of a violation he was committing.

Both guards instantly trained their rifles on Walker, who dropped to one knee and said, "Easy, guys. Just gotta take a piss."

Choi made a two-handed fist and hit the lead guard in the nose with all his strength. As that man struggled to recover, the other guard swung his rifle on Choi, giving Walker an opening. Park also sprang to his feet.

Before long, everyone was out in the sitting room: Park, Walker, Choi, and Mr. Whitfield holding guns on all four crooks, all of whose wrists and ankles were bound just as theirs had been.

"Okay, we're good," said Park. "Choi, you get the Whitfields out of here and we'll call Ragasa and wait for him."

"You got it," said Choi, elated, but only briefly, as that's when he heard a hissing sound. Then another on top of the first, and the air grew cloudy and bitter. It tasted like medicine. Choi whirled around, and the last thing he saw before nodding off was an Asian woman wearing black tactical gear and a gas mask.

***

"Kang stopped by," Dane remarked casually when Asher returned. The muscular accident specialist was sitting behind the monitors at the makeshift data center by the windows, now keeping an exceedingly watchful eye on his captives.

"*What* did you say?" said Asher.

So they had a drink on the balcony while Dane told the whole story. Since it was dark by then, the colored lights of downtown danced on the bay's dark waters below, with the bridge curving its way to the island and the stately hotel lit up like Disneyland.

"Why didn't you shoot her?" asked Asher once he'd heard everything.

"I should have."

"And you're sure she's gone?"

"Definitely. All four of us were still groggy from the knockout gas, but I saw her sit right here on the railing and do a backward somersault. It was crazy. She didn't have a rope or anything," Dane said, finishing the last of his drink. "I gotta go."

Asher nodded, followed him inside, and made sure to lock the balcony door. Then he turned to Dane's three guards and said, "Search every room."

"We already did," one of them protested.

"Do it again. More carefully this time. Then I want you back out here, on your feet and prepared to fight." Asher grabbed his pistol off the bar, verified that it was loaded and ready to fire, then strode over to the workstation to watch the monitors. *One more day*, he told himself as he sat down.

***

It almost worked, Choi thought, shaking his head with profound disappointment. He and the others were back in the same place on the wall, sitting in the same order, with their wrists newly bound and fresh cuts, bruises, and black eyes. They'd all been beaten for their escape attempt, all but Mrs. Whitfield, who rose, helped her husband up, and walked with him to the far right corner. As the Whitfields bowed their heads, it struck Choi as odd that the crooks hadn't burst in and screamed at these humble people to sit down whenever they stood to pray, which the Whitfields had been doing on a regular basis. And this gave him the solution to his earlier dilemma. Now he knew how to get into the HVAC service panel and send his wife a message without his captors seeing him.

***

"Ladies and gentlemen of the jury, good morning," said Cammie. "I sincerely hope you're feeling well today, as you all have a heavy burden—now you must weigh the evidence in a criminal case of the most serious kind and determine the defendant's guilt or innocence. I do not envy you. As you know, starting in October of last year, a long list of financial irregularities was being investigated and they were later brought to court in LA County. In that process, five individuals closely connected to the case were killed under suspicious circumstances, and that resulted in a mistrial. Then, in January of this year, as Southern Trust's actions continued to be scrutinized here in San Diego, two more persons of interest were killed. While eating his dinner at a corporate event, Ronald Green began to feel ill. Suddenly his face and throat swelled up and he couldn't breathe at all. His heart was pounding so fast it hurt, as if someone were stabbing—"

"Okay," said Roche, "It's very good, of course, but I know that's not what you want to hear."

"No, it's not," Cammie replied. She stood near Roche's dining room table, facing him as he fixed dinner in the kitchen. A serving bar stood between the two attorneys.

"The jurors will have just eaten breakfast," he said while stirring the sauce. "So maybe you should tone that last part down."

Cammie's first instinct was to argue; she'd included those technical details for a reason, but on second thought and after a calming breath, she forced herself to consider his point of view.

"If you're going for emotional impact," he went on, "you might want to talk about Green's brokenhearted family instead of describing his death in gory detail."

He was right, Cammie knew, so she scratched that part and began again. By dessert, they'd trimmed the fat off her one-hour speech, while still giving a clear and convincing account of the evidence presented at trial.

The following day would probably be the last one of this legal marathon, and Cammie couldn't stop thinking about it. At least now her closing remarks were in good shape. It wasn't so much that her argument was convincing, but that the facts themselves painted an abundantly clear picture of Dr. Haukea's involvement in the crimes of which she was being accused.

Yet Vincent Tyson, by parading a series of well-paid witnesses before the court, and by excluding key evidence for the prosecution through collusion with Judge Toles, had deprived Cammie and Roche of half their case. Thus, it seemed quite possible, if not highly likely—

"You've done the best you can," said Roche from across the dining table, snapping her out of her anxious thoughts.

"*We've* done the best we can," she returned, catching his sea-green eyes. He grinned warmly, but she looked down at her coffee. A second later, she glanced back up to see him watching her still, with that same handsome smile.

"You're an amazing person, Cammie," he told her. "And a brilliant attorney. You're gonna do great tomorrow. You'll see."

She drew an anxious breath, gathering up the tension of two long months. Then, when she blew it out, she felt ready for the final battle, win or lose. More significantly, she felt supported. Cared for. And wanted. She could sense that last part loud and clear. So as Cammie rose from her seat, Roche also stood, and they came together at one end of the table. He reached for her hand and drew her in close, slowly, so that their lips were inches apart. Swimming in those liquid eyes of his, Cammie let herself go, leaning into a tender, probing kiss. Loving. Unhurried.

Encouraged by his desire, she deepened the press of her mouth, and this moist exploration grew intense as their bodies came tightly together and their hands went roving up and down. Soon they were headed for the bedroom, but Roche's security system broke the spell with an insistent beeping alarm.

They hustled to his study and watched on the computer monitor as a black-clad intruder prowled up to the main breaker box outside.

"He's going to cut the electricity," said Cammie.

"No, he's not," said Roche, darting to a corner to grab his baseball bat. "Choi moved the real breaker box inside and left a surprise in that one."

The prowler was heavily muscled and wore a holstered gun on his hip. This worried Cammie terribly, since she knew Roche was tough, but only compared to other lawyers; he wouldn't stand a chance against a trained fighter or a professional gunman. "I'm calling Taylor," she said.

"Good," said Roche. "But call 911 first. They're closer."

On the monitor, the brawny intruder popped open the old breaker box and got sprayed in the face with some kind of gas.

"I'll be right back," said Roche. "Lock yourself in."

"Please don't go."

But Roche gave her one last kiss and charged out the door.

Cammie locked it behind him and went back to the screen, staring transfixed as the prowler screwed his eyes shut and rubbed them with his palms, blundering around until he froze. Then he hurried off screen—probably to get ready for a fight.

A minute ticked by in silence and with nothing new on the monitors. As Cammie's heart thundered away, her mind showed her a different video feed, shifting between many scenarios, all of them with the same two subjects and variations of the same final scene: Roche's body lying on the ground in a mangled heap and the intruder coming into the house to kill her, too.

The waiting dragged on and on. All she could do was stay ready. Finally she caught the faint sound of sirens in the distance, growing louder by degrees, and then there came a knocking at the door.

"It's me," said Roche on the other side. "He's gone."

Still wary, Cammie moved closer to the door, unlocked it, and pulled it slightly ajar. She gasped as she swung it open.

There stood Roche, beaten so severely that his head had lost its normal shape. With purple eyes swelling shut and blood streaming out of his broken nose, he didn't smile or crack a joke to make her feel better—not through those split lips. He just eased himself into a chair and hung his head.

***

Hypervigilant, Asher sat at the makeshift workstation while Dane's three guards searched every room. The screens showed the prisoners praying again. But it wasn't just the Black couple this time. It was all of them, standing in a tight circle with every head bowed. He thought about putting a stop to this touching little ceremony, since now it was a clear violation of the established rules. *Wait. Is that all of them?* he wondered for a split second just as a muffled thud echoed at the far end of the hallway.

"Sitrep, guys!" he called out immediately.

"Back bedroom's clear," came one guard's voice.

"Library's clear," said another.

One man had failed to report. Asher snatched up the pistol from the table, disengaged the safety, and crept toward the entrance to the hallway. He heard a scraping on the floor back there, like furniture being bumped around, and then a choking gurgle. *The second guard*, Asher figured, positioning himself at the wall's edge, just before the turn, and there he waited, straining his ears. The only possible explanation for these telling sounds was that Kang had somehow slipped back inside after Dane had seen her jump.

A muffled shout broke the heavy silence. *The third guard.* A moment later, soft padding footsteps came toward him in the hall, so Asher popped around the corner and pulled the trigger, missing his target, as she was down in a crouch currently punching him in the testicles. Before the pain even registered, his gun was in her hands. She smacked him in the head with it, and the next thing he knew, he was on lying his back with his wrists and ankles taped together and two strong hands wrapped around his throat.

Asher fought for his life but he couldn't do much. Especially not with her on top of him.

Kang was grinning madly, squeezing even harder, her black hair hanging down in tangled strands.

Asher found it ironic that this was exactly what he had done to her, but then he realized she'd planned it this way. "I can give you Tyson!" he croaked, but she would not relent. His vision grew blurry and his body began to twitch, but he did manage two more syllables: "Money."

At that Kang eased off a bit, just enough to let him speak. "I know where he keeps his stash," Asher gurgled. "They're in a black bag in the trunk of his car."

At the mention of the black bag, Kang's eyes gleamed. "I'm listening," she hissed, while keeping the pressure on.

"He told me he's catching a flight tomorrow morning, and that means—"

"I know what it means," she said, tightening her grip once again. "Now go to hell."

At that instant, Dane came charging out of the kitchen, and Kang was fast enough to scramble out of his way. She raced for the sliding glass door to the balcony, but Dane caught her as she tried to get it open. Yet by punching him repeatedly on a large egg-shaped bump on his head, she managed to fend him off long enough to slip outside and dive over the railing.

Dane followed her out and drew his pistol, but by then she'd fallen almost twenty stories, and her white parachute was popping open. He fired, but she was too far out of range.

Glancing down, he spotted something on the side of the building that he hadn't noticed earlier: two thin beams protruding from the wall, with a cable running between them. *She must have twisted in mid-air*, he reasoned, *catching that wire and waiting for a chance to sneak back in*. He cursed himself for failing to check the façade after she'd jumped the first time. Then he hustled back to his partner in crime.

"One more day," Asher croaked.

32

RELENTLESS PURSUIT

Dulce Garcia did not want to get out of bed. Not at this early hour. And yet, she did, as always. Usually her husband Sean Choi would help with some parts of her morning routine, which over the years they'd trimmed down from two hours to one through the use of assistive devices and permanent fixtures. And through daily practice, whether she felt like it or not.

Today it would take Dulce longer to get ready, since Choi was still unaccounted for. But he'd prepared the house to make it easier for her if she should ever find herself alone for any reason. So she reached up for the hanging trapeze bar and used her considerable upper-body strength to swing her dead legs over the side of the bed. Then she grabbed the floor-to-ceiling transfer pole—the stripper pole, Sean sometimes called it, which would only sometimes make her laugh—and lowered herself into the waiting wheelchair.

In the bathroom she engaged the wheel locks and took hold of a wall-mounted grab bar to move herself onto the toilet. Once seated, Dulce performed self-catheterization to relieve her bladder, and in that process she recalled the accident, which hadn't been an accident at all.

It had happened during the Mazatlan case, as she'd heard Park and Walker refer to it; Choi too, but she hadn't known him at the time. She'd been on a double date with one of Walker's lifeguard buddies, Mark Thompson, along with Walker and Dulce's sister,

Tina. On the way back from a cozy family restaurant up in the hills, Mark's deliberately weakened motorcycle forks had snapped, throwing both him and Dulce into the woods beside the road.

Her throat hurt, her eyes clouded over, and a lonely tear plunged down Dulce's cheek as she relived the trauma for the millionth time, watching Mark die at the foot of a tree. At the time she'd been crying out in excruciating pain, having broken her back at L3.

Another, more current source of distress was that having children would be terribly difficult for her. Raising them, too. Motherhood was a status symbol in the Garcia family; both of her sisters had made their mother proud by having kids. *But what can you do, right?* Dulce thought as she rolled into the shower and turned it on. Under the hot, relaxing stream she reminded herself that if she hadn't been faced with so many challenges, she might not have developed the fighting spirit to accomplish all that she had: earning a B.S. and an M.S. in computer science, summa cum laude, obtaining the OffSec OSCP, becoming CTF champion, even beating Choi. *Twice,* she thought with a smile while getting dressed on the floor.

Finally ready to search for her husband again, she wheeled herself down the hall and into their data center, where she parked at her computer station on the right side of the room. Promising herself she'd put in two hours before breakfast, Dulce started monitoring citywide systems for irregularities, knowing that any out-of-place event could be a clue, but also that Choi was not likely to be able to send her one.

Miserably, she moved on to building management systems and read the fault codes one by one, just as she'd been doing every day with zero luck. This time, though, she spotted a curious error code in an HVAC log. The error had occurred the previous night at 8:14, which she associated with August fourteenth, her wedding anniversary. And when she saw another one timestamped at 10:24

p.m., or 20:24, she knew it couldn't be a coincidence. She and Choi were married in 2024.

A minute later, she'd found out the unit number and the building's address and reported it to Lynn Peters. Then she searched for anything else she could learn about the downtown high-rise building, but all relevant data had been completely wiped—another strong indication that she was on the right track. That done and thus encouraged, Dulce had little else to do but eat breakfast early and hope with all her heart for good news.

***

Less than an hour later, DA Investigator Dom Taylor was flying along the highway, weaving in and out of the early morning traffic in his newly modified Police Interceptor at a much higher rate of speed than the SUV had ever traveled before, even with its new armor plating. As he drove, he pressed a button on the dash and said, "Taylor for Harbor One."

"Go for Harbor One," came the rough baritone of Lieutenant Coffin of the Harbor Police, the coordinator of the raid.

"I'm five minutes out," Taylor said. "Over."

"Roger. Same ETA here. I have to remind you to stay in the parking garage until I give the all clear."

"Copy that," said Taylor.

"I know you're disappointed, but it's out of my hands."

"No problem, sir."

Coffin went on to review the actions and contingency plans established for the tactical operation, which included disabling the elevators, covering the stairs, and storming the penthouse suite. Then he concluded with "Harbor One out."

Shortly thereafter Taylor had shown his credentials to the security guard at the entrance, driven into the parking garage, and now he was standing by. As he sat behind the wheel wearing a tactical vest with a rifle next to him in the passenger-side footwell, it occurred to him to experiment with one of the new high-tech features Choi had installed in the Interceptor. *You never know*, he thought. *It might come in handy.* So he tapped a button on the dash-mounted touchscreen to activate the radar system, which booted up with a hum, and a color picture popped up on the display. It looked like a simplified vertical slice of the twenty floors above him.

Taylor twisted the depth dial until the image came sharply into focus. Astonished by what he saw, he studied it until he was fairly certain he was looking at a secret elevator that wasn't on the floor plan, which was now gliding down from the penthouse with two bodies inside.

He looked through the passenger-side window at a door on the wall of the garage. He'd thought it was a maintenance closet but now realized that it led to the secret elevator. And next to that door were a pair of high-performance motorcycles, one of which was crimson. *Asher!*

Now in combat mode, he hit the mic button while positioning the Interceptor to block the door. "Harbor One, this is Taylor—requesting immediate assistance. Over."

***

"Badges," said Asher from the balcony, looking down at the street. "Let's go."

Dane bolted from the couch and ran to his room. There he made a quick call while grabbing the tactical backpack he'd been keeping ready, which held his payment in gold and several other items he couldn't live without. Then he hustled back out to the kitchen, where Asher was holding open the door to the hidden elevator.

On the way down, Asher pulled up the camera feeds from the garage on his tablet. "Take a look," he told his partner.

Dane peered over Asher's shoulder to see a black SUV blocking the primary exit door. It looked like an armored model, which screamed law enforcement, and this suspicion was confirmed when he recognized Taylor sitting behind the wheel.

Asher and Dane didn't turn to each other to confirm the change of plans; they just tightened the straps on their bags, readied their keys in their hands, and snapped around in sync to face the secondary doors behind them. When the lift hit the basement level, they sprinted around the back way, leapt on their bikes, and roared out of the garage.

***

Taylor heard the motorcycles start up and saw them speed away, so instantly he slammed the turbocharged SUV into gear. His tires squealed on the polished concrete as he took the turns on the way up to the ground floor. Speeding through an aisle with cars on either side, he spotted the crooks up ahead. They were just passing the security station, turning right onto a city street, and racing out of sight. At that instant, a heavy grate crashed down, blocking the exit and the entrance. Taylor slammed on the brakes to avoid a collision and flew out of the SUV toward the guard, who had already known Taylor was law enforcement. "Open the gate immediately!" he bellowed.

The security officer, a balding older man with curly white tufts over his ears, did not get up from his chair. He seemed to be having trouble with the computer at his desk. "I'm sorry, sir!" he blubbered. "It's an automatic function and I don't know how to cancel it."

"*Sure* you don't," Taylor growled.

It took a fair bit of intimidation, both legal and physical, to compel the man to raise the barrier. By then Taylor was five minutes behind the bikes, and he didn't know where they'd gone. He gambled on the highway, which was only two blocks away, making it a very solid bet. The only real dilemma was whether to head north or south, so he used his voiceprint to log on to the onboard AI system, which gave him access to the police intranet with citywide surveillance. By means of voice commands he told it to ping the freeway grid, and this is what he heard through the speakers: *CalTrans sensors have flagged two motorcycles traveling southbound on Interstate Five in excess of one hundred miles per hour at mile marker twenty.*

Taylor had to grin at the voice, which was female, husky, and overtly sexual. *I'll have to get Choi to tone that down*, he thought as he roared up the on-ramp and merged into traffic.

He caught up to the fugitives near Chula Vista. Both were wearing helmets, so he couldn't make a positive ID, but the guy on the crimson bike was probably Asher, the hacker who'd tried to kill him and his friends on multiple occasions. Asher was lagging behind the other rider, so as Taylor moved up behind him and slightly to the right, he was tempted to clip the hacker's back tire and send him crashing into the center divider. But the traffic was heavy, and even if it hadn't been, such a maneuver would have put civilians at risk in addition to Taylor's job and reputation.

Asher swiveled around to fire his pistol twice at Taylor's windshield, causing only minor cracks in the glass. Then he aimed lower, attempting to shoot out the left front tire. No problem there either, Taylor was happy to note, remembering that Choi had ordered the run-flat variety.

Asher faced forward again and hit the throttle, weaving quickly through the cars ahead as only a two-wheeler could, even passing his partner. But Taylor was an excellent pilot, trained in combat driving, and the Interceptor's emergency lights proved helpful as some of the motorists started to veer out of his way.

Taylor was gaining on the other guy now, whose stocky body looked like that of the felon who'd taken Walker and his family hostage; Taylor had seen the video.

The stocky rider reached into his pocket for a grenade which he dropped onto the road. *Whoomp* it went, having been tossed perfectly so that it exploded under the Interceptor, but Taylor just gritted his teeth, tightened his grip on the wheel, and charged on through, saved by underbody IED protection.

The closer they came to the border, the worse the traffic grew, which enabled the fleeing suspects to outdistance Taylor despite his best efforts. *It doesn't matter*, he told himself while roaring along at a hundred and twenty. *With those bikes and backpacks, they'll be stopped for sure. And with my credentials and so many U.S. agents around, I'll have no problem asserting jurisdiction. All I have to do is keep them in sight.*

Yet as he slowed at the Mexican border checkpoint, the crooks just blew on by, disappearing into that foreign country. Worse yet, a masked and heavily armed team of national guardsmen waved him to the side of the road for a "random" inspection.

That's when Taylor knew he'd been had. From the secret elevator with its alternate exit, to the uncooperative security guard in the garage, and now judging by the actions of the Mexican authorities, it was clear that the suspects' evacuation had been planned and activated in advance. As he whipped the Interceptor around and headed back to San Diego, Taylor slammed his palm on the steering wheel and screamed out loud.

He radioed Harbor One on the drive back, giving and receiving a situation report, so he knew MARTAC hadn't found any hostiles in the penthouse suite and therefore that he didn't need to arrive as quickly as possible. When he finally pulled in to the parking garage, the security guard waved him in with an embarrassed expression and more than a little fear. By that time the main elevators were working, so he took one straight up to the penthouse.

At the door to the suite Taylor shook hands with a man in green fatigues posted there—Furious, as everyone called him, was a sturdy African American member of MARTAC, the same tactical team to which Park and Walker belonged.

The expansive sitting room was bustling with forensic technicians, MARTAC operators, and other people including Lieutenant Coffin, who waved Taylor over to where he stood with the five rescued hostages.

"Glad you made it back," said Coffin as Taylor merged into the circle.

"Hey buddy," said Walker, beaming. The fair-haired detective was black and blue in the face, but visibly overjoyed to be reunited with his friend. It was the first time they'd seen each other since before Taylor's coma-inducing disaster. "Long time no see."

Park was equally glad and just as bruised and battered, as was Sean Choi, who took the opportunity to introduce the Whitfields.

Lieutenant Coffin turned to Taylor. "I was just telling them about your short stay in Mexico," he remarked.

"Yeah," said Taylor regretfully, but he nodded with determination. "We'll get 'em, though." This was met with emphatic nods and strong verbal agreement. Then he shifted his gaze to his brilliant partner, whose face was hard for him to look at. "Nice work, Sean. But I can't figure out how you managed to access the HVAC system with no equipment and cameras overhead."

"Well, everyone gathered around me, like they were praying—"

"We really *were* praying," said Mrs. Whitfield.

Choi nodded gratefully. "But at the same time they were blocking the cameras. So while I was out of sight, I popped Tony's watch open and connected the battery to the diagnostic port using some of the other parts."

"Twice, and at very specific moments," said Taylor, nodding appreciatively. "But how did you know what time it was if you'd taken the battery out?"

"There was a clock on the HVAC controls."

"Sir," barked Sergeant Ortiz, MARTAC's team leader, hustling up to his lieutenant. "We found materials and components consistent with recent bomb-making activity."

"How recent?" Coffin asked.

"Twelve hours, give or take."

"That means one or more explosive devices were built here last night," Choi concluded. "By Asher, who just fled the country. So they're in place right now. And where else would Vincent Tyson tell his man to hide them but..."

"The courtroom," said Taylor, who was desperately worried for Cammie, Roche, Lynn Peters, Lieutenant Ragasa, and many other people.

Coffin whipped out his phone. "I'll deploy the K-9 unit and the bomb squad."

"I'll have Tina bring Lulu," said Walker, referring to his dog. "She'll get there faster."

Taylor came running back with a report. "I called the courthouse but didn't get an answer," he said. "And Cammie's cell phone went straight to voicemail. Roche's too."

"Judge Toles' too," said Mr. Whitfield.

"That's even more reason to believe the courtroom's hot," said Choi.

Without another word, Lieutenant Coffin started barking orders at Sergeant Ortiz and his men while Taylor, Choi, Walker, and Park piled into the Interceptor and sped out of the underground garage.

33

A CREDIBLE THREAT

"Ready for your big day, *Doctor*?" sneered a gruff, broad-shouldered correctional officer as she snapped on Millie's restraints.

"Yes, I am," said Millie, dying to add *Fatty* to her reply, but she merely let the woman take her down the hall. It *was* a big day, much bigger than her round-bellied minder knew, and thus the worst possible time for any altercation or delay.

Millie had pulled her brown hair back in a ponytail to let Morgan know she'd be going along with the plan, but when she came to the elevator and saw a waiting group of sheriff's deputies, she didn't recognize a single one. *He'll meet me down in the tunnel*, she supposed.

As the elevator descended, her doubts flashed rapid-fire through her mind, as they'd been doing all night and all morning long. *Can I trust him to get me to safety? Will I die trying to escape? Even if I do manage to escape, will I lose control of myself at the first opportunity? I should just do what I'd already decided on—change my plea to guilty and stay in jail.* She started to let down her hair, but the image of herself on the porch with her children and Morgan fishing in the water popped into her head again, so she left it in a ponytail.

At the entrance to the tunnel she was placed in a group of fifteen female inmates, all scheduled for court that morning. The group was marched through a series of doors that opened and closed in sequences, while deputies confirmed their identities from behind computer screens. None of them looked familiar, either. Still Millie expected Morgan to appear, but she also half-hoped that he wouldn't. Then her fate would be decided for her. Then she'd plead guilty.

By the time she came to the storage room at the middle of the tunnel, where they would have slipped inside to change into civilian clothes, she'd resigned herself to her fate. *It's fine*, she thought. *He's probably lying on the floor somewhere, out of his mind on drugs, so it's a good thing he didn't meet me here like that.*

Minutes later, she emerged on the other side and was taken to a meeting room, told to sit down, and left alone to wait for Tyson. Millie felt cleaner, lighter than before, and eager to know whether after changing her plea she'd be given a lighter sentence than if the jury had found her guilty. But then she was struck by the most enticing fantasy: *What if it's not Tyson who walks in here, but Morgan in his place, and he's planning to help me in the courtroom somehow?*

It was too far-fetched; she'd need a SWAT team on her side to escape from the high-security courthouse. No, the tunnel had been the best option and Morgan had failed to show up, disappointing her once again. And this sobering realization was confirmed as Tyson dropped into a chair across the table from her. It was him. She could tell by the eyes.

"Here's your outfit," the lawyer said, pushing a bag toward her on the table.

"Thanks."

"You're welcome. Now get dressed quick. Court comes to order in twenty minutes. Today we're giving closing arguments."

"I know," she said dryly, letting down her ponytail and shaking it out.

"The jury might find you guilty of some of the charges today. Maybe the break-in at the Hall of Justice. But without the East County evidence, I don't see how they could convict you of murder one."

"Maybe I should just change my plea."

He screwed up his mouth for a moment as if considering her words, but then he shook his head. "It's not a good idea. The way I see it, the jury will either acquit you completely or send you to prison for a few years, and if that happens, I can break you out."

I've heard that before.

"I want to tell you something," he said softly, looking her right in the eyes. "You and I haven't been doing too well lately, and I feel terrible about it. It's just this Southern Trust case. What a mess, right?"

She nodded tentatively.

"But you really put yourself on the line for me, and I'm gonna make it up to you. I promise. One way or another, you'll be released and given a new identity. I know a guy." He smiled. "Then, if you want, we can go our separate ways. Just let me take care of you one last time."

Millie couldn't tell what was going on behind those deep black eyes of his. The words were right, but they still rang hollow. Even so, she wanted to trust him. Needed to. "Okay, Vince," she said, returning his smile. "Thanks for everything."

Since it was time for her to slip out of that orange jumpsuit and into something respectable, they both rose from the table, but instead of reaching for the bag, she just stood there looking at him, sure that he'd give her a hug. And he did. A stiff and hesitant one, but it was enough. At least he was trying.

"See you in there," he said as he left her in the room.

***

Tyson came down the courthouse steps in an unbearable state of disgust. He'd had to wrap his arms around the pervert to complete the illusion, but of course he was not going to "see her in there," and as he crossed the street to sit on a bench at the trolley station, he tried to imagine the look on Millie's face when she realized as much. It would serve her right for lying! After that, she'd get an even bigger surprise, but the explosion would tear her apart too quickly for it to hurt her.

Tyson unfolded a newspaper to hide his face, noting with interest that the average cost of buying a home in California had gone up by eighty-two percent in the last six years.

***

Earlier that morning, before Choi and the other hostages were rescued, Cammie was awoken by the sound of her alarm. She shut it off and rolled toward Johnny Roche. His facial injuries were shockingly bad. "How you feelin'?" she whispered, not wanting to wake him, but court would be called to order in an hour. "Do you still want to go?"

His puffy black eyes came open just a little. "Of course I do," he said.

"Oka-ay," she replied in a sing-song voice that suggested it wasn't what she wanted, nor what she'd have done in his place, but that it was his call to make. Then she smooched him lightly on those busted lips and rolled out of bed in her underwear.

Nothing had happened the night before, not in the sexual sense, because too much had occurred in another. After Roche had come back from his fight with the intruder, several SDPD officers had arrived, secured the premises, taken statements, and insisted that Roche be driven to the hospital. So they'd gotten home late and even if they hadn't, Cammie reflected while soaping up in the shower, Johnny was too banged up for there to have been any kind of romance.

Once they were suited up for battle, Cammie drove to the courthouse, escorted by two police cruisers—one in front, one behind.

"So we're moving for recusal this morning," she said with her eyes on the road. "Right?"

Roche was leaning back in the passenger seat, resting his lumpy head. He didn't turn to look at her as he gave his reply. "Yes we are, but Toles will definitely refuse. He won't step down from the bench voluntarily."

"Then we'll request a continuance."

"He won't grant us one."

"Then we'll just walk out and immediately file for emergency relief," she said. "We can't let the jury deliberate based on what they've seen."

"Or what they haven't seen. I agree. What about Tyson?"

"I say we start with the U.S. Attorney's Office."

"On what grounds?" Roche persisted.

"You're right. There wouldn't be much evidence unless Judge Toles testified against him. Which he wouldn't."

Roche nodded, then winced in pain, so Cammie made no further comment for the rest of the trip.

***

In the courthouse lobby, as Roche passed through the security station, the officers on duty stared at his face. He couldn't blame them. *Maybe Cammie was right*, he thought while picking up his briefcase from the far end of the x-ray machine. *Maybe I should have stayed home.* But it was only his head and face that were affected; the rest of his body was more or less intact, and he'd wanted to be there for Cammie. He'd *had* to be there for her.

Soon they'd taken their places at the People's table on the right side of the well by the jury box. Cammie wore an emerald green blouse under a black skirt suit and matching leather pumps. Her glossy black hair fell almost to her shoulders and it smelled of Roche's shampoo. She was staring straight ahead, ready to pounce.

Lieutenant Ragasa and his men reported to their post, standing along the side walls, while Tyson's associates occupied three padded chairs at the table for the defense. Then Millie Haukea was brought in, looking perfectly innocent as she had been doing throughout the trial. The court reporter and the clerk sat down at their stations, the spectators slid into the pews, and still Vincent Tyson hadn't arrived.

"Morning guys," came a rushed voice from behind Cammie and Roche. "I need to talk to y'all really quick." It was Lynn Peters, also dressed in a skirt suit. Hers was navy blue. She glanced down at Roche in horror. "Oh my gosh! Don't get up," she said. "I've been trying to call you both but I think my cell phone's broken."

"We have to talk to you, too," Cammie said. "I'm moving for recusal. Assuming Toles refuses, if he won't grant a continuance, then we're walking out. We have to stop this trial."

"That's the right call, and you know I've got your back," Peters assured her, then nodded toward Roche. "So what happened?"

"He chased away an intruder," Cammie explained.

"No I didn't," said Roche. "The sirens scared him away."

Cammie set a hand on Roche's shoulder. "Well, at least you kept him away from me." She beamed at him, then turned back to her boss. "And I tried to call you, too. Both last night and an hour ago. Left you a message."

"I didn't get any messages," Peters said slowly, as if trying to make sense of it.

All three of them exchanged worried looks as the bailiff came forward, caught Peters' eye, and nodded toward her place in the gallery.

"I gotta go," Peters said quickly. "But just so you know, I think we found Choi. Maybe Park and Walker, too, and the Whitfields."

"All rise," the bailiff called out as she scurried back to the pews. "The Honorable Andrew Toles presiding."

The imposing form of the judge limped up to his usual high position. Center stage. "Good morning everyone," he said into the microphone, pulling it toward his mouth. With dark sunken circles around his eyes and a sickly yellow tint to his skin, he swept his gaze around the courtroom and stopped it on Roche, peering over his glasses and raising his brows. Roche shook his head. He didn't want to talk about it. So Toles turned his attention to the defense. "Counselors," he boomed, "I see that Mr. Tyson has yet to arrive. Should we give him a moment?"

"Yes, Your Honor," one of them answered. "If it please the court."

"All right. We will stand in recess for fifteen minutes."

A general murmur arose as the gathered crowd relaxed. Some spectators rose and left the room. "Look," said Cammie to Roche, indicating Tyson's associates, who also appeared to be having trouble with their telephones. "Something's definitely wrong."

"Excuse me," someone called out over the buzz of conversation. "Judge Toles?" It was Millie Haukea, standing next to Tyson's associates. "I want to fire my lawyers and change my plea to guilty."

Judge Toles smacked his gavel twice and the room fell quiet. "Court is back in session," he announced. "Let the record reflect that the defendant has made a request to discharge counsel and enter a new plea. Doctor Haukea, before we proceed, I need to be sure that you fully understand what you are asking and that it is your own decision."

"Yes, Your Honor. It is."

"May I ask why?"

Before she could answer, the main doors burst open to admit Taylor, Choi, Park, and Walker, the last of whom had a large black dog on a leash.

"Your Honor! We need to evacuate the courtroom immediately!" Taylor called out, charging past the spectators and up to the bench. He spoke to the judge in an insistent whisper, and at once Toles rapped his gavel again.

"This proceeding is suspended," he said into the microphone. "I need everyone to make their way to the main exit, and cross to the other side of the street. Now!"

***

By force of habit, Vincent Tyson glanced at his bare-skinned wrist to check the time. He chuckled. *A hair past a freckle.* Guessing that court was now in session, he folded up the Union-Tribune and dug from his pocket a prepaid cellular phone, and was glad to see that he'd been right. Eight thirty-five. Millie would be seated at the defense table by then, he assumed, as well as his three associates and the prosecution, plus Judge Toles on the bench, and—if he was lucky—Lynn Peters in the pews. But Tyson proceeded slowly, just in case. He put his phone away. Watched as the Orange Line trolley passed between him and the courthouse twice, one time in either direction. As suits and skirts strode hurriedly along the sidewalk and a shabbily dressed man on a bicycle rode by, looking like he hadn't eaten in a day or two. Only then did Tyson reach into his coat for a small device and click its only button. Supremely relieved, he rose and headed back to his black sedan.

The Southern Trust affair was finally over. It hadn't turned out as well as he'd hoped, but under the circumstances, Tyson felt, the outcome was better than satisfactory. And he'd be rewarded for it. Filled with excitement, he edged into the flow of freeway traffic, bound for the private airfield he always used. Just last night, the Sovereign had called him personally to offer him a job, saying she'd be waiting on the plane to talk about it. So he twisted a dial to turn up the music as he drove on, destined for even greater success.

34

FINALE

"I need everyone to make their way to the main exit, and cross to the other side of the street. Now!" boomed Judge Toles. "Bailiff, escort the defendant to the secure evacuation area."

The spectators were the first to reach the courtroom doors, since all they had to do was stand and turn around. Sean Choi looked that way, saw a little pile-up, and reckoned they might be having some minor problem such as an argument or a stuck hinge. But mainly he was focused on his tablet, turning it on in case he needed to do any bomb-related research.

Meanwhile, Detective Walker was leading his eight-year-old black Labrador retriever to the most likely places for a hidden explosive device. He and Lulu had formerly been a K-9 team, working bomb detection together for several years, and now she was retired and lived with him and his family.

"The doors are locked!" one of the spectators cried out, pounding on them with his fists for help.

"The side door too!" shouted the bailiff. He had custody of Millie Haukea, who was now in handcuffs.

"And the fire door's jammed!" hollered Roche at the rear exit, standing there with Cammie. He grimaced in pain and brought his hand to his head.

Cammie picked up where he'd left off. "We think it's been tampered with!"

The people started crying out and screaming for help, some running around with no clear aim. It wasn't a large crowd—about thirty in total—since the jury was elsewhere, waiting to be called in.

Judge Toles smacked his gavel repeatedly. "Anyone who's not working on a solution, sit down and stay out of the way!" he yelled, doing little to suppress the mounting sense of panic.

As Walker and Lulu were sweeping the jury box, the black dog leapt onto a chair and sat on her hind legs under the wall-mounted air conditioning unit, fixing her handler with a pointed look.

"Good dog," said Walker. "Good job." He rubbed her head and sent her away. "Are any of y'all certified bomb technicians?" he asked Lieutenant Ragasa and Ragasa's men as they converged upon the jury box together with Choi, Park, and Taylor.

"No," said Ragasa, shaking his head like the rest of them.

So it fell upon DA Investigator Taylor to carefully remove the unit's housing with a new set of tools he'd found in the Interceptor. This revealed a gray metal box with protruding wires that ran into the AC unit's internal hardware. Sunken into the top of the metal box was a digital display showing a countdown in blood-red digits.

Choi's heart slammed into overdrive when he saw the timer reading one minute thirty. One minute twenty-nine. One minute twenty-eight...

***

Earlier, when Millie had been brought into the courtroom and seen Tyson's empty chair, a sinking feeling had come over her, a dawning realization that he wouldn't appear. *No, it was before that*, she decided as she stood by the rear fire exit, watching the prosecutors and the bailiff try to get it unstuck. *I knew it when he gave me that empty hug. But maybe that was his way of being honest, of finally showing me what he was—a piece of garbage. Maybe not. In any case, why am I surprised?*

Deep down, Millie had always known what Tyson and Morgan were made of. Sadly, she had vast experience with disappointing men: the father who'd left her, her Nazi granddad, her high school "friends" who'd raped her, Captain Victor Lager, and others. Then there was the selfish glutton of her mother. Breathing hard by then and balling her fists, Millie stewed over each one of these betrayals in an endless loop, growing more indignant, her anger burning hotter with each mental revolution. She felt compelled to punish someone—anyone—everyone!—for what they'd done to her.

But there was no time for it. As Millie glanced over at the jury box and saw the bomb, she knew for sure that everyone in the courtroom was seconds away from being torn apart by a sudden storm of fire. *Asher's an irritating little weasel, but he's the smartest guy I know. If none of these cops are bomb technicians, then we're dead.*

***

Now halfway to the private airfield, Vincent Tyson drove his shiny sedan at a moderate rate of speed, while singing along with the music he'd put on. He didn't know or care what had become of Asher and Dane or their prisoners. Soon his appearance would be surgically altered, and with the gold, the gems, all the cash, and the rest of the valuables in the trunk of his car, he could easily live out the rest of his days on the warm sandy beaches of some non-extradition country. *Maybe Cuba*, he mused. *My Spanish is fairly good. But first let's see what the Sovereign has to say. It'll have to be a hell of a job offer to make me put that off.*

On arrival, he was stopped at a security gate, where his face, his ID, and his license plates were scrutinized by armed guards before being allowed to enter, so now, on the other side of that secure barrier, he felt even more confident that his plans would come to fruition. But when he walked back to the trunk and popped it open, all that delightful anticipation vanished like a bubble burst.

"Hands up," said a familiar voice behind him. "Turn around."

Tyson closed his eyes against such great disillusion and sucked in a breath, seething as he blew it out. Only then did he comply.

It was Kang, dressed in black tactical stretch pants and a ballistic vest. "Did you miss me?" she asked, targeting his chest with a silenced pistol. "I heard you have a big bag in there." She nodded toward the trunk. "It must be the one I left at your house."

"Help!" he called out, but there was no one around, and by the time he'd said it, Kang had flown forward to press the gun into his forehead.

Tyson shut his mouth and dropped to his knees.

"Give me the bag and I'll let you live," she told him.

"I have a better idea."

"I'm sure you do."

"There's about six million in there, but that's market value. *You* might be able to get three or four when you sell it, assuming you can make it out of here with such a heavy load. But it's yours if you want it."

"It is?" she asked in mock astonishment, still holding the gun to his head.

"Do you see that jet over there?" he asked, gesturing over his shoulder with his thumb. "The richest person in the world is on it, waiting for me."

"Sebastian Cross?"

"Cross?" Tyson barked a laugh. "He's just the guy they put on stage. His net worth is in the billions, or so we're told. I'm talking about *trillions*."

"Go on."

"Can I get up?"

"Yes," she said, backing away but with the weapon still trained on his head.

Tyson kept his hands up as he stood. "She's offered me a job and I'm sure she could use your services as well. What do you say we have a chat with her? No strings attached. If you don't like what she says or you don't want to proceed for whatever reason, you just walk off the plane and keep the bag. Otherwise, we'll split it."

Kang pressed her lips together, looking deadly in that tight-fitting tactical gear, Tyson thought, and then she lowered the pistol. "Agreed," she said. "But I will carry the bag."

"Of course. And yes, I did miss you, babe."

"Ugh."

***

"Just hang on! We're working on it!" hollered a sheriff's deputy from the other side of the main courtroom doors.

"Understood!" Lynn Peters called out in reply. Then she whirled back toward the terrified group of spectators, clerks, and attorneys behind her and said, "We need to get as far from that air conditioner as we can. Over in the corner. Come on!"

So she helped them get settled behind the farthest pews, packing them tightly together in a sitting position, hugging their knees. Some of Ragasa's men hustled over to assist, while Cammie, Roche, and the bailiff still worked on the fire door in the rear, close to the judge's bench.

"Are you sure it's supposed to open?" Cammie asked the bailiff.

Taylor could be heard counting down the remaining time: "One ten. One oh nine. One oh eight..."

"Yes, ma'am," the bailiff replied. "It's the only door in the room that can't be locked by the central security system."

"So someone definitely tampered with it," she mused out loud, while Roche put his full weight on the crash bar, jumping and falling on it with his rear end, finally popping something loose.

"I got it!" he shouted, prompting a cautious trickle of folks to walk and then run in his direction. One of those people was Judge Toles, who leapt down from the bench but dropped instantly to the floor, clutching his knee.

"Dammit!" he roared. "It's dislocated."

But before the trickle could become a full-fledged stampede, Choi saw the blood-red digits cycling backward at a much faster rate. *Classic Asher.* The timer read forty seconds then, and by the time he could scream at Roche to pull the door closed and Roche had quickly done so, the clock was down to twenty-five.

Choi stood front and center, surrounded by Taylor, Park, Walker, and Ragasa, all of whom were staring at him intensely, while he was doing his best to relax and ignore them, studying the explosive device. By then the metal casing had been removed to expose a block of light-gray putty beneath two green circuit boards with a red wire connected to the timer. But behind the main board, Choi also noticed a secondary circuit powered by a battery pack. He'd tried to use his tablet to learn more about this particular configuration, but Asher was blocking all wireless signals. Choi didn't know what to do.

Nineteen. Eighteen. Seventeen...

***

"What the *hell* are you doing?!" exploded Tyson. A well-armed, well-trained, and heavily muscled security team was patting him down, placing Kang in handcuffs, and searching their bags.

"It's just a precautionary measure, sir," the team leader told him.

Seconds later, a blacked-out SUV came rolling over to where they stood, and a bald man in a dark-blue suit stepped out of the driver's side, introducing himself as the Sovereign's executive assistant. He asked for and listened to Tyson's quickly fabricated explanation as to how someone who was not on the list had slipped past the security guards, and why that person was now attempting to come aboard.

"Would you just let me speak to her?" Tyson sputtered in frustration.

Sure enough, after being handed a radio and giving it back, he and Kang were driven to the plane. They stepped through a wide airlock-style doorway into the custom-built aircraft, marveling at its spacious interior—a masterful blend of modern design and cutting-edge tech with no expense spared in its construction. The same dark-suited man guided them through a reception room full of Italian leather and lined with dynamic artwork on flat LED screens, and showed them into the main entertainment area. There he indicated a polished-stone table and said, "Please. Make yourselves comfortable. The Sovereign will join you in a moment." Then he gave them a formal nod that was almost a bow and left them to themselves.

"See?" said Tyson as they slid into their seats, gazing about the room in awe. It didn't look like any plane he'd ever come aboard, and he'd flown on many private jets.

Before long, a well-dressed waitress appeared with a pair of champagne flutes and a bottle made of diamond-studded glass. By the brand, Tyson recognized it as a ten-thousand-dollar liter of water.

The young woman reverently set aside the cut-crystal cap and poured them each a small amount. "Please enjoy," she said with a smile.

Five minutes later, Tyson and Kang were slumped face down on the polished-stone table, and the Sovereign was standing over them. Tall and blonde, in her mid-forties yet impeccably maintained throughout her life, the woman looked much like Lynn Peters—but with ice in her blue eyes and not a trace of joy in her expression.

Soon the ultra-luxury jet was soaring over the Pacific Ocean at ten thousand feet and the Sovereign's security team was dragging two dead bodies to the edge of the open rear cargo hatch. She looked on with cruel indifference as they tossed Tyson and Kang into the sea like toilet paper into a great big bowl.

"Where to, ma'am?" her executive assistant asked.

"Somewhere cold," she said. "Surprise me."

***

Choi's heart was racing out of control. His fingers shook as he dug through the mass of multicolored wires, following each one from origin to endpoint. Some of the people in the corner were shrieking with fright, and the men surrounding him were desperately impatient. *Okay*, he thought. *Why shouldn't I cut the red one running from the timer to the main circuit board? Because Asher wouldn't make the solution obvious unless it's another trap. So why is there a secondary circuit hidden in the back?*

Fifteen. Fourteen. Thirteen.

And why does it have its own power source?

Twelve. Eleven. Ten.

Because it's a backup trigger. If I cut the red wire first, the bomb will go off since it'll still be powered by the secondary circuit.

Nine. Eight. Seven.

And the purpose of that circuit is to detonate the explosive immediately. So let's say someone came in and snipped the red wire with one minute still to go—

"Sean!" barked Taylor, holding out a pair of pliers with fervent insistence.

Choi nodded, then carefully removed the backup battery with the entire courtroom watching. His pulse was pounding in his ears.

Six. Five. Four.

He took the pliers and cut the red wire.

Three. And there the timer stayed.

Choi lowered his head and closed his eyes, blowing out a chest full of air as a raucous cheer erupted in the room. His buddies mussed his hair, the policemen clapped him on the back, and everyone wanted to shake his hand as he stood and turned to face them. The spectators were applauding wildly.

All except for Judge Toles, who was sprawled out on the floor between the bench and the rear fire exit. "Somebody help me!" he boomed, but no one came to his aid.

***

Millie Haukea was one of the few people not swept away by the celebration. Still in handcuffs, she glanced at the rear exit out of the corner of her eye. It was unlocked, she knew. *Should I make a run for it? No. I'll be caught.* The bailiff was standing next to her.

Clearly Tyson had intended to kill her with the bomb, so Millie's pent-up anger over the many betrayals in her life and the desire to punish someone for them grew even stronger, swelling into an irresistible wrath. As if she were a puppet being operated by some unseen master, she watched herself edge closer to the bailiff's holstered pistol. Then, in a single motion, she hit the thumb release button and drew the lawman's gun, backing away as she targeted him.

Millie's rage was so complete that she was unable to consider the consequences of this choice, nor evaluate any other course of action. With her mind bent on murder and her heart pounding like a tribal drum in a ritual sacrifice, all she could think of was who to shoot first. She imagined how it might feel to put a bullet in Jeff Walker's head, finally finishing what had begun in Hawaii, or to claim the life of Cammie O'Mara, since she knew the prosecutor was Jewish and still hated Jews. Then there was Roche. Boy, would she like to straddle him and choke the confidence right out of those blue-green eyes. Who should it be? One of Tyson's three useless associates? Judge Toles? A cop?

Driven by the relentless power of hate, Millie strode toward the last person she'd thought of—Lieutenant Ragasa—with the pistol aimed between his eyes and her finger on the trigger. But even in the throes of wrath, caught as she was in evil's iron grip, her better self told her "no." And she listened. Millie slipped her finger out of the trigger guard, but still strode forward, lining up her sights on the SWAT team leader, and this gave him no choice but to snap his rifle into firing position and take her wretched life.

35

EPILOGUE

Over Detective Jeff Walker's back yard wafted the irresistible aroma of steak and chicken cooking on the grill, the joyful shrieks of children playing in the pool, toasts being made, glasses clinking, and sudden bouts of hearty laughter.

"Good dog, Lulu. Good job. Who's the pretty dog?" said Walker, dropping to his knees before the ninety-pound canine. They held their foreheads together in a mutual display of fondness, then Walker rose to slice up a juicy steak and feed it to his loyal companion.

He swept his gaze across the yard, settling it on the bench beside the night-lit pool, where his buddy Dom Taylor and Kate Harris, Taylor's new girlfriend, were sitting. She wore her auburn hair done up and a casual black dress, and he was keeping her fully entertained.

*****

Harris threw back her head as she laughed, each joyful peal a crystal ringing sound.

When she settled her sweet gaze on Taylor again, he asked, "So what do you like best about San Diego?"

"You mean besides being with you?"

"Yes."

"Oh, I don't know," she said, scrunching up her mouth in thought. "Maybe meeting the team at lifeguard headquarters."

"*That's* interesting." He searched her twinkling eyes for deeper meaning and found it there. Apparently, she was considering a more permanent stay. Given her experience as the senior lifeguard on the North Shore and his strong ties to her professional equivalents in San Diego, she'd have no problem landing a job, and certainly wouldn't be starting at the bottom.

Thrilled by that idea, Taylor leaned in to kiss her, closing his eyes, and the world disappeared for a soft and blissful moment. Beaming at each other, they turned to the shimmering water straight ahead. He caressed the back of her hand with his thumb, she laid her head on his shoulder, and the rest of the group reveled on at the outdoor table nearby.

***

Behind the bouts of roaring laughter at the table, where Park was holding court with one of the many classic stories in his repertoire, a consistent pocking sound could be heard, that of a hollow plastic ball with each whack of a ping-pong paddle and every bounce on the playing surface. Under floodlights, Cammie and Roche were in the middle of a rally.

"Well," she said, "it's over." *Pock.*

"Yep," he replied. *Pock.* "No news about Tyson?"

"No, and I can't stop thinking about it."

"He'll get what he deserves."

"In this life or the next," Cammie quoted from a film she'd hated, but knew Roche loved.

"That's one of my favorite movies! We should watch it sometime."

"Yes!" she said, smiling with delight. "For sure." *Pock*.

"Hey, speaking of the Southern Trust case," he said, catching the ball in mid-air. "I can't believe how well you did. You're the most talented lawyer I've ever met."

"It was a team effort, Johnny."

"I mean it. You're next-level smart. And beautiful, too."

Their eyes locked on with soft intensity. "So are you," she told him.

"To be honest, I prefer 'barbaric' or 'warrior-like.' Something like that. You know, scary. Guys can't be beautiful." Then he served the ball to begin another rally, and a giggle spilled out from between her lips.

"What?" he said. *Pock*.

"You're scary," she said, glancing pointedly at his battered face.

"Har de har har."

After another minute of spirited play, she asked, "So are you gonna go back to Economic Crimes? I'm sure you could stay with me in the MVU."

Roche nodded sadly and didn't reply. Reminiscing about Dea Bladet, Cammie suspected.

"I guess that's up to Lynn," he finally said, returning her shot with a tricky spin.

Cammie could have hit it, but she let the ball bounce past her as if she'd been confounded, so it hit the ground and rolled into the bushes. She turned and dropped to her knees, pretending to search for it, and soon, as she'd hoped, he appeared beside her in the same position. The ping-pong table stood between them and their friends, making this a private moment.

"I found it," he said, pulling out the ball.

"And I found *you*," she replied, planting a slow kiss on his lips. "You don't know how happy that makes me."

"Yes I do," he declared, with real warmth in those sea-green eyes. "It's mutual, Cammie."

***

Chief Deputy Lynn Peters opened a sliding-glass door and went into the kitchen for a glass of water and a Tylenol. She sat on a stool at the serving bar in the kitchen, where she swallowed the pill, and through the same glass door she'd just pulled shut, she had an unobstructed view of the party outside.

Peters was alone, as she had been for most of her life. *But that's how you like it, right?* she asked herself. While waiting for the medicine to work, she set her elbows on the bar, rested her chin on her hands, and looked out at Dom Taylor and Kate Harris on the bench by the pool. She missed him. Who wouldn't? But now that she'd reverted to her default status, she was free to tackle the city's toughest and most demanding cases, and frankly, she knew deep down, Taylor was better off without her. Peters tore her gaze away from the lovebirds only to brood over David Goode, her first love, but he was up in heaven, as they'd say at his church, Hillside Baptist. *Maybe I need to go back there*, she thought. *Would they take me in without him?* She reckoned they would.

"Looks like someone could use a drink," said Dulce Garcia, who came wheeling up from another part of the house. Her sister Maggie was walking beside her.

"More like a vacation," Peters grumbled.

"Speaking of vacations," said Maggie cheerily, "did you hear about the judge?" She unfolded the front section of the Union-Tribune and set it before Lynn Peters. A bold headline announced: "TOLES RESIGNS AMID ALLEGATIONS OF MISCONDUCT."

Peters nodded. "Yeah, everyone's talking about it. There's a rumor going around that the ethics board will strip him of his pension."

"Perfect," said Dulce sharply.

Peters shrugged. "He's not really a bad guy. When I saw him yesterday, he was extremely apologetic."

"But it wasn't his fault, or was it?" Maggie asked. "I heard Tyson was blackmailing him or something."

"He should have turned Tyson in," Peters replied. "But like I said, he's not that bad. He said he's finally getting that knee fixed." Then, at the sudden sound of music, Peters turned to look outside, where Maggie's husband, Marcus Crawford, was singing and strumming his guitar. Now that her headache had subsided, the chief prosecutor turned to her friends and said, "Maybe I *will* have that drink after all."

Dulce and Maggie exchanged a smile.

***

From his seat at the outdoor table, Sean Choi saw Peters stepping out of the house with Dulce (his wife) and Maggie (his sister-in-law), who seated herself next to Crawford. Yet another brawny policeman among the many in attendance, Crawford grinned at Choi as he continued to entertain the group, and when the song was over he asked if anyone felt like singing.

"Sure," Choi said. "Let's do 'La Bamba.'"

So Crawford launched into the well-known opening of that classic tune, and as Choi prepared to belt out the melody, he swept his eyes around the gathered circle, starting with his gorgeous wife, whose heart-stopping smile and exotic dark eyes never failed to mesmerize him.

He and Dulce were different than the others; she for obvious reasons and he for his singular constitution—heavy on brains, light on physical strength. Despite this and also because of it, Choi had finally found a place where he belonged, where something that had always made him odd was now considered a special gift.

As it came time for him to sing, he moved on from his wife's warm, cheerful face to those of his closest friends and family, one by one. At each stop he felt fuller. Recharged. Ready for anything. And grateful most of all.

***

A few months later, Dane and Asher were still in Tijuana, Mexico, speeding side by side on two newly acquired motorcycles. They weren't fancy machines, at least not in appearance, though Asher had been working on them over the past few weeks, improving their performance as only a technical genius can.

In the meantime, Dane had been busy making connections. He'd discovered a local bar called "El Acantilado," where, with its unmarked entrance, cash-only business model, and rotating location, criminals tended to gather to conduct their business. That's where they were headed at the moment. Soon they pulled their rides to a stop in an alley, dismounted, popped off their helmets, and bounded up a set of concrete stairs. At the second-floor landing, Asher paused to take in the sweeping view of the Pacific Ocean. It was exactly the same as that of San Diego since Tijuana lies just across the border.

For a variety of reasons, reconstructive surgery is a thriving industry in that Mexican town. As a result, Asher and Dane had been able to choose from among several top physicians who practiced that specialty, so now they looked different than before. Asher's jawline was sharper, his nose thinner, and his eyes and hair a lighter color. Dane's face had been hollowed out, and his nose made broader and more prominent. This, in addition to fresh identities and plenty of cash, had set them up perfectly to implement Asher's new business plan, but someone else had had a better idea.

They grabbed chairs at a table facing a wall of tinted windows, providing themselves with that same spectacular view, and before long, the man who'd wanted to meet Asher arrived.

"Here he is," said Dane, who stood to shake the hand of a lanky Latin American man in his mid-thirties, whose extraordinarily large hands and long fingers were adorned with grisly tattoos, as were his arms, neck, face, and forehead. His features were reminiscent of Dane's new look—gaunt and hollow but more so, and his head was shaven practically bald.

The most interesting of this man's permanent marks was a running tally of some sort on his lean-muscled arm; it was kept in sets of five, each set constituted by four vertical lines joined by a diagonal slash. There were more than fifty of these grouped symbols.

Asher also rose, and the tall, wiry Latino looked him square in the eyes, searching his gaze as if trying to detect a weakness. This went on long enough for three waves to crash down on the beach. Finally he nodded in approval, introduced himself as "Chasquas," and everyone took a seat.

They drank and talked, mostly about Asher's and Dane's experience and their particular skills. Toward the end of the interview, Chasquas looked satisfied with what he'd heard. "Okay guys," he said with a heavy accent. "I am constructing an empire, and if you want a part of it—a big part—then you can come to work for me."

And so it was agreed: The newest members of the SoCal Syndicate shook Chasquas's hand, another round was ordered, and a toast made to the success of their partnership. Asher had been right: Life really *was* looking better now, for the both of them.

Afterword

Dear Reader,

Well, that's "the end" of my best work so far. I hope you really enjoyed it. If you did, I'd love it if you left me a review—just a line or two would suffice. And if you haven't read them already, be sure to check out the two free prequels to *The Southern Trust Conspiracy*: "A Hell of a Spring Break" and "Relentless," both of which are available on my website, patrickweill.com.

"Do you have any other work available, Pat?" you might ask.

"Yes!" I'd reply. "But if what you want is a sequel to the one you just read, it might be a while. What I *can* offer you right away is an action thriller trilogy starring Jeff Walker and Tony Park."

"Sounds too macho for me."

"Yeah, maybe. It's got more guns, more guys, and less romance, but all three books in the trilogy do have a heart, and two of them won awards. The easiest way to learn more about *The Park and Walker Action Thriller Series* is to visit my website."

Wishing you a good day,

Pat Weill

www.ingramcontent.com/pod-product-compliance
Lightning Source LLC
Chambersburg PA
CBHW021137310726
48971CB00002B/364